I0576157

STABLE HAND

The Braided Crop Ranch, Book One

AE Lister

A NineStar Press Publication

www.ninestarpress.com

Stable Hand

Printed in the USA

Print ISBN: 978-1-64890-131-7

First Edition, November, 2020

Also available in eBook, ISBN: 978-1-64890-130-0

WARNING:
This book contains sexually explicit content, which may only be suitable for mature readers.

The Braided Crop Ranch is looking for stable hands. But this is no ordinary horse ranch. They cater to men with a certain interest. An interest involving harnesses, tails, and trainers.

Managed and expertly run by registered psychologist, Adam Marsland, the Ranch is a safe place for the expression of sex positive and kink positive needs and fantasies.

Jensen Moriarty is desperate for a job. He can handle horses. In fact, he's a pro at it. Too bad the BCR doesn't deal with real horses. But they do have "ponies".

If Jensen can wrap his head around what the BCR actually stands for, he may have the opportunity to expand his resumé and experience something completely unexpected in the process.

This novel is dedicated to my family, who know of what I write but don't look too closely. They are my behind-the-scenes cheerleaders.

Chapter One

Horses. They were what I knew. What I'd grown up knowing, riding, grooming, tacking in the small Alberta town where I'd lived.

I missed small-town life. Ottawa wasn't a huge city, but it was big enough, crowded enough, it made me crave the peace and quiet of a smaller life.

My friend Mitchell hadn't told me much about the Braided Crop Ranch except to say the place was secluded deep in the heart of the Muskokas in Northern Ontario, which turned out to be an understatement.

From my calculations I was only about twenty minutes away, but the brush had thickened, and the GPS wasn't making sense. There wasn't even a proper road. Out of desperation, I pulled my car over to the gravel on the side of the dirt track. I left the car on, air conditioner blasting, while I looked up the name of the man who'd interviewed me over the phone: a Mr. Adam Marsland. I found the number quickly in my contacts and hit call.

"BCR, Connor speaking," a chipper male voice announced after a few rings.

The voice didn't belong to Mr. Marsland.

"Uh," I hesitated. "Hi. I'm trying to reach Adam Marsland?"

"Who's calling, please?"

I cleared my throat, feeling like an idiot. Nothing like starting a new job and not being able to find the place.

"This is Jensen Moriarty. I'm supposed to be there at noon, but I—"

"Oh, hi, Jensen. I'm Mr. Marsland's personal assistant. Would you like me to get him for you?"

"I just need directions. My GPS isn't making sense."

Connor laughed. "He should have told you not to rely on the GPS. You should be using the map from the email."

Email? "What email?"

There was a pause. "You didn't get the welcome email? The one outlining our policies and practices? I'm sure I sent the form to you a few days ago..."

I wracked my brain but didn't remember seeing an email. Unless the message had gone into my spam folder. "No, I didn't get it. A map would be...helpful."

"Sure, yeah, let me text the map to you. Hold on a second."

"You might as well text me the other info as well."

Connor cleared his throat. "Yes, well, I'll let Mr. Marsland explain everything when you get here."

I heard a notification and saw the map had come through. I opened the file quickly and had a look.

"Looks like I'm not too far."

"Okay, come to the main building when you get here. You'll see the BCR sign on the wall."

"BCR?" I asked, wiping a crushed mosquito off the dash.

"The Braided Crop Ranch. That is where you're trying to get to, right?"

"Yes. I just— Yes, that's where I'm headed." God, could I make a worse first impression?

"I'll make sure Adam is here to greet you."

"Thanks," I said.

As I'd suspected, I wasn't far out. If I followed this dirt road and turned onto another called Rattler's Revenge in about three miles, I'd be there.

Would they put me to work right away, cleaning stalls and looking after the horses? Mr. Marsland hadn't described my exact duties during our phone interview, but Mitchell had said they were looking for a stable hand.

Marsland had seemed like a nice guy. He'd appeared more interested in the kind of person I was rather than in any experience I'd had. I'd explained I needed a job that would give me some direction along with a decent salary so I could pay off my student loans.

The business degree had been a waste of money, no matter what my parents said. Turned out I hated accounting. Yeah, I was good with numbers, but working with them all day and night was too much to ask.

I needed to be outside. I needed to be interacting with other beings, human or animal. I needed hard work and adventure.

Now I had no idea what I wanted to do. Except for horses. I wanted to work with horses. Living on a ranch with a bunch of other cowboys wouldn't be so bad either. Even if they didn't share my orientation, the eye candy would be heavenly.

I'd been surprised when Adam told me the salary I'd be earning. The level was high for a stable hand. He'd also mentioned something about the *special stock at the BCR* so maybe they only housed Arabians or something. That would be a treat. I'd never seen a full-blood Arabian horse up close.

After following the serpentine curve of Rattler's Revenge for about fifteen minutes, the brush thinned, and I emerged into a large clearing with the impressive outline of the ranch spread before me. The path took me to a set of steel black gates with BCR in big iron letters affixed to the bars.

A black intercom box perched on the stone wall to the left of the gates. I pulled in close, lowered my window, and pressed the button.

There was a crackle and then Connor's voice. "Name please."

"Jensen Moriarty. We spoke on the phone."

"Awesome. I'll buzz you in."

An electrical humming noise sounded as the gates unlocked and slowly swung open.

"Welcome to the BCR, Jensen," Connor said.

I drove forward and rolled up the window to keep the heat out.

An array of bright red and brown buildings crowded the far distance. In front of me stood an imposing clapboarded farmhouse with these words, painted in black, spanning the wall:

THE BRAIDED CROP RANCH STABLES

~ Pony shows every month ~

Pony shows every month, huh? Looked like I'd have my work cut out for me.

I parked in the small lot to the left of the front door and turned the car off. I wondered if driving all the way out here had been the right thing to do. At any rate, the job provided a new beginning and somewhere to spend the summer. If I enjoyed the work and found the people to be friendly and helpful, maybe I'd stay for a while.

There wasn't much for me back home in Ottawa. Growing up in small-town Alberta, I'd become habituated to being outdoors among the trees, shrubs and farmlands, not surrounded by tall buildings and concrete. Except for the lack of mountains, heading up north into Muskoka country reminded me of home. If I couldn't have mountains, I'd take forests and lakes any day.

I opened the door and stepped out, boots scuffing on gravel. As I stretched my aching legs and yawned, I wondered if the weather would be this hot all season. The muck and mud of spring had gone, but the dry heat and dust of high summer could be equally as troublesome, especially if I was expected to keep the horses and stables clean and tidy.

Grabbing my worn grey cowboy hat from the passenger seat, I placed it carefully on my head, dusted off my jeans and the blue button-down I'd ironed that morning, and walked purposefully to the large wrap-around porch. My boots thumped on the old wood as I climbed the three steps and grabbed the handle of the main door, opening it quickly, ignoring the butterflies in my belly. Starting over was always difficult. But I wasn't scared. I was excited.

The image greeting me when I stepped inside stopped me in my tracks. I'd never seen a farm building this clean, and it unsettled me.

The wood floors were polished to a sheen; there was no dust I could see, or dirt stains from hands that had been to the stables and back; and the hallway in which I stood was airy and bright with modern fixtures. It threw me because usually places where people dealt with animals were less polished than offices you'd see in the city. But this place—well, I could have been back in downtown Ottawa instead of the middle of nowhere.

A sign with the word ADMINISTRATION was visible, with an arrow pointing down the hall to a large desk, fronting what appeared to be a line of offices.

A young guy about my age, whom I assumed to be Connor, looked up and blinked, eyes scanning me from head to foot while his face lost some of its color. I looked down at my shirt, in case I'd dripped some sauce on the front while I'd eaten my fast-food lunch on the go. But my shirt looked as clean as when I'd dressed that morning.

C'mon Jensen. Fake it till you make it.

"Hi. I'm Jensen Moriarty," I said, removing my hat and striding forward as I extended my right hand.

Connor stood up, covering his uncertainty with a smile, and glanced over his shoulder as an older man came out of the office directly behind Connor's desk and gazed at me with similar confusion.

I stood there awkwardly, my hand extended.

The older man glanced at Connor before recovering. He flashed me a warm smile as he shook my hand.

"Welcome to the BCR, Jensen. I'm Adam Marsland. It's nice to meet you in person. Connor said there was a mix-up with the email?"

"Yeah, I guess so. I never got the email. You said you'd try me out. A probationary period to see if I'm suited to the position." I swallowed, feeling unprepared. "I can show you references..."

"No, no. It's all right. Your credentials are excellent. But I just realized, I never explained what the job actually entailed. Those details would have been in the email you didn't get."

I grinned, putting my hat back on. "Well, I'm assuming it'll entail a lot of shoveling dirty hay and manure and grooming your horses, Sir."

Mr. Marsland looked away and cleared his throat. "I had assumed, since Mitchell recommended you for the position, he would have gone into what we do here in some detail?"

I frowned. "No, not really. He just told me you were looking for a stable hand."

Mr. Marsland exchanged a brief glance with Connor, who looked as though he wanted to be somewhere—anywhere—else. Then he smiled at me and gestured toward the room he'd recently exited.

"Why don't we sit down in my office for a moment."

He gestured for me to precede him. "Connor, please hold my calls. I don't want to be interrupted while I brief Mr. Moriarty on his duties."

"Yes, Mr. Marsland. I'm sorry about the mix-up."

"It wasn't your fault, Connor. Hopefully, we can straighten everything out."

There wasn't much conviction to his words, which made me nervous. What was going on here?

"I'm sure whatever your requirements are, I can meet them, Mr. Marsland. I'm young, strong, and highly motivated. And not afraid to get dirty."

Mr. Marsland made a sound halfway between a laugh and a choke as he sat in the large leather chair behind the desk. "Sit down, Mr. Moriarty. I'm afraid there may have been a slight miscommunication."

My stomach did a flip. I knew it. I fucking knew this position was too good to be true. I'd driven all the way out here, assuming they had a job for me. I wasn't about to give up easily.

"I can *do* the job, Mr. Marsland. I won't let you down," I said, trying not to show how desperate I felt. If not for the air-conditioned office, though, I would have become a puddle of sweat on the floor.

I watched Mr. Marsland shuffle through some papers on his desk until he drew one out. "Mr. Moriarty—Jensen. Can I call you Jensen?"

"Yes, of course."

"Jensen, this isn't about you not being willing to work for me. I can see you *are* very motivated, and you look strong and fit."

I nodded, feeling some relief. "I thought I had a good chance of getting the permanent position from the way we spoke on the phone," I admitted, turning my hat over in my hands and rubbing my calloused finger along the edge of the brim.

Mr. Marsland held up his hand. "Jensen, you still have a good chance. But... I might have left out some very important details about the kind of ranch I'm running here. You might not want the position once you learn more about us."

Marsland's deep-brown eyes conveyed a genuine warmth, which I found comforting, since his words didn't give me much confidence. An inch taller than me and at least a decade older, Mr. Marsland seemed the kind of distinguished-looking man I could imagine as the lead in a romantic film. But I banished those thoughts and focused on my objective.

"I've never worked with Arabians before. But I know I can handle the challenge."

He stared at me, lips twitching as though he was trying not to smile, or laugh. He ran a hand through his short, slightly greying hair. "I'm sure you could," he said, leaning back in his chair, assessing me. "But we don't have any Arabians at the moment."

"Oh. Lipizzaner horses, then? Obviously, you must have some rare horses here." I was scrambling. I had no idea what was going on.

Mr. Marsland used the tip of his finger to push the paper containing my information slightly forward as he gazed down at the form and said, "Jensen, we don't have horses here...at all."

I blinked. *No horses? But, I applied for a job as a stable hand.* "Uh, I'm not sure what you mean. This *is* a ranch, right?"

Mr. Marsland inclined his chin, trying to maintain a straight face. "Yes, but—"

"I don't see what's funny about this," I said. Part of me wanted to stand up and walk out. But I needed this job.

Mr. Marsland nodded, clearing his throat and forcing a serious look onto his handsome face. "I'm sorry. You're right. I never foresaw this situation, and now it's actually occurred, I'm not sure how to deal with it."

"Why don't you show me some of the livestock you *do* have on hand? And I'll let you know if I think I can be an effective stable hand here." I wouldn't leave without a fight.

Mr. Marsland stared at me for a long moment, then nodded. He stood and opened the glass door of the cabinet behind him, pulling out a large leather-bound book.

Okay, now we're getting somewhere.

Marsland dumped the heavy-looking album on the table in front of me, making me jump, and opened the book to the first page.

I think I stopped breathing, though I didn't know what I was looking at for several moments. When the meaning of the image began to come clear to my startled brain, I wasn't sure I'd ever breathe again.

"That's a— That's a—" I stuttered, eyes flying up to Mr. Marsland's sympathetic features and then back to the photo. My body was in full-blown DEFCON 1 mode. "I need to sit."

"You are sitting."

Horses. There were supposed to be horses. What the fuck was this?

I pushed the chair out and stood. I took off my cowboy hat and waved it at the desk, eyes wide and skin suddenly clammy. "What? I mean! That's a...guy!"

Marsland nodded.

I took a step back and stared wildly into Mr. Marsland's calm eyes, then glanced down at the photo again. I took a step forward and looked more closely. I glanced up at Marsland.

"I mean. Jesus Christ."

"Breathe, Jensen."

I took a breath and then another. I couldn't stop staring at the photo.

"You okay?" Mr. Marsland asked.

Was I? I shook my head. "Sure." *I might never be okay again.*

"You don't look okay."

I froze, realizing the impression I was making. *Get yourself together.* I swallowed and took a deep breath, then put my hat back on and sat down in the chair.

After a few moments, during which I stared at the photo in front of me, I nodded. "I'm fine."

"I told you we don't deal with horses here at the Braided Crop Ranch. What you're looking at is a pony. A human pony. A man."

Oh, my fucking God. "I mean, shit. I mean, is *this* what you do here?"

Mr. Marsland smiled an understanding smile. "And much more."

"Holy fuck." I was going to murder Mitchell! Why hadn't he told me? But I knew the answer to that question. Because if Mitchell had told me the truth about this job, I would never have come.

There in the photo was a man. A beautiful, black-haired, blue-eyed man, about my age, naked except for scuffed, black Docs, a leather BDSM body harness, and a bridle with a silver bit spreading his red lips and white teeth. His muscled torso shone with sweat and dirt; his black hair stuck to his broad forehead. His arms were bound behind him, forcing his chest out. The man's erection, contained in some kind of cage causing the flesh to bulge between the steel bars, jutted out.

Jutted out!

I started to hyperventilate.

"Let me get you some water," Mr. Marsland said, moving to the door. "Connor, please bring Mr. Moriarty a glass of water."

"Of course."

Mr. Marsland resumed his seat and leaned forward, placing a calming hand on my shoulder. "Are you okay?"

No. I will never be okay again.

I nodded. I wouldn't screw this up, no matter what might be going on here. I was open-minded. I could handle this. But, *Jesus Christ*.

"Take a deep breath. Count to ten," Mr. Marsland said, closing the album.

When Connor brought the water, I downed it quickly and leaned back in the chair, taking my hat off again and fanning myself with the brim. "I'm sorry, I just...wow. I was expecting horses. Real horses, you know?"

"Is he okay?" Connor asked. "He looks like he might pass out."

I sat up straight. "I'm okay. I'm fine. I didn't know this wasn't a regular ranch. I thought it was a *ranch* ranch." My voice sounded strangled.

"I'm sorry the email didn't go through. I didn't get a notification," Connor said, closing the door and taking the seat beside me.

"It's okay," I said, staring at Connor and finding it hard to believe both he and Mr. Marsland were running a stable of...human ponyboys. For what reason exactly? God, I had so many questions.

"I'm still confused. Do you need a—" I swallowed. "—a stable hand?" I tried, unsuccessfully, to meet Marsland's eyes. "Or not?"

Mr. Marsland smiled. "We need a stable hand, Jensen. And your qualifications are excellent. But you have to be aware you won't be grooming horses. You'll be grooming men."

Grooming men.

I made a half laugh, half gasp. A bloom of heat, which had begun in my cheeks, expanded over my entire face and neck.

Connor smiled. "I think he's still in shock."

Mr. Marsland said, "Our stable hands are responsible for the same things they'd be doing if we did house real horses. Keeping the barns and equipment tidy and clean, maintaining the grounds, and making sure the stock is clean and fed."

I blinked. "The stock?"

Mr. Marsland leaned forward. "Do you have any issues with nudity, Jensen?"

I thought for a moment. Was getting aroused at the sight of a naked man in pony gear a problem? I cleared my throat. "No, Sir."

"You don't have a problem being around naked men or women?"

I coughed. "Uh. Nope. Not a problem, exactly." I fiddled with the edge of my hat, looking down at the bulge in my pants. Maybe getting aroused was a problem.

"You like looking at naked men and women?"

My gaze drifted up to meet the frank expression on Mr. Marsland's face. "I, uh." I cleared my throat again and nodded curtly. "Men."

"I'm not allowed to ask you about your orientation, Jensen. But being gay or bi might make your job easier and more enjoyable."

I shifted in my seat, trying to make my dick behave. "Are you fucking serious?"

"About what?"

"About the fact my job would be looking after...gorgeous, athletic men, and cleaning them, and, like, grooming them, and...um...keeping them pretty?" My voice went up three octaves at the end of the sentence.

"I think we've got ourselves a new stable hand, Connor."

"Yeah, I'd say so. Much as I thought I'd completely screwed up when I took a look at Mr. Moriarty here."

I blinked at Connor, then at Mr. Marsland.

"You look like a cowboy, Jensen," Connor said with a grin.

I looked down at myself and at the hat in my hand. My voice sounded faint and faraway when I spoke. "Yeah. I guess I kind of am one. Always been with horses. My whole life."

Mr. Marsland shook his head, smiling at me. "I'm sorry. I assumed, since you were referred by Mitchell Garr, he'd explained everything."

I shrugged. "He only said your ranch was a great place to work."

"Well, we certainly think so," said Mr. Marsland. "And I'm pretty sure at least a couple of our ponyboys will get a kick out of being tended to by a real cowboy."

Home, home on the range. Where the kinksters and the ponyboys play.

I smiled weakly. "Well, if you're not prejudiced against real cowboys, I guess I'm not bothered by not looking after real horses. At least, I can try the job out."

Was I nuts? Was I really going to do this?

I looked at the photo again, feeling my cock swell more and my brain explode.

Yes. Yes, I was.

Mr. Marsland looked like a huge weight had been lifted from him. He sank back in his chair and let out a relieved laugh. "Okay, I need a goddamn drink."

"Me too," Connor said, standing up and heading for a cupboard in the corner of the office.

"Same," I said weakly.

"Scotch?" Connor said as he peered into the cupboard.

"The good stuff, Connor."

When we each had a glass of Mr. Marsland's Macallan in hand, Mr. Marsland raised his, clinked it with mine, and then Connor's.

"To our new employee, Jensen Moriarty. May he find looking after our ponyboys to be as rewarding as tending to the beautiful Arabians of his imagination. And much more stimulating."

I almost choked on the potent liquor as my mind swirled with images of handsome, rugged men in nothing but cock cages and scuffed Doc Martens.

Chapter Two

"I want to explain the business model behind the ranch. It's important for you to know because we all have a place and you'll see how the BCR makes money."

"Okay."

The pleasing burn from the aged scotch tickled the back of my nose as Mr. Marsland, who had told me to call him Adam, explained how the ranch was set up.

"I manage the ranch. I'm an employee under the owner, who visits occasionally but not often. We keep in touch through email and an occasional phone call. I employ four trainers and four stable hands—you'll make a fifth until Brian leaves for his master's degree. We're paid a yearly salary. I believe I already quoted you a level."

I nodded.

"We are employees of the Braided Crop Ranch. The ponyboys, the men who come here to be treated like animals, are actually members of the BCR. We operate as a private club. We have service members—the ponyboys—and guest members."

"I mean, I have seen some of this stuff online. I never thought I'd actually..."

"Encounter pony play in reality? Jensen, this is going to blow your mind." Adam looked me over, taking in my traditional cowboy get-up. "If your mind is open enough to take it."

I smiled weakly. "Here's hoping."

I knew my mind was open enough, but I worried my body would betray me every step of the way. Now the shock had worn off, and the scotch had mellowed my nerves, the appeal of the job began to come into focus.

I'd hoped to be privy to the benefits of watching some hot cowboys working around the ranch and getting down and dirty with some honest labor. But those faceless men of my imagination had been clothed and not voluntarily submitting to the treatments offered here at the BCR. I didn't know what those activities were exactly, but I could guess.

The situation was so strange and unexpected. I was a little surprised I took this stuff in so eagerly and adapted so readily to the thought of this new reality. *Go figure. I keep surprising myself.*

"Our guest members pay a yearly fee based on how often they want to visit. There's a well-appointed resort with twelve large suites facing the lake. The resort is open daily, but the ranch and stables are only accessible to our guest members on weekends. It's enough to attract a regular clientele who enjoy being pampered during the week and experiencing the unique nature of the ranch on weekends.

"If they only want to come twice a year, they pay the lowest fee. If they want to come for four weeks per year, they pay at the next level. Our blue-ribbon members can stay up to eight weeks per year, meals included. We pride ourselves on offering both a unique and elite experience," Marsland explained with pragmatic frankness.

I blinked, trying to wrap my head around the idea. "Okay. So, when they are here, what can they do?"

Marsland smiled. "You mean besides enjoy the beauty of the lake and the luxury of their accommodations?"

I smiled. I liked Marsland and the way he obviously enjoyed explaining how the BCR functioned.

"Ah, so, we have to obey certain legalities in order to stay in business. Our service members are not sex workers. Which means, our guest members are limited to observation only."

"A voyeuristic vacation like no other," Connor said, a dreamy look in his eyes.

I could believe it but I'd never realized places like the BCR actually existed.

"Exactly. Sometimes we invite them to watch the trainers put the ponyboys through their regular routines. Once a month we put on pony shows, in either the indoor or outdoor arenas."

My eyebrows lifted. "Pony shows?"

"Yes."

"If you stay, you'll see one in a few weeks," Connor added. He glanced at Marsland, then smiled at me. "The ponyboys show off their skills at various physical activities, and the trainers try to outdo each other. Very entertaining. And the outfits are a little fancier than the ones used on weekdays."

"But no sex, right?" I said, trying to understand.

Marsland blushed and gave a small laugh. "Well, not exactly."

Mother of God. Not exactly?

"Our trainers, being employees of the BCR, and our ponyboys, being members, can legally cross the line if it's consensual."

I sat up straighter. "So...the guests can pay to observe a trainer and a ponyboy..." I looked back and forth between Marsland and Connor.

Marsland held up a hand. "Engaging in various forms of dominance and submission, often to the point of orgasm. Not intercourse. Most of our ponyboys and trainers wouldn't be open to that kind of public display and intercourse isn't permitted between trainers and ponyboys, even if it's consensual."

"But...other kinds of public displays?"

"Sure. A certain amount of exhibitionism is a part of the experience for our ponyboys. We have contracts for each of them, containing detailed information on what they will and will not consent to. They have safewords they can use at any time."

"Jesus fucking Christ," Jensen said softly. This place was like a Disneyland for fetishists. It was fucking brilliant.

Marsland grinned. "What's yours?"

"What?"

"Your safeword. Jensen, if this is all too much for you, say so."

"It's not. It's not too much for me. I just—" I looked around the office at the ordinariness of everything and at Marsland and Connor. "I feel like I'm having a really intense dream."

"Dream?" Marsland asked. "Or kinky nightmare?"

I laughed. Marsland really was quite charming. I tipped my hat further back on my head and sat up straighter, licking my lips as I met Marsland's gaze. "Wet dream?"

Marsland stared at me. I threw him a wide smile and a shy look. I was embarrassed, and I felt like a total newb. I still wasn't sure I could...handle...everything. But I had to see this for my own eyes.

Connor laughed. "Wait until you see—"

"Connor, you should get back to the phones. I'll take Jensen around the stables," Adam said, flashing Connor a stern look.

"Yes, Sir. Thanks for the scotch." Connor stood and placed his empty glass on the tray with the decanter.

"Connor? Next time, make sure the email goes through, will you?" Adam said.

"Yes, Adam. Sorry."

"No worries. It appears to have worked out all right this time."

*

As we headed across the grass toward the large red barn, Adam ran a hand through the hair at the back of his neck. "Maybe we should start with the arena. Give you a feel for what we do here at the BCR. We can get into the specifics of your job later on."

"Sure," I said. It was a wonder I could talk at all right now. My brain felt like it was alternately exploding into fireworks and folding in on itself at the same time.

The scent of the dry grass, the dirt, and the wood of the buildings soaking in the summer sun reminded me of all the ranches I'd been to, except for one overwhelming factor. The pervasive and pungent smell of sweaty horses and manure was absent, and the lack of that familiar scent threw me. More than anything I'd seen or discussed in Marsland's office, that olfactory omission told me this was *not* a standard ranch.

My stomach felt tight as we approached a sizable barn, and I wondered at something so familiar feeling so threatening. There were no horses inside, or anywhere nearby, and the thought alone made my palms sweat and my head feel light.

Adam stopped in front of the large wooden door. He turned to me and raised his eyebrows. "Ready?"

I swallowed, hoping Marsland couldn't see how panicked I felt as I nodded. "Sure."

Adam laughed softly and opened the door.

The odor of human sweat and thumping of boots on hardwood assaulted me as we entered the brightly lit space before the sharp crack of a whip sliced the air.

"Five more rounds, please," someone ordered in a loud, confident voice that stroked over me like a firm hand. "Luke, if you don't keep your head up this time, I'm taking you for extra training after supper. Ben, you need to work on your foot placement, but you're coming along."

My heart thumped in my ears as we walked along the grey wood wall toward a bearded man dressed in jeans and a T-shirt, wielding a bullwhip in one hand and a riding crop in the other. For a moment, I became transfixed by the man's olive skin and the curve of his forearm as he hefted the whip. Then my eyes found the others.

I inhaled so deeply and suddenly I barely avoided swallowing my tongue. The photo in Marsland's album didn't do justice to the ponyboys in the arena. The accoutrements were slightly different, but the sight of the three almost-naked young men in Doc Martens, thick leather body harnesses and collars made my blood rush through my veins and my breath come quickly. Especially when I noticed they wore the same metal cages on their penises as the man in the photo. Also, like the photo, their muscular arms were held behind them, crossed over the small of their backs, in broad leather cuffs running from wrist to elbow and buckled together, forcing their chests out and keeping their backs straight.

One of the ponyboys turned his head to glance over and stumbled.

The handsome trainer cracked his whip against the floor. "Face forward. Keep your stride." He appeared to be of Middle Eastern descent with a neatly trimmed goatee and thick, arched eyebrows above deep-brown eyes. He was fucking hot.

"Kamal." Adam greeted the whip-wielding man. "How are they doing today?"

Kamal shrugged, gaze roaming his charges as they jogged around the arena. "Not bad. They're coming along."

Adam motioned in my direction. "Kamal, I'd like you to meet our new stable hand, Jensen Moriarty."

I forced my eyes away from the ponyboys and remembered myself. I yanked the dusty hat off my head and nodded at Kamal. "Good to meet you."

"Pleased to meet you as well, cowboy," Kamal said with a wink. "Welcome to the BCR." He looped the crop over his wrist and held out his hand.

Kamal's hand was warm and rough, his handshake firm and friendly. I tried not to let my gaze wander to the whip, but it was useless. Kamal noticed. "The whip is to get their attention, really. And a bit of a threat besides, although I'd never actually use the bull whip on them. Only they don't know that for sure."

I cleared my throat and let go of Kamal's hand, replacing the hat on my head. It made me feel better, more like myself, when I wore it. I needed the comfort more than ever in such strange circumstances.

Adam grinned. "Jensen is under the usual probationary guidelines to see if he fits in here and if he can do the job. He assures me he can. Even though he only recently became aware of what the job might entail."

Kamal raised a dark brow. "Oh?"

I felt my cheeks flush. "It's fine. I'm fine."

"There was a slight mix-up with the emails, and I might have neglected to mention during the phone interview that the BCR wasn't an ordinary horse ranch," Adam clarified.

Kamal blinked at Adam, looked at me, then barked a deep laugh. "So, you're a real cowboy? Not just pretending?"

I shrugged, wanting to run but standing my ground. Kamal must have sensed my unease.

"Sorry." Kamal peered at his charges, who obediently kept jogging the outside wall of the arena, but couldn't help stealing curious glances my way. "Well, the boys are gonna love this. A real cowboy to tend them. Don't you think, Marsland?"

Adam chuckled. "Oh, I imagine."

Kamal narrowed his dark eyes at me. "So, you thought you'd be looking after animals?"

I nodded curtly. "I did. I have a lot of experience with regular...livestock."

Kamal gestured toward the men in the arena. "They aren't so different. In fact, if you can treat them the way you'd treat an actual animal, with certain subtle differences, you'll keep them, and us, very happy."

I tilted the hat back on my head, watching the way the men moved gracefully in their restraints.

"What do you think?" Adam asked me.

What did I think? They were extraordinary.

I followed them with my eyes. "They're magnificent," I said finally, glancing at Kamal.

Adam laughed and patted my shoulder. "Yeah, you're gonna do fine here, Jensen."

Kamal grinned his approval. His eyes drifted down to my crotch. I glanced down at myself, then back up at Kamal. "Oh shit, sorry."

Kamal shook his head quickly. "Happens all the time with newbies. Means I'm doing my job and they—" He gestured with the whip at the ponyboys. "—are doing theirs."

"We pride ourselves on a very open and inclusive philosophy toward sexuality because our job is to satisfy the voyeuristic fantasies of guest members and the submissive fantasies of our service members," Adam said.

He leaned against the wood wall and shoved his hands in his pockets, watching the ponyboys. "You'll find, Jensen, your first few days here will be difficult, but in a good way, I think. In the regular course of your duties you will be in direct physical contact with the ponyboys. It is understood by our service members that in order to enrich their experience they will be on the receiving end of some very intimate physical care from our stable hands."

Intimate. Physical. Care.

I cleared my throat and adjusted my hat. "Right. Sure."

Kamal grinned. "They all have contracts, and there is a safeword they are free to use at any time. You will know of any hard limits restricting the intimacy of your care, although I can't think of any of our current members whose limits affect the stable hands. More so what they do with the trainers, which can be more extreme. But you'll find out soon enough."

My brain spun in circles and my palms sweated as I imagined what my duties might entail.

"Call one of them over, Kamal," Adam said.

My body vibrated with excitement and terror. Excitement at seeing one of the beautiful men up close and terror I would embarrass myself, and they would know how innocent I was, how out of depth I felt.

Kamal cracked his whip. "Luke! Come forward. The rest of you, take a break."

I took an instinctive step back as the blond-haired ponyboy broke from the group and approached us. God, he was something.

I couldn't keep my eyes from roaming over Luke's heaving chest, down his belly, over his captured cock and down his long, powerful legs, then back to his collared throat, where his Adam's apple bobbed seductively and his blue eyes gleamed with intelligence and curiosity.

I stared at Luke, and then out of instinct, removed my cowboy hat and nodded a greeting. Luke's broad lips curved into a smile before Kamal touched the tip of his crop to Luke's stubbled chin, forcing him to raise it. The smile vanished.

"Head. Up," he ordered. "If I have to put you in the brace again, you'll feel this crop on your beautiful ass. You hear me?"

Luke blushed. His gaze flew to me for a moment before moving back to Kamal as if drawn by some powerful magnet to those of his authoritative trainer.

"This is Jensen. He's a..." Kamal leaned in to whisper loudly in Luke's ear. "A real cowboy. He's used to breaking horses, so I'm sure a spoiled pony like you won't be much of a problem, hmm?"

I held my breath as the full force of Luke's intense gaze met mine. Luke's eyes were a deep ocean blue, which stood out against his platinum faux hawk. His features, except for the piercing sharpness of his intelligent eyes, were soft and boy-next-door handsome. Luke nodded in polite response to Kamal's question, but he didn't smile, which challenged me in a way that made my cock throb.

Kamal withdrew from his intimate closeness with Luke and stood aside, leaving a firm hand on the back of the ponyboy's neck as if to remind him of his presence.

"Why don't you give our pretty pony a pet, Jensen?" Kamal said.

Luke's whole body shuddered as something flashed in his blue eyes. A warning? Or a dare?

I licked my dry lips but couldn't think of a thing to say, mesmerized by the gorgeous creature in front of me.

"You're going to have to touch them, you know. If you're going to be a stable hand," Adam said, a smile in his voice.

I closed my eyes and replaced the hat on my head to take a moment to disconnect from Luke's gaze and gather myself. I opened my eyes with renewed intention.

I was the stable hand and Luke was the pony. My job would be to have hands all over these ponyboys, and as much as the responsibility excited me, it challenged me too. I could do this job. And I wouldn't be a slave to my baser impulses, no matter how much they wanted to rule me at the moment. They—Adam, Kamal, Luke and the rest of the ponyboys—needed me to be professional. And I would be professional if it killed me.

Fake it till you make it.

I took a step forward and regarded Luke with what I hoped was an assessing manner. I tried to pretend Luke was an actual horse in my care and did what I would do if it were so. I placed a hand on Luke's shoulder and squeezed gently, then ran my hand down Luke's arm to his wrist, where I circled it as if taking his measure. The man's skin was warm and covered with a sheen of sweat, but I felt a humming of energy beneath. He was electric.

"How old?" I asked, releasing Luke's wrist and bending to run a knowledgeable hand slowly up the man's leg from the top of his boot to his knee.

Luke made a huffing noise and struggled to stay still, exactly like a horse might, and I tried not to smile. Maybe this job wouldn't be much different after all.

Kamal nodded. "Twenty-eight. Healthy as a h—" His eyes met mine, and he tried not to laugh at his error. "Well, he's very healthy. A bit too headstrong for his own good, but we're working on his behaviour."

I straightened as I moved my hand along Luke's naked flank to the dusting of soft hair on his belly, where I laid my hand flat and looked upward, meeting Luke's gaze. I felt the power and the energy contained within this incredible specimen of a young man, and a thrill rushed through me. Luke blinked, eyes wide, and gazed back at me with something like respect. At least for a moment. Then he shook his head and snorted, moving away from my touch and closer to Kamal.

"Easy there, you devil. You'll stand for him in the grooming barn, or I'll hear of it and punish you for such bad manners, understand?" Kamal said, the hand on the back of Luke's neck tightening. "Understand?"

Luke coughed and nodded, his face the caricature of a sulky teen.

"Very good, Jensen," Adam said. "You have exactly the manner of a perfunctory stable hand the ponyboys enjoy and we demand. The more you can think of them as lesser creatures than yourself, yet still respect them in all the ways they deserve, the better you'll be."

Kamal snapped the tip of his crop against Luke's thigh, very close to where the ponyboy's penis swelled in its steel cage.

"Getting a bit tight there, Luke? You like our new stable hand."

Luke whined and shifted his feet, then let his eyes run over me as I felt an electric jolt go through me.

"Oh, shit," I couldn't help muttering as my hand instinctively came down to rub against the aching cock in my jeans. I blushed and let my hand fall to the side, embarrassed.

Luke's chest rose and fell as his eyes pierced mine with obvious interest and white-hot desire.

"Luke's a little pent-up these days," Kamal said. "You'll have to excuse him."

"Why? He not performing adequately?" Adam asked, looking critically over the blond ponyboy.

"Nothing I can't handle." Kamal grinned. "I've been giving him some motivation in the form of deliberate neglect of certain needs until he gives me what I'm after."

"I see. An excellent technique."

"I've always had good results with orgasm denial."

"Except he looks like he wants to fuck our new stable hand into the ground right now."

"Jesus," I breathed. "Christ."

A loud guffaw and a curse word broke the silence. Kamal turned and cracked his bullwhip in one fluid motion. "Enough! I expect you two to be able to stand in silence while I'm otherwise occupied!" he said, boots stomping on the wood floor as he marched over to the others.

"Both of you, turn and place your forelocks to the wall. Spread your legs." The men were quick to obey.

"You'll wear your tails for the rest of the afternoon. That should help you to remember your manners."

I glanced at Luke and Adam. Luke watched Kamal with interest as Adam stroked the ponyboy's blond hair absently. Neither evinced any surprise at Kamal's declaration.

Kamal threw the whip and the crop to the side and walked to a wooden table set up against the wall of the arena.

"Why not get Jensen to assist you? We'll see if he can handle the job. We might as well find out now," Adam said.

Oh hell no. What?

"Jensen, come over here, please," Kamal ordered.

Heart pounding in my throat, I took one last longing look at Luke and walked to where Kamal had opened one of the drawers of the cabinet.

Kamal took two objects from the drawer and placed them on a clean table beside the cabinet. Then he plunked a large jar beside the objects and opened the lid.

"Cover them with the stuff. I want these to slide in easily," he said, glancing at the ponyboys. "Well, as easily as possible, anyway."

I stared at the objects.

"You've seen a butt plug before, Jensen?"

"Sure," I lied, feeling out of my depth but determined to fake it. I'd heard of them, but never seen one.

Kamal passed me a box full of latex gloves, and I pulled two out. As I drew them onto my shaking hands, I watched Kamal do the same.

Then I looked at the objects again. "Are you going to—"

"Yes." Kamal said bluntly. "Hurry up. I haven't got all day."

I nodded, scooping a handful of white cream from the jar and coating one of the large plugs with the stuff, trying not to touch the handsome tail. They really were quite clever, and I could imagine what they would look like once inserted. When I'd finished coating both with generous amounts of lube, Kamal picked one up.

"Bring the other and follow me. I'll do one and you'll do the other. Part of your job will be preparing the ponyboys for special performances where they will need to be fully decked out. As you can imagine, these plugs aren't exactly comfortable, especially when the ponyboys are required to be active. But they look so very pretty." Kamal grinned at me as he moved to the nearest ponyboy and placed a gloved hand on his pale backside. "This is Ben."

I resisted the urge to laugh hysterically as I stood beside Kamal, holding a lubed butt plug horse tail. "Uh-huh. He's very...well-proportioned."

Kamal grinned as he slid the tip of the plug down the man's ass crack as the man in question made a whimpering sound. "Open for me, Pony."

If I thought too much about this, I wouldn't be able to continue. I had to distance myself from the reality of what I was about to do. Never in a million years would I have believed I would be called upon to insert a butt-plug horse tail into a complete stranger's ass, by another complete stranger, *during a job interview.*

I had to think like a stable hand and believe I was learning new skills as a handler of a very unique breed of human horse. Sure, the act was sexual. It couldn't *not* be sexual, considering I was attracted to men and here were two magnificent specimens of manhood, certainly. But at this moment, the two attractive men wanted to be horses, and who was I to deny them? This was their space, and I'd come into this environment unexpectedly and a little naively. But I wouldn't ruin the experience because I was too conventional to think outside the box.

Because I most certainly wasn't. I could see what was going on here, and I supported everything I'd observed. I certainly didn't believe there was anything wrong with the expression of a fetish. In fact, this fetish fascinated and aroused me, but if I thought about *that* too much, I wouldn't be able to function either. So, I watched Kamal's actions and pretended to be a stable hand learning a new skill, instead of the participant in a strange sexual ritual. Even though both were true.

Ben widened his stance as Kamal moved the tip of the well-lubed device to the wrinkled skin of Ben's anus. "Firm but gentle," he said, rubbing the nub against the man's hole and nudging steadily until the object began to push in. He kept up an even pressure as the rubber tip sank deeper and deeper into the man's backside. Ben gasped as the largest part went in and groaned as his hole closed around the neck of the flange, holding everything inside. The black horsehair cascaded from the pale globes of Ben's ass down over his muscular thighs.

Kamal removed his gloves and arranged the fall of hair carefully, tickling the delicate skin of his charge with deliberate intent as he did. "Very nice. Now go stand beside Luke and Adam."

Ben groaned as he straightened and walked slowly to the other side of the arena.

"Okay, Jensen. Your turn. While I'm sure you never had to do anything like this in your previous employment, you might as well learn what being a stable hand at the BCR is all about. And decide if you really want to be here."

I nodded. "Right. Sure." There was no way I was backing down, though this was the weirdest fucking job interview I'd ever had.

"This is Hunter. He's from New York."

"Hey Hunter. I apologize in advance if this bothers you at all. I'll be careful." I was as shocked as anyone at the calm and competent tone of my voice, but it reassured me I could do this job and do it well. I was still faking my comfort level, but I was determined to succeed.

The ponyboy named Hunter chuckled and stuck his ass out farther as if he couldn't wait to be the object of my inexperience.

Kamal nodded. "Nice. Okay, put one hand on his ass, so he knows where you are."

Hunter's skin was warm and comforting. Before Kamal said anything else, I repeated the trainer's actions and slid the tip of the plug down Hunter's crack until it rested against his pink pucker. I knew my way around a guy's asshole, at least, even if I'd never done exactly *this*. My breathing picked up as I carefully pressed the plug against the strong muscle.

Hunter sighed as the muscle yielded and the plug began to sink in. I kept a firm pressure, as I'd seen Kamal do, and managed to seat the plug smoothly while the muscles of Hunter's buttocks quivered in a fascinating way.

I looked at Kamal for approval and saw the handsome man staring at me in some surprise. "Have you done this before? Have you plugged a man before?"

I gulped and blushed. "Not exactly. But the technique seems straightforward."

Kamal let out a huge guffaw, turning to Adam. "I like this cowboy. I think he'll work out fine."

I found myself grinning as I removed the gloves and arranged the silky horsehair so the strands fell in attractive waves over Hunter's thighs. I patted the ponyboy on the rear as he backed away and admired my handiwork.

Kamal put a hand on my shoulder as he told Hunter to stand and join the others. He held a hand out to me. "Welcome aboard, Jensen. I look forward to working with you."

I took Kamal's warm hand, shaking firmly but feeling less confident all of a sudden. What had I gotten myself into? A lot of hard work and torturous arousal was in store for me over the next few weeks. I'd be jerking off three times a night at this rate if I could keep control of myself during my daily duties.

"Come on, I'll show you where you'll be sleeping, Jensen," Adam said. "Stable hands sleep with the ponyboys in the bunkhouse."

I had started walking toward Adam and Luke, but halted in my tracks. My eyes met the gazes of three handsome ponyboys as I stuttered my surprise.

"I'm—what?"

"Luke, Ben, Hunter, ten more laps around the ring please. Keep your knees up, especially you two with the beautiful tails," Kamal ordered as Adam led me out of the arena and shut the door behind us.

I suddenly felt light-headed and took off my hat, fanning myself and leaning heavily against the arena wall.

"You okay? I know this place is a lot to take in, especially when you were expecting something completely different."

I nodded, suddenly wanting to be alone. I cleared my throat. "Can I... Can I think things over? Or do I have to make a decision right now?"

Adam's forehead wrinkled. "You could take a walk up to the resort if you want. It's about twenty minutes along the path, and the site is pretty impressive. There's a café if you want to sit and have a drink before you walk back."

I felt relief wash over me. "Yeah, that would be fantastic." I needed a minute to breathe and assess the situation with a clear head.

Adam put a hand on my back. "You were like a natural in there, by the way. I do think you have great potential here. But I know this was a pretty big shock."

"I mean, yeah. For sure. But, honestly, my head is filled with what I've seen over the past hour and I need to sort it out before I make such a big commitment."

"I'm glad you're taking this offer seriously because our stable hand position is an important job and crucial to what we do here. It takes a certain kind of person to do the job well, and I think you really have the touch, Jensen. But you're the only one who can decide."

Adam showed me the path to the resort hotel and spa and assured me there wasn't anything kinky about the restaurant and establishment.

"Just a run-of-the-mill high-end hotel. One of about fifty in this neck of the woods."

I raised my eyebrow.

"Well, we needed something to make us stand out." Adam laughed. "Be back here in an hour or so and tell me what you've decided. I'll take you to the bunkhouse then."

"Why do the stable hands stay in the bunkhouse with the ponyboys?" I asked, curious as to the unusual set-up.

"Why does a real stable hand stay in the barn with the horses when one of them is ill or not-quite-right?"

"Well, to keep close and make sure the horse knows it's being looked after. Oh," I said, illumination dawning.

"We find the intimacy of bunking together facilitates and enhances the bond between stable hand and ponyboy. You all get to know one another as people, and the things going on in the grooming barn don't seem so unusual," Adam said. "Sometimes a—" Adam struggled to find the right words. "—more usual kind of intimate relationship develops between ponyboys, or between a stable hand and a ponyboy. We don't have any rules against sexual relations in those circumstances, in case you're wondering. But be careful. Some of the ponyboys can be jerks when it comes to personal relationships." Adam shrugged. "Like anyone else."

*

The paved path to the BCR resort began behind the main offices, skirted around the barns and outbuildings, and weaved through the forest until the landscape opened up beside a magnificent lake.

Welcome to the Braided Crop Ranch Resort and Spa.

Adam Marsland hadn't been kidding when he'd said the ranch resort was a high-end hotel. The large three-story building was painted a bright white with grey trim. A massive porch wrapped around the building, on which were scattered a number of deck chairs and small tables, with decorative lighting draped over the railings and hanging from the roof.

My eyes were drawn to the large beach fronting the lake, where numerous adults enjoyed the strong afternoon sun, dressed in swimwear and light clothing, stretched out on towels or on lounge chairs with umbrellas blocking the worst of the heat. The entire scene wouldn't have been out of place on the French Riviera; luxury and wealth seeped from everything.

I wandered up to the cheery café called the Saddlery, ignoring the feel of several gazes upon me. I opened the glass door and stepped inside, gazing around the pleasant open space of the small eatery filled with light from a number of skylights and large windows. The room was devoid of other customers at the moment.

"Afternoon," said a young woman with a ponytail, dressed in black slacks, a crisp white cotton shirt with vest and bow tie. "Welcome to The Saddlery. What can I get you?"

I removed my hat and approached the counter. "I could use a drink."

Understatement of the year.

"Absolutely." The woman smiled and looked me over. "We don't see too many cowboys here. Very refreshing. I take it you're being introduced to the ranch, and Adam sent you up here to check out the resort?"

"Yeah, something like that."

"You look a bit dazed. The first day on the job here can confuse the most seasoned kinksters."

I nodded. "I haven't actually accepted the job yet."

"Hmm. What are you up for? Trainer?"

I shook my head and blushed. "Stable hand."

The woman put down her cloth and extended her hand. "My name is Alison."

"Jensen."

We shook hands and I ordered a beer. As Alison poured my drink, she continued talking. "Ask me anything. I'm sure you're full of questions."

"So...I guess you know what goes on down at the ranch..." I said, wanting to make sure before I mentioned any of my concerns.

"Oh yes. I help with the pony shows."

"Oh. Okay then. Yeah. Well."

"Are you freaking out, Jensen? You look a bit like you're freaking out right now."

Definitely freaking out.

"You can tell?"

"Here. Drink this. Let's talk." Alison gave me the beer and poured a seltzer for herself. "Cheers."

We clinked glasses and I took a much-needed swallow. The Scotch I'd had in Marsland's office had dissipated eons ago.

"Oh fuck. What am I going to do?" I moaned, rubbing my face with my hands.

"You don't want the job?" Alison speculated, staring at me kindly with a smile.

I shook my head. "No, I do want the job. I just...didn't really expect...the kind of intimate activities...the job involves."

"What do you mean?"

"I thought there would be horses. Real horses." I mumbled, swallowing another drink. "I grew up in Alberta. On a ranch. An actual ranch, not a sexy, blow-my-mind-all-over-the-fucking-place fetish ranch. With grown men dressed as...dressed as..."

"Ponies."

"Right. Ponies. Goddamn sexy ponies."

Alison laughed. "Uh-huh. Damn sexy ponies." She wiped the bar down with a wet towel. "That must have been a shock. Sounds like quite a mix-up."

I grinned. "So, not only me then? They turn you on?"

"Oh, honey," Alison murmured, licking her lips and raising her eyebrows. "You'd have to be a pretty cold fish not to react to those beautiful boys prancing about in their harnesses, preening and currying favor with their trainers and the stable hands."

"I don't know how I'm supposed to...control myself. Pretty tough doing any job with a raging hard-on in your pants."

Alison laughed. "Well, I wouldn't know. But I suppose I can imagine."

"I'm not sure you can, actually."

"Look, the job will be hard at first—pun intended—but you'll get used to seeing and touching the ponyboys up close. You'll be amazed at how everything becomes business as usual in a few days. And if you remember you are doing a job and remember to be professional about your activities, you won't have any problems, Jensen."

"Yeah. Maybe." The job requirements still felt intimidating as fuck.

"Well, the only way you'll find out is if you try. Right?"

I finished my beer, stood the empty glass on the counter, and shrugged. "I just—"

"Look, let me ask you this. If you walk out of here, go back to Mr. Marsland, politely decline this position, and drive back to your little rental apartment in—"

"Ottawa."

"In Ottawa. Where you do all kinds of boring, normal chores, day in and day out, and you get a run-of-the-mill job that kills a little bit of your soul every day, do you think you might regret not giving this place at least a shot?"

"You have a point." She had a point.

"I've got plenty. I can tell you Marsland is a wonderful man to work for; the ranch is pretty fucking special, and the kind of men we attract who enjoy playing pony? They're pretty fucking special too. You should think very carefully before you pass this up."

Chapter Three

I walked back to the ranch with renewed determination and my decision made. I gave a nod to Connor as I entered the main building.

"Is Mr. Marsland free?"

Before Connor could reply, Adam came out of his office as if he'd been waiting for me. "Come on in, Jensen."

I removed my hat. "I've decided to take the job. But I have some questions."

Adam laughed. "I'm sure you do. Connor, can you put on some coffee?" He turned to me. "Do you drink coffee?"

I nodded. "I could use one."

"Perfect. Connor, we'll be in my office. Jensen has a few questions about the position but it looks like he's going to work out. Kamal is impressed with him."

Connor stood. "Kamal is impressed? Wow, that's a first."

As soon as I sat in the chair in front of Adam's desk, I started to feel better. I took a few deep breaths and wiped the sweat from my brow before replacing my hat. "Do you mind?"

Adam's forehead creased. "Hmm?"

"If I keep my hat on? It...comforts me. It's familiar."

Adam laughed. "I don't mind in the least. I think you'll find the cowboy hat attracts mostly positive attention here at the ranch. If my instincts are correct, and they usually are." Adam crossed his arms on the wood desk and gazed at me. "You were right at home in there, helping Kamal," Adam commented. "You have a steady hand."

I shrugged. "When I'm dealing with real horses, I have to. Animals can sense a lack of confidence, and they will exploit it."

Adam grinned. "Yes, well such a skill translates well to the human men you'll be dealing with, believe it or not. Confidence is everything. A sure hand elicits obedience and respect."

Connor came into the room with two mugs of coffee on a tray with sugar and creamer.

"Thank you," Adam said as Connor placed the tray on the desk and pulled up a chair. "Connor worked as a stable hand for a while. Until I needed to fill the reception position, and he decided he was better suited to representing the BCR at the front desk. Connor, maybe you can help answer some of Jensen's questions."

"Sure. Let me get another coffee."

Adam leaned forward. "We try to keep our employees happy here, Jensen. If you're not happy in the position you're assigned, we'll see what we can do. We don't like to lose good people."

I nodded. His words were...reassuring.

Connor came back and sat in the chair beside mine. "I didn't mind being a stable hand. But I've had issues with my back since I was a kid and the job is very physically demanding. I still help out now and then."

"The job *is* very physical, Jensen. Although if you're used to working on an actual horse ranch, I'm sure you're prepared for those types of demands, if not for anything else here at the BCR."

I pursed my lips and nodded. "I enjoy working up a good sweat. Cleans out the pores and does the heart a lot of good."

Adam stared at me as if he were considering something. "I like you, Jensen. I'm really excited to have you on board."

I felt a sense of welcome and appreciation I hadn't experienced in a very long time, and my cheeks flushed. "Thank you, Mr. Marsland."

"Please call me Adam. We'll be working together, and I can't have you being so formal."

"Thank you, Adam."

"You're welcome." Adam folded his hands and leaned forward. "So, we generally have four stable hands although you'll make five right now until Brian leaves. He'll be helping to train you. We usually have two on the day shift and two on the night shift, and we rotate the teams every couple of weeks. The day shift is responsible for grooming the ponyboys and preparing them for the trainers, dealing with any issues that arise during the day, and keeping the grooming center clean. The night shift takes over at four and also cleans the arena and the barns. Day shift is eight to four, night shift is four to midnight."

I nodded. "Okay."

"You'll be on the day shift with Brian to start. Then I'll put you on the night shift with Adrian and Enzo, so you can see what needs to be done to clean the facilities."

My brain spun, but I forced my thoughts to still and examined the questions I'd come up with earlier. "How many men—I mean ponies—I mean ponyboys, will I be dealing with?" I was still getting used to the terminology of this place.

"We house six ponyboys at a time for a period of six weeks. Then they leave and we have another six ponyboys come in. We find the six-week period allows our trainers to get the best out of the ponyboys and allows them to get what they need from the immersive experience. Six weeks is also a reasonable time frame for them to leave their regular lives and jobs."

I nodded. "So, the ponyboys I saw today... Are they starting or have they been here awhile?"

Adam's mouth twitched. "They're on their first week. But most of them have been to the BCR before. Like Luke. He's a regular."

I nodded as if this was a casual piece of information I needed and not something I had been desperately curious to know. So, I'd be looking after Luke for at least another five weeks. Something about the fact made me very happy. I noticed Adam watching me carefully.

"Luke is amazing. He's one of our best ponyboys," Connor interjected.

"Really? Because he was learning to keep his head up at the right angle," I said, looking from Connor to Adam.

They grinned. "Luke is not exactly a naturally submissive animal."

"He's not?"

"Oh no. It takes a firm hand to keep him in line, which is the reason I put him with Kamal whenever he's here. Few of the other trainers can handle him."

I was confused. "But he comes here for submission. Doesn't he?"

Adam grinned. "Oh, he comes here for submission. But he fights Kamal's dominance every step of the way. Right, Connor?"

Connor nodded. "I think his obstinance is what's so fascinating about him. And why he does so well. Most of our guest members like seeing a ponyboy get into trouble. Go figure."

"Luke is a brat," Adam said dismissively. "But at least he keeps the trainers on their toes."

I nodded. "Okay. So, most of the others—they behave themselves? I'm not sure I believe you. I mean, I saw—"

Adam turned to Connor. "He saw Ben and Hunter get their tails because they were being too loud while Kamal was talking to us."

"Ooh, lucky," Connor said, sipping his coffee.

"Anyway, that sort of thing is de rigueur here. You haven't seen a ponyboy actually punished yet," Adam informed him.

My breathing ramped up at the thought of what Adam might mean. "Well, I...okay, well, I see I've got a lot to learn. Can I see where I'll be staying? I have a duffel bag in my car."

*

Past the two red barns, down a gravel path snaking its way through the long grass at the edge of the heavy forest, stood a large grey building with the word BUNKHOUSE burnt into a slab of brown wood attached beside the door.

I followed Adam inside.

"This is the bunkhouse where the service members and the stable hands are housed."

I nodded, hoisting my duffel bag and looking around at the tidy space. The bunkhouse smelled clean and looked cozy. Bunkbeds lined the opposite walls of the small room. Straight ahead of me a ladder led up to a loft area where a few mattresses could be seen. Personal items were scattered on some bunks, and others were tightly made up and looked like no one had claimed them for a time.

"There's room for up to twelve people to sleep comfortably in here although usually there are only six ponyboys and four stable hands." He pointed past the last of the bunkbeds to the left. "See the door?"

"Yeah."

"Those are the showers. There are toilets and urinals in there as well. It's kept well-stocked with shampoo and all the necessities. We have cleaners in here every day to keep the showers clean, and they sweep and tidy the main room every few days."

I hadn't expected anything fancier than this. But I also hadn't prepared to be in close contact with so many kinky and athletic young men. I wondered at the wisdom of housing us all under one roof.

Something suddenly occurred to me. "Are there any female ponyboys here? I mean, pony*girls*?"

Adam shook his head. "Not here. At our sister ranch. The woman behind our ranch and our sister ranch decided it was safer and made more sense to set up two different clubs, one with male ponyboys and one with female ponygirls. Mixing the two together didn't seem wise and left us open to some legal vulnerabilities we didn't want to deal with. In a stable of only male ponyboys or only female ponygirls, we don't have to worry about unexpected biological events occurring, if you get my meaning."

"Ah. Yes, I see." Housing young men and women together might be tricky in all sorts of ways, and I admired the BCR for finding a solution. Why own one kinky ranch when you could own two?

"We normally only hire male stable hands for this reason. However, right now we do have a wonderful female stable hand with us. She stays at the house."

I felt tempted to ask if I could stay at the house too. But Adam had already been very accommodating, and I didn't need any more favors. I could handle the bunkhouse. I'd have to adapt.

"We have both male and female trainers. The trainers are not encouraged to fraternize with the ponyboys although they do perform some sexual functions as part of the job. These functions do not involve intercourse, which is strictly off limits. For the trainers."

"Oh." Adam had implied that as a stable hand I was free to pursue a sexual or romantic relationship with another stable hand or a ponyboy. My head began to swim again, and I needed to sit down.

"Anyway, you've taken in a lot of information, Jensen. I'm sure you're exhausted from the drive and from all you've learned today. Take some time to settle in. Supper is at the main house at six. I'll see you then." Adam turned to leave and then swiveled. "Oh, one other thing. I need your phone."

I blinked. "Huh?"

Adam smiled. "BCR policy. No one carries personal devices. Everyone's phones are kept locked up at the main house, and may be accessed whenever needed, but only within the main house."

I fished in my back pocket and handed my phone over. I'd been dying to call Mitchell, but that conversation could wait. I'd already said I would stay and give the job a try, which was what I expected Mitchell had wanted all along. I knew my friend wouldn't have recommended the place if he hadn't thought I would do well here. But I looked forward to chewing the guy out at some point for keeping all this a secret.

Adam took the phone and nodded. "The staff communicates with walkie-talkies," he said, tapping the black device hooked on his belt. "I'll have one for you when you take over from Brian. You won't need one before then because you'll be working under close supervision."

"Okay."

"There are too many security and privacy issues to worry about photos and videos getting out. Plus, the ponyboys like to fully immerse themselves in the goings-on at the ranch and prefer not to have the distractions of their home lives."

I nodded. "Fair enough."

"See you at supper."

I dropped my duffel bag to the floor, gathered my resources, and then held out my hand. "Thank you for this opportunity, Adam. I won't let you down."

Adam smiled and shook my hand. "I'm not worried. I think you'll fit in quite nicely."

Finally, I was alone in the quiet of the bunkhouse. There were two things I absolutely needed to do in the next hour. One, I needed to jerk off. And two, I needed to lie down. Then, if I could snag a half-hour nap, I'd be ready to face the rest of the day.

I set my bag on the nearest unoccupied bunk and headed for the door Adam had said led to the showers and toilets.

The huge room held six toilet stalls, eight showers, a bank of shelves containing towels and washcloths, and underneath them, benches to place clothes on. There was a long urinal trough against one wall and a row of sinks and hand dryers on the other.

The scent of powerful cleaning products assailed my nostrils as I walked to the urinal and relieved myself.

I imagined what it would be like to work here. By the time I'd finished and shook myself off, I'd already started to swell, thinking about what had happened in the training barn today. The ponyboy named Luke fascinated and aroused me, and I remembered helping Kamal insert the butt-plug tails into the two misbehaving ponyboys. By the time I'd stripped and stepped into the shower, turning the water on and reveling in the strong burst of heat, my cock had hardened and now throbbed for attention.

"Easy there," I murmured, taking my dick in hand and giving myself a few strokes. "You've been very patient." I noticed the bottle of body wash on the ledge so poured some into my hand and wrapped myself in slippery warmth.

"Oh God," I moaned, moving my hand slowly at first and then more quickly. The sliding pressure felt amazing and so needed.

Ever since I'd seen the photo in Adam's office, I'd been fighting this. Ever since seeing Luke in the flesh, caged in the steel device and collared. Ever since helping Kamal plug those two naughty ponyboys with their fine tails...

And I was coming, dripping onto the wet floor of the shower as I groaned with the release.

"Oh, fuck me. Fuck me," I whispered, leaning my wet forehead against the tile and continuing to stroke myself gently. "I am such a goner."

*

I was dreaming of handsome ponyboys when I heard voices.

"Shh. Don't wake him up."

"What's his name?"

"Must be the new stable hand."

"He gave me a 'hand' earlier."

Laughter.

My eyes snapped open. I stared up at several handsome faces looking down at me.

"Hey there, sleeping beauty," said one man with grey eyes and brown hair.

I pushed myself up to a sitting position. My hat, which had rested on my chest, fell to the floor. I bent to get it but the brown-haired man grabbed my hat and held it out to me.

"Sorry, am I in someone's bunk?" I asked, voice deep and husky from sleep.

"No, but you can come to mine if you want." The brown-haired man flashed me an inviting smile. "You don't recognize me, do you?"

I paled. "Oh hell. Did I—"

"Push a tail up my ass earlier? Yeah, you did. Quite efficiently, I might add."

The other men guffawed.

"Doesn't take much to put something up your ass, Hunter," a dark-skinned man with close-cropped black hair laughed, his white teeth contrasting against the deep brown of his skin.

"Shut the fuck up, Trey." Hunter turned back to me. "Hiya. I'm Hunter. We, uh...met...earlier."

I felt my cheeks flush. "Sorry, I didn't really see your face..."

The other men laughed loudly again. Someone said, "You didn't miss anything. His ass is prettier."

"They think they're pretty funny, y'know. When they don't have their harnesses on and their tails in," Hunter said.

I gazed up at the group of attractive men, in jeans and T-shirts now, watching me curiously. My position was both unnerving and, in a way, incredible.

"Fuck," I said.

"If you play your cards right," Trey winked. "You're awfully cute. Are you a real cowboy?"

"Well I—"

"If I heard correctly, he thought we'd be real horses. Right?"

I wondered for a second if I should deny this fact. But I hated lying, and what Trey said was the truth. I shrugged. "Yeah, I did. Thought I'd be mucking stalls and shoveling horseshit."

Hunter closed his eyes as if he couldn't bear to look at me. "Stop it, you tease. You're making me hard."

"I'm sure Hunter wouldn't mind being treated like a real horse. Likes to be ridden hard, anyway."

"Jesus Christ," I said.

Hunter opened his eyes and stared at me with some intensity. "True, I'm afraid. I'm a sucker for cowboys. You put the hat on, I'll let you do anything you want to me."

I stared at him, wondering if he was serious. When Hunter's deadpan expression suddenly vanished, and he erupted into loud laughter, I had my answer.

"Stop teasing the poor kid, H."

"Where the hell is Luke, anyway?" Trey asked.

Hunter stood up, gazing down with affection and good humor at me. He winked, and I didn't feel the least bit offended.

"Kamal kept him in for some extra attention."

"Yeah, I bet. Luke's been pushing all his buttons lately."

"That ponyboy is gonna get seriously boned by Kamal if he doesn't watch his sass. A guy can only take so much."

"No way. Kamal knows he can't fuck Luke. He can do everything else though. Over and over and over again until Luke's a quivering, shaking mess. Which is exactly what Luke wants."

Hunter nodded. "You should have seen Luke looking at this cowboy earlier. Like he wanted to eat him for dinner."

Trey laughed and gazed at me. "Well, kid, you better hope Kamal wears him out before he comes back here. We can't be responsible for Luke once he takes a liking to someone."

Hunter snorted. "Very funny. You're gonna scare the kid."

"I'm not a goddamned kid," I said, feeling awake now and overcome with indignation. "I'm fucking twenty-five years old. And I can look after myself, thank you very much," I said, standing up from my spot on the bunk, forcing the men to move back and give me some space. "And I can look after all of you too. Taking care of you is my job, right?"

"Oh, fuck, I hope so," said a short guy with a goatee, wearing a Sex Pistols T-shirt. "You look like you could give me one hell of a rub-down. Especially if you're used to grooming horses."

The door opened and someone came in. The group of men turned to look.

"Oh, hey, Adrian. Have you met the new stable hand?" Hunter asked, moving back so the man named Adrian could come forward. "This is Jensen... Oh shit, I don't know your last name," he said, the teasing tone gone as he tried to introduce me properly.

"Moriarty. Jensen Moriarty," I said.

Adrian, a tall man in sweatpants, runners, and a tank top, who looked like he'd just got back from a run, came close and extended his hand. "Good to meet you, Jensen. I'm Adrian. You'll be working with me and Enzo next week once Brian trains you on the day shift. These guys treating you okay? Let me know if they get out of hand. They can be a bit much before they get to know you."

I nodded, trying to act like I attracted this much attention on a regular day. "Nice to meet you. It's fine. They're fine."

Trey whistled. "Did you hear what he said? No truer word was ever spoken. We are fine! We are *so fine!*" He sashayed past me and headed up the ladder to the loft area, followed by the guy with the Sex Pistols shirt and goatee. The rest of the men dispersed to their own bunks, leaving Adrian and me together.

"So, how are you finding things? Did they get you working yet?"

"Not yet. I think I start tomorrow morning? I'm supposed to go to the main house for supper at six."

"Yeah, everyone eats there. Except the suckers who are on the night shift. Which is me this week and next. We bring something to the barn and take our half hour break in the middle of the shift."

"Oh."

Adrian lifted a hand over his head and grabbed the material of his shirt, pulling it up and off. "I need a shower before my shift starts."

Somebody whistled, and Adrian held his hand out with his middle finger up, without looking around. "Shut up, you assholes. God, you're a horny bunch tonight."

"Tonight?"

Laughter.

Adrian raised an eyebrow at me. "They can be a bit much sometimes. If they don't get any physical release during the day you can kind of tell when they get back here. The trainers work them up like crazy and then send them back here. In fact, I have a feeling Trey and Callum are getting busy up in the loft right now."

Oh, hell.

I tried not to look at the loft where suspicious rustling noises and muffled groans could be heard.

"Where's Noah?" Adrian asked of no one in particular. "Did he meet Jensen yet?"

"Not yet," a steady voice said.

It belonged to a slim, boyish looking individual in skinny jeans and a grey button-down who sat quietly on the bunk opposite mine.

"Noah! There you are. Come here and meet Jensen."

The young man named Noah stood and walked over to us. He gazed at me under his lashes. "Hi."

"Hi," I said, my voice sounding breathier than I'd intended. I cleared it nervously and tried for something deeper, manlier. Something not expressing as much of a *wow, you are superhot, and I want to fuck you* vibe. Because, holy hell, this man was hot. As hot as Luke, but in a completely different way. "Hi."

"Jensen, this is Noah. He's twenty-one, shy as shit unless he's in harness, and one of our best performers. He always gets an A+ in the ready-to-please department."

"Adrian." Noah blushed beet red and shook his head. "Don't embarrass me."

"Kind of hard to avoid embarrassing you, kid. You're fucking adorable."

Noah bravely raised his eyes to meet mine. They were sky blue and sparked with intelligence. "I hope the others haven't scared you off. We're not all assholes."

I felt myself warming to the shy man immediately. "Not a chance. I like a challenge."

"Then you'll do great," Adrian said. "Anyway, I gotta go shower. Maybe Noah can entertain you for a bit."

Noah looked at the floor. Noises from the loft had become more urgent, and it wasn't difficult to figure out what was going on.

"You might as well get used to the sex sounds," Noah commented. "The testosterone in this place is off the charts."

"Yeah, I guess." I looked down at my feet and tried not to listen to the impassioned noises from the loft.

"I like your hat, by the way. We don't get many real cowboys here."

I grinned. "Thanks. I feel a bit conspicuous. Maybe I should get rid of it." I turned the old hat over in my hands and wondered if I was capable of making such a sacrifice.

"Don't. The hat's a part of you. I can tell."

*

Noah had retreated to read in his bunk so I dug my copy of *On the Road* out of my rucksack and did the same. The noises from the loft had ceased after some rather loud exclamations, and now all we could hear was snoring.

The door suddenly creaked open and shoes scuffed on the painted wood floor.

I glanced up and felt my pulse quicken as I recognized Luke at the same time he came to a stop and stared right at me.

Noah glanced at Luke and looked back down at his book, not even offering a greeting. There was something off there, like Noah didn't think he was worth Luke's notice. Maybe I wasn't either. The man, now in street clothes, was fucking intimidating and incredibly good-looking. He stood out, even in this group of very handsome men.

But when I glanced at Luke again, I found the blond man still staring at me with an intense curiosity. As I locked gazes with the intimidating man, the corner of Luke's mouth slowly curved, and he nodded. "Cowboy."

"Cowboy" was a word I had heard often in reference to me during the day, but the way the syllables curled out of Luke's mouth and hung in the air between us was something else entirely.

I cleared my throat and stood, extending my hand. "Jensen."

Luke nodded, ignoring my hand, which dropped slowly to my side. "Luke. But you know my name."

"Yeah."

We stood there, not saying anything. I had no idea what I should say and felt uncomfortable under Luke's intense gaze. But the way he watched me aroused me tremendously.

"Did you actually come here thinking this was a horse ranch?" Luke asked, moving forward and collapsing onto my bunk. "Sorry, I need to sit. I just got off—" Luke looked down at the floor and smiled. "—an intense session." He looked up at me.

I could only imagine what he meant as I slowly sank down beside him. I wasn't sure if I should, but my knees were about to give out. Luke smelled like sweat and sex and leather. It was a heady mix, and I had to fight to keep my eyes from closing as I inhaled his odour.

"Yes," I said simply.

"Grooming horses what you're used to?"

I nodded. "Yes."

Luke licked his lips and grinned. "Well. You're going to have your hands full with us."

I opened my mouth but didn't speak for a moment. Then I said, unexpectedly, "Hopefully."

Luke raised his eyebrows.

"I like a challenge?" I continued.

Luke gave me a slow smile and leaned back against the bed post. "Mm-hmm. I think you like more than challenges."

We stared at each other, my heart going a mile a minute. I felt intensely drawn to this man and couldn't hide my interest. "Yeah...well...maybe you're right."

Luke glanced down at where my jeans had become tight and then met my eyes again. "I know I am." He stretched his long arms over his head and yawned, looking me over. "It's a good fucking thing Kamal took care of me before he sent me home today, is all I'm gonna say. It's going to be an absolute pleasure working with you, Jensen, and watching you discover every aspect of the Braided Crop Ranch."

"Uh-huh," was all I could say in response.

"Hopefully you'll enjoy sleeping under me." Luke lifted his hand and pointed upward. "Did you know this was my bunk?"

I shook my head, reaching for my duffel bag. "Sorry. I can find another one."

"Relax, cowboy. I only use the top. Mostly." He looked me over from my socks to the top of my head. "If I have a hankering to use the bottom, I'll let you know."

The double entendre just about had the top of my head popping off. I watched as Luke climbed the ladder and flopped down, groaning with pleasure as he stretched out.

Then my dazed eyes met Noah's. Noah smiled and winked, then mouthed, *He likes you,* and I shrugged, embarrassed and not really sure Noah's conviction was valid. Luke felt something for me. But was this feeling affection or something else? The idea both scared and tempted me.

And the answer might make my stay at the BCR even more interesting. Or a bigger challenge than I'd bargained for.

Chapter Four

Supper at the main house was a casual affair. There were a few grills going. Connor and another man were cooking burgers and dogs, and there were salads and buns laid out on three large tables on the back porch. The food smelled and looked like a regular country barbecue, making my belly rumble.

I'd walked up with Noah from the bunkhouse, finding the young man's unthreatening presence a comfort. Noah seemed happy to befriend the new employee and determined to put me at ease.

I heard my name called from the open door of the house and looked up, surprised to see Kamal leaning against the frame, holding an open beer.

"Jensen, come over here."

"Excuse me," I said to Noah, who nodded.

I walked over to Kamal, removing my hat and nodding. "Hi."

"Nice hat."

"Thanks," I said as I replaced it on my head. "This looks like a good spread."

Kamal nodded. "The guys treating you okay?"

I shrugged. "Sure."

"They're a little excited and nervous about you."

"Nervous about me?"

Kamal nodded. He winked at me. "You may not realize exactly what's in store for you tomorrow, but they do."

I looked down at my boots, blushing. "Oh. Right. Shit."

"You'll do fine. But you and the other stable hands will be in charge in the grooming barn, in case nobody's mentioned that pertinent fact. You have any trouble, you call me, or one of the other trainers."

I nodded, glancing over to the group of men who would be submitting themselves to my treatment tomorrow. Yeah, no wonder they were teasing me. Was their behaviour because I was new? Or did all the stable hands get ribbed when they weren't under the protection of the trainers? Was the teasing a natural defense mechanism for the men to take advantage of the close living quarters?

I cleared my throat. "So...what exactly are my duties when I'm on the day shift?"

I felt a warm hand on my shoulder and glanced around, to find myself staring into the vibrant green eyes of a small red-haired woman. "You come with me and I'll fill you in. You'll be working with me and Brian this week." She moved beside me and offered her small hand. "Olivia Muir. But you can call me Liv."

I found myself grinning without effort at the attractive redhead as I doffed my hat.

She was the second female member of the BCR I'd encountered, and I felt a good amount of relief. Thank God, there were a few women here. Adam had referred to some female trainers, and now I saw Adam speaking with a tall brown-skinned woman beside one of the grills.

I shook Liv's hand. "Jensen. Nice to meet you, Liv."

"Same. You're quite the celebrity this evening. News travels fast."

I blushed and shoved my hands in the pockets of my jeans after replacing my hat. "Celebrity?"

Liv took my elbow and steered me away from Kamal, who was now speaking to someone else. "Rumor has it you have more experience with four-legged animals than you do with the world of human pony play."

"Is that what it's called?"

Liv nodded, regarding me curiously. "Yeah. That's what it's called. Jesus, you *are* a greenhorn." She stared at me for a moment. "Are you kinky at all?"

I was taken aback. Here was the least intimidating person I'd met so far, yet she had put me on the spot.

I coughed. "I mean, sure. Yeah, I can be kinky." Can I? I certainly hoped so. I was about to get very kinky with a group of ponyboys tomorrow.

Liv raised her eyebrows.

I said the only thing I could think of, out of desperation. "I mean, I know my way around a rope and some knots." This was true. I'd never tried using those skills on a guy. But I couldn't deny I'd imagined roping a wrist or two to my bedposts.

Liv barked out a laugh. "Yeah, I bet you do. These guys would be all over the boy scout skills, by the way."

I blushed. "Anyway, I'm a quick study, and I have an open mind."

Liv stared at me, her green eyes filled with sudden humor. She laughed and clapped me on the back. "I think we're gonna get along fine, Jensen. Why don't you grab yourself a burger and come sit with me. I'll fill you in on a few things so you're not completely blindsided tomorrow."

*

"What would you be required to do in a regular stable?" Liv asked, taking a big bite of her burger and a sip of beer.

"You know, take care of the horses, mostly. Brush and groom them, exercise them, make sure nothing's wrong with them, treat minor cuts and bruises. And muck the stalls and keep them clean."

Liv nodded. "Okay, so, same deal. Only...you're dealing with slightly different animals."

Uh, right.

I raised an eyebrow. "Slightly?"

"They're not so different. You ever dealt with a stubborn horse, Jensen? Y'know, one who doesn't want to behave, no matter how nice you are?"

"Sure."

Liv gestured with her plastic fork to a group of men by the grill. "The blond, with the shaved sides. That's Luke. He's your stubborn horse. So, you use the same techniques you'd use on a stubborn horse. You let him know you mean business. You don't let him get away with bad behavior."

I chewed my cheeseburger with slow, thoughtful motions, then swallowed and licked my lips. "He's arrogant."

Liv chuckled. "He's arrogant as fuck. But when he's under my hand he'd better behave himself. And he does. Usually."

"Usually?"

Liv rolled her eyes. "Most of them are pretty sensible. But him? He'll put up a ruckus because he feels off that day. I don't think he even knows why he's so oppositional."

"Hmm." I stared at Luke, who glanced back and grinned at me before turning around.

"Holy shit. Did he smile at you?" She looked at me like I was a fluffy pink unicorn or something.

I could hardly believe Luke's smile either. "Yes?"

Liv grinned, looking between me and Luke. "Oh, Jensen. You are in a world of trouble."

"But I just got here. And I haven't even started doing the job yet."

Trey came out of nowhere and plunked himself down beside Liv. "Hey, gorgeous. How is my favorite massage therapist?"

Liv gave him an affectionate smile. "Simply lovely. How are those beautiful muscles of yours? Feeling good?"

Trey sighed, winking at me. "Very, very good. Thanks to you, Liv. Why does that bastard always work me so hard?"

"Careful, T. You don't want me to tell Michael that's how you refer to him, do you?"

"Oh God, Liv, don't fucking tell him. He'll run me ragged again."

"You know why he works you so hard, T?"

"Why, Liv, darling?"

"Because you look beautiful all harnessed up, working hard, doing his bidding. If I was a trainer, I'd work you hard too."

"Ah, Liv. You mean it?"

She leaned into Trey's broad shoulder. "I would. And then I'd reward you handsomely."

Trey quickly glanced at me, and I saw his brown skin darken. "Shh. There are uninitiated ears listening."

"Well, he's gonna learn soon enough, isn't he?"

I couldn't help watching the two of them closely. I was deadly curious and fascinated by their easy intimacy although I was sure I had been privy to Trey's efficient conquest of Callum an hour earlier.

"How would you reward me, Liv, darling?" Trey murmured, nuzzling into her neck and kissing her freckled skin.

"I'd turn you to the wall, wrap my hand around your big, black cock, and jerk you off so slowly you'd about die before I let you come." Her sweet, sugary voice saying those words made my cock twitch and throb.

"Oh, fucking hell," Trey moaned, dropping his forehead to her shoulder. "You little tease."

Liv giggled, flashing a smile my way.

I was hard in my pants again. I gulped, shifting on the bench, and took a bite of my burger. This place made me feel like a sixteen-year-old virgin.

"May I join you?" said a voice—deep and close by. Trey swore, turning away and trying to stand, except Liv took hold of his T-shirt and made him stay.

"Trey."

"Michael," Trey muttered, turning back to the table, pouting and sulking before picking up his burger.

"Michael, what?" the man said.

Trey spoke with his mouth full of meat. "Michael, Sir."

"Better." The man named Michael reminded me of a retired football player—big in the shoulders and upper body, slim from the hips down. His short brown hair had started to grey, but he looked like he could bench-press all three of us.

Liv giggled as Michael took a seat across from me and nodded. "You're the new stable hand, aren't you?"

I nodded. "Jensen Moriarty. Yes, Sir."

One corner of Michael's broad mouth flicked up. "You don't have to call me Sir. *He* does." Michael gestured at Trey. "He's being punished."

"Yeah, for nothing," Trey muttered under his breath.

Michael kept looking at me. "Trey, do you want me to march you back to the stable right now for another lesson in restraint?"

Trey's eyes popped wide, and he was quick to recant. "No, Sir. Sorry, Sir."

Then Michael waited for me to say something.

"I'm still trying to wrap my head around this place," I admitted.

"Yes, Adam told me you—"

"Thought I'd be looking after real horses. Yeah, that's the big joke around here." I was getting a little tired of having attracted so much attention to my innocent blunder. Couldn't they all give a guy a break?

Michael regarded me carefully. "I don't think your previous experience is a joke to the ponyboys. They're wondering what it will be like being cared for by a man who's used to dealing with large, unruly beasts." He took a large bite of his hot dog and wiped some mustard off his chin. "Will you be rough and unyielding, or gentle and soothing? Will you relate to them like you'd relate to a beautiful, dumb animal?" He smiled, glancing at Trey and running his tongue over his bottom lip with deliberate intention. "They're beside themselves to find out."

I coughed, almost choking on my burger. Trey shivered from his head to his feet, glancing at me and then looking at Michael. "You want another weiner? Sir?" Trey said.

"Oh, Trey, you sexy little fuck. I'll deal with you tomorrow. No doubt you've already enjoyed yourself and taken the edge off my lesson."

"I...what...come on, Michael. What do you think I am?" Trey looked genuinely offended. But both Michael and Liv raised their eyebrows at him. "Okay fine. Have it your way. You know I'm a horny little slut. I don't deny being one."

I dropped what remained of my burger into my lap by mistake and swore, standing to clean myself off.

Trey moaned, glancing at my crotch.

Michael gave Trey a stern look. "Stand down." He looked at me. "You watch out for this one. He'll convince you he's going to die without a hand job at breakfast, lunch, and dinner."

"Jesus," I said, suddenly feeling light-headed.

"You okay, sweetie?" Liv asked. "Maybe you should go to bed. You've got a busy day ahead of you."

I nodded, picking up my hat from the table and putting it on. "Not a bad idea. Glad to meet you, Liv, Michael."

Michael, Liv, and Trey looked at me as if I had ketchup all over my face.

Oh God, now what?

"What?" I said, so tired and wanting to be out of everyone's sight for the next twelve hours.

"You...uh...you've got the *good 'ole boy*, naive cowboy thing going on right now. The way you handle yourself is even making me wonder." Michael said slowly.

"Wonder what?" I asked, knowing I'd regret the question even as I asked it.

"Whether you're as competent as you seem. Whether you have the right touch. Whether this wasn't your destiny all along." He stood up and nodded. "And I can't wait to find out."

*

Walking back alone on the gravel path to the bunkhouse, I admired the beauty of the grounds, listening to the whine of the cicadas and the melodic song of the blackbirds as they heralded the evening light. The intense heat of early afternoon had dissipated, but the air still clung warm around me. My skin felt damp with sweat, but the solitude gave me the peace and quiet I needed after such a tumultuous day.

I wondered why I wasn't more shocked at what I'd discovered here at the Braided Crop Ranch. I had always been interested in the kinky side of sexuality, but I'd never had any opportunity to express more than a passing curiosity in any of my brief dalliances with other men. I'd never been in a steady relationship, and outside of the safe confines of an establishment like this one, I wasn't comfortable experimenting with strangers.

Everything about the BCR screamed safety and consent. The setup allowed people to have their most secret fetishes indulged and celebrated. Some might think this kind of sex play was a hair's breadth from bestiality. But I knew it had nothing to do with animals and everything to do with the submission of one human to another, the domination over a person's innate tendency to overthink, so a person could exist purely in their most primal form. And sex was very primal. Sex was perhaps *the most* primal urge, behind the tendency to violence and aggression. And to harness that energy this way, subvert it by treating the person as the animal they essentially were, seemed like a revelation.

I mulled these thoughts as I opened the door to the bunkhouse, listening to the creak of the dusty hinges. The silence welcomed me like an old friend. I tossed my hat onto my bunk and walked around slowly, even climbed the ladder to peek into the loft, to make sure I was, indeed, alone. Because there was something I wanted to do although I'd already succumbed to the need once.

After kicking off my boots, I lay on the bunk I'd claimed as my own and stared at the bottom of Luke's bunk, sliding a hand down to touch myself. I closed my eyes as I rubbed my swollen cock through my jeans with sublime relief.

"If I have to put you in the brace again, you'll feel this crop on your beautiful ass." Kamal's voice echoed in my brain.

And this: *"Getting a bit tight there, Luke? You like our new stable hand, hmm?"*

I pictured Luke in his body harness and collar, his penis bulging and vulnerable in the metal cage, his arms bound behind him.

Those goddamn harnesses. Made of thick, black leather and studded with grommets, they crossed the chest and back, circled the shoulders, and extended down the sides of the torso to attach onto a pelvic piece that looked like a leather jock strap without a jock. Two broad leather straps framed the ponyboy's buttocks and crossed just above the pubic bone. I had never imagined anything so sexy in my wildest dreams.

I undid the button of my jeans and pulled down the zipper. I slid my hands beneath the waistband of my cotton boxer briefs until my fingers wrapped around the hot pulsing flesh there.

God, I thought I might come thinking about Luke being disciplined by Kamal. What I would give to actually see that!

I stroked myself back and forth, thinking of other things I'd heard.

"I'd turn you to the wall, wrap my hand around your big, black cock, and jerk you off so slowly you'd about die before I let you come."

I groaned and stroked myself harder. I almost didn't hear the hinges creak as the door opened.

I froze. The frantic beating of my heart filled the large space.

I was in plain sight of whomever had come in. Still, part of me thought if I kept my eyes closed whoever was there would ignore what was going on and graciously move on to his own bunk.

So I breathed as quietly as I could, but I was already so close to orgasm I couldn't control my stuttering inhales. After several moments, I started to wonder if I'd imagined the noise.

I opened my eyes. Only to find myself staring directly up into Luke's bright blue ones.

My breath caught. I thought I might actually die. Not the *little death* of an explosive orgasm, but an actual, final death—of embarrassment.

Luke drank me in as if I were a pool of cool water and Luke a thirsty animal in the desert, and one side of his lip quirked up. "You know, you don't have to do that yourself."

My mouth opened. I tried to speak but couldn't form words. I clutched my dick for dear life and realized one or two more strokes, while I gazed into Luke's blue eyes, would have me erupting all over myself.

Luke looked around at the empty room. "No one else here, hmm? So, you thought you'd take the edge off?"

Still, I couldn't speak. Couldn't move.

Luke took over. "Take your hand out of your pants, cowboy."

I found myself obeying. I released my cock and slid my hand out of my pants, not sure what to do, my body a taut wire of expectation.

"Stand up."

I slowly sat, then swung my legs over the edge of the bunk, placing my stocking feet on the wood floor. I made myself stand to face Luke. We were almost the same height, although Luke was a fraction taller. I gasped softly as the friction of my pants teased me. I stood shakily beside my bunk, eyes on the floor, cheeks flushed with arousal and shame.

"Hot damn, cowboy. You are fucking hot."

"So are you," I said, voice almost a whisper. I sounded about sixteen. I cleared my throat. "So are you," I said in stronger voice, keeping my eyes down.

Luke reached out and touched the zipper on the open front of my jeans. "How old are you?"

"Twenty-five."

"I'm twenty-eight. So, you're younger than I am." Luke muttered, running his finger along the zipper. "And greener."

I couldn't think of anything to say, so I shrugged. And bravely raised my eyes to meet Luke's bold gaze.

The expression on his face ripped me apart. And so did the words he said next.

"Take off your shirt, cowboy."

I nodded, moving to obey, feeling like the air in the bunkhouse was burning me up. I undid the buttons of my best shirt and pulled it off, letting it fall. I remembered getting dressed in the morning, but that was a million miles away and an eon ago. Never in my wildest dreams did I imagine anything like this happening.

Luke looked me over slowly and licked his lips. I watched him press the palm of his hand to the front of his jeans.

"Now put your hat on."

Huh?

I stared down at my cowboy hat, then looked at Luke.

"You heard me. Do it."

Something in Luke's voice took all my self-direction away. He had secret powers, and I was a slave to them.

I swallowed hard. I reached down and took my cowboy hat from the bunk, putting it on and staring at Luke, saying nothing.

"Hold onto the rail. Both hands."

I didn't move. I was paralyzed again. I still couldn't believe what was happening.

Luke stared at me. He virtually vibrated with anticipation. "If you don't want to, say no."

My chest rose and fell with my excited breaths. There was no way I could say no because every part of me wanted this. Yet I appreciated his magnanimity. I slowly lifted my hands to clutch the wood frame of the bunk, wondering what Luke was going to do.

Luke let out an animalistic groan as he pulled off his T-shirt and dropped to his knees. His hands went to the opening of my jeans. He glanced up and when our eyes met, I thought I might have a heart attack if Luke didn't hurry the fuck up. I thought the anticipation might kill me.

"I'm going to suck your cock, cowboy. You want me to stop, say so."

I nodded, holding my breath as Luke's fingers pushed my jeans and boxers down so my throbbing erection bobbed free in the stuffy room.

Luke licked his soft lips as he eyed my penis like a ravenous dog looking at prime rib. My hips thrust forward of their own volition, so the head of my cock kissed his stubbled cheek and left a spot of moisture there.

"Sorry," I gasped.

But he smiled and grabbed my cock by the root, lifting his eyes to meet mine as he opened his lips and engulfed the head in his warm, wet mouth.

Oh, mother of God!

I cried out—a reflex sound of surprise and pleasure—as my eyes widened. I lost myself in Luke's blue gaze as his talented tongue moved over my glans, slowly, savoring every curve.

I groaned, holding the bars of the bunk for dear life and praying no one else would come to the bunkhouse in the next few seconds. Because that was all it would take. I felt my balls draw tight as Luke wrapped a hand around me and plunged down again.

I tried to stutter a warning as my body took over, but only groaned as I came epically in Luke's mouth, body jerking, cock spurting endlessly, hands gripping the rail for dear life. My eyes closed as Luke kept going, sucking every last drop from me.

"God, I'm sorry," I muttered finally, panting, watching my wet cock slide from Luke's beautiful lips. "I couldn't help it." I'd come fast as a fucking teenager and had not given the other man any warning at all.

Luke gazed up at me, a satisfied look on his face, lips gleaming with the remnants of my release, eyes blazing a heat that turned the air in the bunkhouse Arctic cold. He cocked his head to the side. "What are you sorry for, cowboy?"

I blinked at him. My mouth dropped open as Luke wiped semen from his chin, then snaked his tongue out and licked my softening cock from root to tip, making it jerk and quiver.

He stood up slowly, standing in front of me, eyes roaming over me again, and smiled. "I like the way you taste."

I didn't know what to do. I was still gripping the frame of the top bunk, my chest moving up and down as my breaths evened out. I wasn't sure I could let go. That bar was the only thing keeping me upright.

"Oh, fuck yes. Don't move, cowboy. You look like a goddamn jerk-off fantasy," Luke said, undoing his pants while I watched. He dug his very hard and erect cock out, gave it a few pulls, and aimed the thing at me.

Suddenly, I gathered my wits and stared right at Luke—in challenge. "Go ahead."

Luke's eyes widened. Then the corner of his mouth quirked up.

"Oh, cowboy, I intend to. I'm gonna come all over that belly and cock of yours if it kills me. And it might."

I groaned again as Luke spit into his hand and gripped himself, stroking and pulling, closing and opening his eyes. His hand moved faster and faster.

"Oh God," I gasped. I felt renewed stirrings of lust as I watched Luke's eyebrows knit together, his mouth drop open, and his cock shoot streams of white onto my bare belly.

Luke groaned as he came, eyes closing, hand moving on himself, milking the last drops from his spent cock.

I gazed down at the liquid on my belly and felt my cock twitch with interest. When I dared to look up, Luke's eyes were open, and he was staring at the mess he'd made.

As I watched, Luke reached out and fingered the warm liquid, rubbing it gently into my skin as if his spunk was expensive lotion. "Fuck, what am I gonna do?"

I didn't know what he meant. Did he mean about the mess? Did he mean he was going to do something else to me?

I couldn't help myself. I let go of the rail with one hand and reached down, circling Luke's wrist and bringing Luke's hand to my cheek.

Luke's eyes widened. His lips parted as I rubbed his wet fingers over my stubbled chin, my cheek, and then my lips. The smell of Luke's semen filled my nostrils and made me giddy. I guided Luke's hand down over my throat and chest, to my belly where the rest of Luke's spunk had claimed me.

"God," Luke sighed as a remnant tremor passed through him. "How am I going to keep my hands off you?" Luke whispered as if I had the answer to that astonishing question.

"Don't keep them off me. I want them on me. All the time." Truth.

Luke smiled a slow, sweet smile at my words. He moved close, his wet fingers sliding up to gently clasp my chin as he bent his lips to mine.

I was surprised but opened my lips under his gentle assault, welcoming Luke's tongue and the pungent scent of his release.

Too quickly, he pulled away. He used his dry hand to fix my hat where he had knocked the brim askew and gazed into my eyes sadly. "But I'm a ponyboy, and you're a stable hand."

"But," I protested. "But when you're not being a ponyboy..."

Luke turned away, and it felt like a warm blanket had been pulled abruptly from me.

He shook his head slowly and tucked himself away. "You're not gonna want me after tomorrow. You're gonna see all the other sexy ponyboys doing their thing, the ones who don't cause a fuss and listen to their trainers and prance around happy as shit and thrilled to submit. You won't want to deal with me after you see them. You'll have your pick of them all, cowboy; you wait and see. You won't want me anymore."

I wanted to say his declaration was bullshit. That I already felt more for Luke than for anyone else I'd met at the ranch. For anyone I'd met in the past *year*.

But Luke had already gone. He'd opened the door and left, shutting it behind him, leaving me still holding the rail with one hand as my belly dried and the pleasure of Luke's passionate assault faded.

Chapter Five

I stood there for several minutes, trying to figure out what had happened. My naked arms folded around my chest. I felt rejected even though Luke's admiration had been obvious.

The absurdity of my situation had me feeling unsteady. I normally picked things up fast and paid attention to details. But because I'd not been prepared for any of this, I had a difficult time gaining my equilibrium.

Niggling doubt crept into my brain. I did up my jeans and put my shirt back on, hands trembling and heart trying to settle itself after being ripped open and sucker-punched by a guy with blue eyes and a narcissism complex.

I looked at the duffel bag at the end of my bunk, contemplating how I would feel if I left now. The entire experience would seem like a dream. A crazy, horny, wet dream I'd stumbled upon like the neophyte I was. I hadn't imagined a place like the Braided Crop Ranch existed.

I went as far as grabbing the handles of my bag and hefting them to my shoulder. Then I became conscious of the sticky skin of my belly where Luke's release still marked me. I needed another fucking shower. Maybe I'd shower first and then leave.

I put the bag down, knowing I wouldn't go. My outright curiosity, my love of a challenge, my complicated feelings about Luke and the other ponyboys, all of it was too fascinating and goddamn fucking arousing to abandon. I had to see this through. I needed to see if I could handle this unexpected job. Needed to see if I could be as good a stable hand to a group of human ponyboys as I had been to the real horses I'd always cared for.

And I wanted to see exactly what being a human ponyboy was like.

The evening hadn't begun to wane. Hopefully, the others would hang out at the main house for another hour or so and I could shower in private. I'd clean myself quickly and go to bed, though I might not be able to sleep.

I stripped to my boxer briefs and brought a clean pair to the showers, hanging them on a toilet stall partition while I turned on the warm spray and ducked beneath. The water felt astonishingly good on my sweaty skin, and I sighed, letting the rivulets trickle over my face as I soaked my hair.

I squeezed some shampoo into my hand and washed my hair, wondering if I should've gotten a trim before coming up yesterday. My ash brown hair was getting long and curling at the edges where the sides grew past the tops of my ears and the back reached the collar of my shirt.

I'd told my friends I'd be out of touch for a while, that I was going away to clear my head and get back to some old-fashioned manual labor. I needed a break from everything, from the meaningless routine of my life. There wasn't one person I'd actually started to miss, except maybe Mitchell. And missing him was tied up with a small sense of betrayal. Or had he saved me? Maybe he'd figured I could do with a crazy adventure. Maybe he knew me better than I did.

Well, there was nothing I could do about my hair now. And why would I think to make myself pretty for a bunch of livestock? I found myself grinning. The mix-up was pretty funny, all things considered. No wonder I was the talk of the ranch tonight.

I'd surprised them all by staying. And damn if I was going to give them the satisfaction of seeing me leave with my tail between my legs.

I rinsed my hair clean and lathered up with a body wash smelling of fresh hay and sunshine. Was the scent intentional or a happy accident? At any rate, I liked it. I was already getting hard again. This place was doing crazy things to my libido. Not that I'd been slacking in the jerking-off department. I orgasmed once a day on average and sometimes more. This would make number three, which wasn't so unusual. Maybe getting off would help me sleep.

I glanced at the door to the showers, listening carefully for any noise in the main bunkhouse. I didn't hear anything, so I wrapped a soap-covered hand around my swelling cock and teased myself, thinking of Luke's mouth on me and remembering Luke's cock spurting fluid on my belly.

It didn't take long for me to come, and I wondered if I would ever be able to stave off an orgasm again. I had no control, faced with the blatant sexuality of this place. Putting a hand on the wall opposite me, I enjoyed the remnant shudders of my release as the water washed my thin spunk down the drain.

Then I noticed movement out of the corner of my eye and turned.

Not Luke this time, and I couldn't decide if I was disappointed or relieved. Standing by the entrance to the showers was Noah in his boxer briefs with a towel in hand, as taken aback as I was.

"Sorry. I didn't think anyone had come back yet," Noah said, his eyes travelling curiously over my naked form.

"I'm all done," I grinned, turning off the taps and grabbing the towel I had placed nearby. I dried my hair and then swiped the towel over my body quickly, grabbing my briefs and pulling them on. When I looked up, I noticed Noah was still there, watching me.

I nodded politely and went to move past when his hand came out and gently wrapped around my damp bicep. Similar to when Luke touched me, or, let's be honest, pinned me with his sex stare, my body lit up like tiny fireworks. I swear there was deep, dark magic going on here.

"The bunkhouse takes some getting used to," Noah said quietly, pushing his briefs down and stepping out of them.

My breathing quickened as I glanced over Noah's slim, swimmer's body and imagined him in a ponyboy harness and collar.

"I'm still getting used to this place." He released my arm and moved forward, turning on a showerhead and ducking under the spray

I stood, mesmerized, watching the hot water course over Noah's body and pool at his feet.

"Thanks," I said, genuinely grateful. Because, unlike Luke, Noah appeared genuinely kind and thoughtful.

He nodded and grabbed the shampoo. "Good night, Jensen. Sleep tight."

I wondered if I would sleep at all with the memories of slick, muscled ponyboys and Luke's eager mouth.

*

Sometime in the late evening after everyone else had come in, I heard Luke enter the bunkhouse. I pretended to be asleep, but I slit my eyes enough to see what he was doing. To my surprise, instead of using the straight chair nearby, he sat on the corner of my bunk, right by my feet under the blanket, and bent to untie his shoes. Even though the room was dark, strips of moonlight kissed the floor and the walls, coming in through small gaps in the curtains. I could see well enough.

I had noticed the ponyboys only wore Doc Martens in the stable and arena. When they were in street clothes, they wore either runners or flip flops. Luke had on a pair of black-and-white Vans like an urban skater boy. And maybe that's exactly what he was when he wasn't at the ranch.

He took them off, while my heart beat a mile a minute, kicked them under the bed, and sat there.

I pretended to be asleep although I was hyperaware of everything. Luke's hand drifted over the bedclothes along my calf and rested gently on my knee. I stiffened all over, wondering what would happen next. But then his hand was gone, and I heard him climb the ladder to the top bunk.

Had I expected him to kiss me again? Maybe. I'd hoped for more. But I should have known better.

My heart beat frantically for a good thirty minutes before I decided Luke wasn't going to do anything but go to sleep. It took me forever, but I drifted off and dreamed of blue eyes and warm tongues.

*

I'd been warned mornings started early at the bunkhouse.

The sun was barely up when, through a haze of sleep, I heard rustling and voices as the men prepared for their day.

I was tired, and since it seemed as if I'd only just gone under, I really wanted to stay asleep. Rolling over to face the wall, I pulled the blankets over my head. I needed another couple of hours.

"You gonna wake him up, Luke? The kid was moaning all night; what the fuck did you say to him?"

"I didn't say anything. He must be looking forward to getting a good look at the inner workings of the BCR. I'd be moaning too."

"Fuck off, Luke. Pretty sure you're so jaded by now nothing gets you off but Kamal and the crop."

"Yeah? Well, don't knock the crop till you've tried it, T. Kamal uses a riding crop like an extension of his cock. If he could beat me with his cock, I'm pretty sure he would."

"Fuck, listen, he's moaning again. He's not gonna last four hours in the stables. They'll be mopping his spunk off the floor."

There was laughter and then I felt the blankets ripped off me. The cool morning air of the bunkhouse shocked me into flipping over and glaring at the men surrounding me.

Luke stood closest and had obviously been the one to uncover me.

"What the fuck are you doing?" I asked.

"You've got to get up, cowboy. Don't you have to be at the grooming barn by seven thirty?"

I resisted the urge to cover myself because I was lying there with a morning erection in nothing but snug boxer briefs. Did I have to be at the grooming barn by seven thirty? I couldn't remember.

"Nobody told me." *Or had they?* "What time is it?"

"Time to get up. Six."

"Six o'clock? AM?" Jesus, it was earlier than I'd thought.

"You said you worked as a regular stable hand. Pretty sure you have to be up bright and early to do that job. Maybe you're all talk. Maybe you haven't had any experience with horses." Luke said.

"It's been a while." I rubbed my face with my hand, feeling the day-old stubble and wondering if I should shave. "And I hardly slept last night."

The other men had dispersed to get on with their preparations, but Luke stood there watching me. His gaze was unnerving but, at the same time, reassuring.

"You were making a lot of noise," Luke said.

"Sorry. I snore."

"I'm pretty sure it was moaning I heard, like Trey said." Luke sat on the edge of my mattress. He was wearing a pair of grey sweats and a black T-shirt. His feet were bare.

He looked around to see if anyone was near. Noah's bunk and the one above had been neatly made, and their owners were nowhere to be seen.

His eyes returned to mine with a mischievous glint. "What were you dreaming about, cowboy?"

Heat flushed my cheeks and my cock twitched. "Nothing."

Our eyes held for a long moment. Then Luke's gaze flicked down to my crotch and back up. "You want me to take care of that for you?" he whispered.

I coughed, unprepared for Luke to say anything so direct. I wished we were alone so I could say yes.

"Uh, not right now." I glanced toward the other end of the bunkhouse where the men were moving around, getting dressed, etc. "I'm not much of an exhibitionist."

Luke smiled and licked his lips. "What a shame. Because I am. In fact, you'll find most of us ponyboys are. I guess that's why we're here, right?"

My chest rose and fell with my breaths, and now I wanted Luke to leave so I could get my body under control. "I guess."

Luke stood up and covered me with the blankets again. "Don't be too long. You don't want to be late on your first day."

Chapter Six

The grooming barn sat about thirty meters away from the arena, slightly smaller but painted the same bright-red color. All the buildings were so clean and new. They looked like horse barns but with no smell of hay or manure, or animal. It was taking me a long time to acclimate.

When I got to the nearest door, I grabbed the metal handle and pulled. Three of the men from the bunkhouse were right there, in the act of undressing.

"Wrong door, cowboy," Trey said.

Noah regarded me with an indulgent smile. "Stable hands go in the other entrance. Marked door's around back."

"Thanks," I muttered, flustered, trying not to stare at Noah. God, he was cute.

I closed the door. Only then did I see it was marked PONIES. Would I ever get used to this place?

The other door marked STAFF was around the other side of the building. God, I could be such an idiot. I took a deep breath, and pushed this door open a little warily, in case I came upon anything else unexpected.

This side of the grooming barn looked spacious and airy, with wide polished pine boards over most of the floor. There was a tiled section at the far end with three evenly spaced showerheads and a narrow doorway to the changing area I'd unwittingly stumbled upon earlier.

As I stood there, taking this in, Callum came through the doorway completely naked and walked calmly to stand beneath a showerhead. He winked at me before crossing his hands behind his back and inclining his head. Although I'd expected this to happen, the sight of a naked man in my vicinity was a shock to the senses.

"Good morning, Jensen."

I tore my gaze from the naked man in the shower stall and met that of Liv, whose eyes sparkled with amusement. She leaned against the corner of a broad table, dressed in black leggings, flip flops and a tank top. "Did you sleep well in a bunkhouse full of barely contained testosterone?"

I removed my hat politely, rubbing the edge of the brim with nervous fingers. I nodded. "As well as can be expected, I guess."

Liv grinned. "Yeah. I'm happy I get to miss all the shenanigans and dick jokes. They're much better behaved here."

I tried to concentrate on Liv as Trey and Noah came through the doorway, also naked. Noah shot me a sweet smile before putting himself in place.

"They're such good ponyboys," Liv cooed.

They sure were pretty. The Braided Crop Ranch knew how to pick attractive men to play ponyboy; that was for damn sure. The BCR wanted to attract paying guests to watch the spectacle and their ponyboys needed to be fit and healthy in order to fulfill the physical demands of performing. Whatever the performances entailed, they would probably be similar to a regular horse show. Running, jumping, pulling carts etc.

I decided I should stop trying to imagine the ponyboys I knew doing those things.

"You can put your hat on the table there. Your jeans are fine for today, but you'll probably want to wear some shorts and flip-flops when you're here. I can guarantee you're going to get a little wet and more than a little dirty. And though it's air-conditioned in here, it gets hot when we're working."

I nodded, reluctantly removing my hat and placing it on the table. I'd packed lots of jeans and T-shirts, but no shorts or flip-flops. I'd grown up wearing jeans and boots all through summer, and it was a tough habit to break.

"For today, you'll have to take off your boots and go barefoot. Everything is cleaned regularly by the guys on night shift, don't worry. But be careful not to slip."

"Okay," I said, leaning over to take off my boots and socks. I spent a few seconds rolling the sleeves of my blue-checked cotton shirt.

The stable hand entrance opened as a man with shoulder-length blond hair wearing flip-flops, bike shorts, and a long T-shirt came into the room with a flashy grin and abundant energy for so early in the morning. "Hey, Liv, sorry I'm late. I was off-site last night."

"No problem. We're just getting started. Brian, meet Jensen. Jensen, Brian."

Brian didn't notice the three men standing motionless in the shower area. I hoped I never got so used to the ranch I didn't even glance at naked men anymore.

"You must be my replacement!" he said, moving forward and offering his hand. "Welcome to the BCR."

I stuffed the socks I'd removed into my boot and shook Brian's hand. "Yeah." I offered a hesitant smile.

Brian glanced at Liv, who shrugged.

"Usually, the stable hands are more excited on their first day. Hard for them to keep their hands off the livestock." Brian waggled his eyebrows.

"Jensen's a bit of a wild card," Liv said. "He didn't realize the BCR housed human ponyboys for sex play."

Brian's face became the picture of confusion. I wanted to turn around and walk out. Instead, I bent to roll up my jeans.

Liv explained. "He thought the BCR was a regular horse ranch."

Brian stared at Liv, then looked at me. I'd finished with my pant legs and stood awkwardly in my bare feet, rubbing the back of my neck.

"Well, fuck me. That's a new one."

"I can do the job," I stated, schooling my expression into one of good-natured determination. "Just show me how."

I might look like a hick, but I wanted to surprise my co-workers with the skills I knew I possessed. I mean, I could gentle a horse in about three seconds and make the animal behave for me. Why not a man?

"Okay," Brian said. "You'll do."

"Jensen," Liv said. "See the whiteboard on the wall?"

I lifted my eyes to where she pointed. "Yep."

"You want to look up there first thing when you come in here. The trainers let us know how they want each ponyboy to be turned out on a specific day."

Each of the ponyboy's names was written at the top of a column. The current date was written underneath, to the left, and beside the date under each ponyboy's name, were instructions.

Performance gear xcpt bridle was written under all the ponyboy's names for this date.

Liv and Brian ran through a list of what we'd be doing for the ponyboys this morning. "We always start with a rubdown and wash in the showers. The ponyboys are expected to douche at the bunkhouse first thing in the morning, so they need to be cleaned well before the trainers deal with them. Today they want them fitted with collars, body harnesses, cages and tails. The whole shebang, basically, except for bridles."

Brian lifted something up to Callum's mouth. "We always use ball gags in the grooming stables. Open."

Callum opened his mouth so Brian could place the black ball gag between his teeth. "Good boy," Brian crooned, fastening the straps behind Callum's head. He touched Callum's wrist. "Arms up. Jensen, come over here."

I moved forward as I watched Callum stretch his arms towards the ceiling. Brian grabbed a pair of cuffs hanging there, which I hadn't noticed before, and fastened them around the muscular ponyboy's wrists.

Okay, well, restraints are efficient. And handy.

"The gags help them get into the headspace for the rest of the day."

Liv walked over to Noah while Brian placed the young man's gag and fastened Noah's slim wrists to the ceiling. I watched closely, trying to focus on the technique and not on Noah's tantalizing form.

Brian then placed Trey's gag and stepped back, observing the three bound men. "Dammit. I am sure going to miss this. Okay," Brian said, looking at me, "I'll do T's left wrist and you do his right."

I had to mentally shake myself out of the trance I was falling into and concentrate on what Brian was saying. I moved between Callum and Trey and helped Brian attach the man's wrists to the ceiling. I tried to ignore the three semi-erect penises, waving free and ready at the moment.

But I soon had to look at them while Liv and Brian coaxed them into the steel cages, snug enough to keep them from becoming fully erect, but loose enough so their semi-hardness became a tantalizing visual, and the metal ring around their testicles kept them high and tight.

Seeing the three men caged and swelling through the bars was enough to give me a pretty good erection of my own.

"These can be tricky. I'll have you put one on Callum tomorrow, but we're a little behind this morning," Brian said cheerily. "Though they are expected to shave their faces at the bunkhouse before their shift, we shave this area every few days because pubic hair caught in the bars can be painful."

I pointed at the devices. "I've never seen anything like that before."

Brian grinned. "Well, besides looking amazing, these help the trainers maintain control. We always put them on, but the trainers can remove them whenever they want. The ponyboys—well, most of them—do as they're told, hoping the cage comes off sooner rather than later."

My mind tried to wrap around this concept while my body let me know exactly what it thought about the whole idea of trapping a man's genitals to motivate him to behave. I gulped and nodded. I figured I'd be introduced to many things I'd never seen before here at the BCR.

Liv gave Noah a soft pat on the backside, then turned on the showerhead above him while Brian did the same for the others. The ponyboys sighed and tilted their heads back under the running water, enjoying the sensuous feeling.

I couldn't help staring at the three gagged men, with their arms extended, genitals captured in the steel cages, and hot water running over their athletic bodies, while I tried to get my own unruly cock under control. Thank God I had jeans on today. What would I do when I only had a pair of athletic shorts on in the grooming barn? Maybe they sold cock cages in the gift shop, and I could get one for myself.

"Here, you work with Callum today. He won't mind an unpracticed hand."

Liv chuckled. "Knowing Callum, he'll love it."

Brian laughed and passed me an oval loofah with a strap on the back for my hand. "Oh definitely. Okay, Jensen, now loofah the crap out of him, staying away from his delicate bits, of course. We'll do those later with a soft cloth."

Following Liv's lead, I poured a generous amount of body wash over Callum's wide shoulders that dripped down his body, spreading over him while I soaked the loofah in the hot water before I pressed it gently against his broad back.

Callum gazed at me with wary brown eyes and shifted, giving me easier access. Interesting to see the loudmouthed man from the bunkhouse submitting willingly to my careful treatment. I imagined this was the very reason for Callum's behavior in a place where he was free to be himself. His arrogance had been a defense mechanism in the sense he'd known today would involve a different dynamic he was helpless to avoid.

I felt invigorated as I began moving the loofah in circular motions against Callum's skin. This part of my job felt familiar though this activity involved naked men rather than horses. I concentrated on finding the right pressure and making sure I gave my charge the pleasure of a thorough grooming. This appeared to be a cherished part of the daily ritual and must feel very good at the beginning of a long day during which you might be expected to do a number of not-so-pleasant activities.

I glanced beside me and saw Brian and Liv working hard at rubbing down Trey and Noah. I began to feel more confident as I finished with Callum's back and moved onto his chest and belly area. It was impossible not to examine the man closely while I worked, and my cock throbbed in response to the seductive visuals and the scent of testosterone and clean bodies.

"You're doing very well, Jensen," Liv commented. I glanced over to see Noah practically leaning into Liv's practiced caresses.

"Thanks. I mean, it's not a curry comb, but I can deal."

Callum shifted in his cuffs, his eyes coming up to meet mine and then darting away again. Unlike Luke's, Callum's eyes were a deep, dark brown. My heart skipped a beat, but I concentrated on bringing Callum's backside to a beautiful shade of pink. I wasn't gentle. I figured a man would be as inclined to love a strong workover as much as a horse would. I moved the loofah back and forth, enjoying the jiggle of Callum's glutes and the rising color of his skin

When I'd achieved this to my satisfaction, I brought the loofah around to begin on Callum's long legs.

The work proved tiring but not unpleasant, and some of the tension left me as I rubbed the attractive ponyboy down. If this was how my mornings would begin, I really couldn't complain. When I was finished, I stepped back to admire my handiwork, and found Brian, Liv and Callum staring at me.

"You're very thorough," Liv said.

"Yeah, Jesus. He's fucking glowing pink all over. Good job." Brian added, giving Trey a few more passes with his loofah.

"Is that okay? Did I go at him too hard?"

Horses could take a pretty rough hand, but maybe human ponyboys didn't like being manhandled.

I heard Liv's bubbly laughter. "Oh God, Jensen. Look at him. He's ready to explode."

She pointed to Callum's cock, bulging between the bars of the cage, leaking at the tip. "I kind of feel sorry for him right now. But, honestly, that's what we're going for. The trainers want them randy and motivated to behave, so good job."

My chest puffed out at this praise. It was a weird thing to hear, but yay me!

My next task was more of a mindfuck since it was a definite departure from my familiar stable-hand duties. I picked up the washcloth, soaking it thoroughly and soaping up with body wash. Then took a deep breath, cleared my mind of wayward thoughts and went at Callum's privates with gentle determination. I worked quickly and efficiently, so as not to further torment the man. Again, I feared my touch might be a tad too rough.

The ingenious design of the cock cages allowed the men's genitals to be cleaned without removing the device, which came in handy for any extended wear, I figured. Although, the men were only expected to wear the devices during their training hours.

Callum appeared resigned to the fact he would be unintentionally teased by the new stable hand for the duration of his grooming session. He huffed and made delicate noises of enjoyment while I tended him. Since I didn't—thank God—have any hang-ups regarding either nudity or bodily secretions, I didn't have an issue washing other men in the most intimate of places. Something that rather surprised me.

Once all three ponyboys were thoroughly clean, I helped Liv and Brian dress them in the required tack. The collar was straightforward but Liv showed me how to fit the body harness on Callum, putting the leather straps around his buttocks and across his pelvis first, then applying the chest piece and attaching the side straps that fastened under the arm and to the pelvis belt.

She ran her fingers under the snug leather strap around Callum's lower waist. "These are jock straps, but we don't use the leather cod piece because we want their caged cocks to be visible. The leather frames their buttocks nicely though," she said, slapping Callum on the rear, making him shift his feet and sigh.

The thick studded leather sitting snugly on Callum's pale skin, outlining his chest and abdomen, then framing his cock and buttocks, made him look like a sexy-as-fuck sex slave out of a Mad Max film.

"Boots are on the shelf here," Liv said, walking over to where six pairs of scuffed Doc Marten boots were arranged side by side. "Their names are on the heel of the left boot and we tie the two boots together when they're put away." She picked up two sets and brought them over, handing the larger pair to me. "These are Callum's."

"Thanks."

"You're taking all of this in stride." Liv commented, giving me a wink.

"So far so good," I said, shrugging.

Callum moaned loudly, rolling his eyes and thrusting his hips.

Liv and Brian laughed. "Callum is taking the brunt of your inexperience very personally, I'd say," Liv muttered. "Seems to make him very happy. Or, at least, frustrated."

Callum whimpered and rubbed his forehead against the skin of his arm, panting softly and huffing in resignation. The other two ponyboys regarded him with sympathy.

"Place the boots beside him. They put those on themselves." She tossed me a pair of grey work socks. "Now take his gag out, and undo the wrist cuffs. Once they've got their boots on, we'll do the tails."

I did as instructed, except I forgot the sequence of events and unbuckled Callum's restraints ahead of removing the gag. The tall man pulled me into a tight embrace and rubbed his face against mine, leaving drool from his chin and the gag all over me. Something about the gesture made me feel praised and appreciated. Like I was on the right track, anyway. I couldn't help a small smile forming before Liv chastised him.

"Hey, Callum. Back off. You don't behave that way in the grooming stables, and you know it. I don't care how delicious the new stable hand is."

Liv clapped her hands loudly and Callum released me regretfully, placing his hands behind his back and lifting his chin as if to say the infraction was worth getting called out.

I stood there, shocked, hiding the pleasure I'd felt being embraced by the naked man I'd polished to a high sheen and decked out in fetish gear. I wiped the moisture from my neck and beckoned Callum with a smile. "I'll take your gag out. Turn around."

Callum obeyed and I gently removed the gag, wiping some drool from his soaked beard. "Good boy. There you go. Now put on your boots, and we'll do your tail."

Everyone was staring at me again. Was I royally screwing this up, or was I doing okay?

Callum swore softly, then bent to put on his socks with trembling hands. Liv and Brian exchanged a look. Noah and Trey laced their boots and tried not to look at me.

Yeah, maybe screwing everything up. But I was doing my best.

Brian slowly walked over to a set of drawers by the table. "Okay. Tails. Come over here, Jensen."

As I dried my hands and padded over, I slipped on the wet tiles, skillfully righting myself before I fell. "Jesus."

"Yeah. Next time, wear flip-flops."

"I didn't bring any."

"I'm sure Adam can get some in your size. I'll let him know."

Brian pulled open the top drawer. Inside, six familiar rubber plugs with horsehair tails nestled in divided partitions with each ponyboy's name on a label.

"Adam told me you got some hands-on experience with one of these yesterday."

"Yep," I said, taking out the one in Callum's box. I turned the tail over in my hand, examining the workmanship closely. "These are pretty awesome."

"Yeah, they are. They look nice and they sure give the guys something to think about."

"Yep," I repeated, feeling my cock throb at the memory of Callum's spontaneous embrace and the thought of fitting the handsome ponyboy with his tail. I put the plug back in the box.

"Gloves are here, lube is here, coat it thick. We'll get them to come over one by one."

Brian put on some gloves and picked up Trey's tail. "Trey, get over here. Bend over and grip the edge of the counter. You know the drill."

Trey obliged, shoving his ass out right beside me and swaying his hips back and forth in readiness while I stared at the perfect globes and tried not to moan.

Which was when Brian slapped one cheek, hard. The sound rang out in the quiet of the room and Trey gasped. I jumped at the sound.

"Behave yourself, Trey. Don't you want to show Jensen what a good ponyboy you are?"

Trey moaned, nodded, and stilled his movements so Brian could insert the rubber object. I tried not to watch as the plug went into Trey but found it almost impossible to keep my gaze away. I swallowed and tried to breathe as Brian skillfully seated and arranged the tail.

"Wow."

"Yep," Liv agreed. "Pretty much the piece de resistance of their get-up." She called Noah over and soon had his tail in place, a gentle yet efficient process I found utterly transfixing.

Then it was Callum's turn. I pulled on some gloves and picked up his tail from the drawer. Callum came forward without any instruction and assumed the position.

I've done this before. Piece of cake. I coated the plug with lube. The entire process went smoothly, and Callum appeared to welcome his tail. I tried to concentrate on technique so I could forget the fact I was inserting an object into a very attractive man's ass.

Once I'd completed my task and fluffed the tail, I held my breath and remained motionless. If I moved the slightest bit after seeing what I'd seen, the friction from my jeans would tip me over the edge, and I'd come in my pants like an adolescent.

Once I'd collected myself, I rocked the plug to make sure the device was fully seated, then removed my gloves, cheeks flushed and eyes not knowing where to land.

"Good job, kid," Brian said. "You've earned yourself a twenty-minute break. We'll take them to the training barn while you sit down."

Oh, thank God.

I nodded, staring at the table after the others had left, wondering what to do with myself while they were gone, and wondering how I'd ever get used to this.

"I'm not a fucking kid," I whispered, wiping my forehead with trembling fingers.

Chapter Seven

I was assigned a number of menial chores for the remainder of the morning, which suited me fine.

I hosed the showers and wiped the tiles, rinsed the cloths and loofahs, and cleaned some leather tack, a task so familiar I could relax for the first time in at least twenty-four hours. It was a relief to lose myself in mindless manual labor. It allowed me to let my thoughts flow and drift while I expended a build-up of restless energy and focused on the jobs at hand. Plus, it gave my dick a chance to settle down and regroup.

I enjoyed cleaning things—whether horses or human ponyboys, real stable gear or fetish wear. The world was a better place when things were clean and orderly, and it made me feel in control and able to contribute.

When Liv and Brian returned before lunch and praised me for what I had done in their absence, I felt validated. I was doing the job for which I'd been hired, no matter how unprepared I might have been at first.

When the ponyboys returned to the grooming stable, I helped Liv and Brian remove their gear. Noah was the only ponyboy who returned to the grooming barn without his cock cage. The others were still restrained, the steel bars wet and dripping with the result of hours of sexual frustration. The sight was enough to get me hard again.

Liv ruffled Noah's short hair affectionately. "You were a good boy again today, weren't you? You always get your reward. Or maybe it's because Lorraine likes to make you happy? Hmm?"

Noah smiled shyly and rubbed his forehead against Liv's shoulder, like a real pony. But his eyes sparkled, and he sent a shy glance my way.

I stared at Callum's sizeable penis and wondered how to remove the cage without teasing the aroused man. This proved impossible, and Callum squirmed and grunted as I undid the clasp and pulled the device off him. I stepped back, watching Callum's penis swell while the ponyboy groaned with relief.

Brian cleared his throat. "Okay, so, Jensen. You have a couple of options here. You can leave him alone and send him home."

Callum whimpered and pulled at his wrist cuffs. I met his pleading eyes while Brian kept speaking.

"Or, you can choose to help him out before you hose him down for the day."

The idea tempted me. But I wanted to make sure I'd heard Brian correctly. "You mean...um...jerk him off?"

"Yeah, jerk him off. If you want. Let me be clear: All you're required to do is hose him down and send him to the bunkhouse. The rest is up to you."

Brian took a black nytril glove from a box on the table and pulled it onto his right hand. Then he ran his gloved hand down Trey's muscled abdomen and wrapped it around the ponyboy's engorged cock, stroking it a few times.

Whoa. I waited for the cheesy porno music to start and was a little surprised when it didn't.

I looked at Callum's cock, and then back up to his desperate brown eyes, then turned and walked away, closing my eyes for a second and making my hands into fists.

When I opened my eyes and grabbed the bottle of lube from the table, Callum made an excited sound behind his ball gag. I grabbed a glove from the box and squirted some lube into Brian's outstretched hand. Orgasms were good for people, and after three hours of working hard for their trainers, these ponyboys deserved a break. At least, I figured they did.

I pulled on the glove, snapping it deliberately as Callum jerked in surprise and Brian chuckled.

"Work it, Jensen. God, you're gonna drive these ponyboys crazy with your attitude."

Then, as Brian began to jerk Trey in earnest, now he had a slippery hand to work with, I moved in close to Callum and wrapped my hand around him firmly. "Let's watch for a sec."

Callum moaned, trying to thrust into my grip, but I let him go and chastised him. "No. You stay still if you want my attention. We're going to watch. Then, maybe I'll give you what you want."

I was starting to get off on this whole dominance/submission angle. I kinda liked it.

Liv chuckled as I wrapped my hand around his cock again, and Callum struggled not to thrust his hips. "Very good, Jensen. Show him who's boss."

We watched as Brian efficiently brought Trey to his release. The ponyboy shuddered as his cock spurted white semen over Brian's gloved fist, satisfied groans echoing off the barn walls.

Callum whimpered against his restraints, frantic from trying not to shove his cock into my grip. Finally, I gave him a soft kiss on the shoulder and began to stroke him.

"What a good boy. Now you can move. Fuck my hand, and I'll make you come, ponyboy."

It wasn't like I'd never jerked off another guy. And it wasn't like it took much to jerk off a guy who'd been desperate to come for hours. But I was surprised by how quickly I was able to get Callum ready to shoot.

After a few strokes, Callum groaned and spurted over my hand, closing his eyes and grimacing with relief. The fluid kept coming, and I kept stroking until I'd drained him. He shuddered and sagged in his bindings. His eyelids fluttered, and he gazed at me with something approaching reverence.

"Holy fuck, kid. I think you're a natural," Brian muttered, picking up the hose and turning the nozzle to produce a wide spray. "I can see I'm leaving the ponyboys in good hands." He nodded at my dripping glove. "Literally."

I released Callum's spent prick and disposed of the glove while Brian sprayed warm water over the three ponyboys and hosed them clean from their day's work.

"We hose them? No soap or rubdowns?" I asked.

"No," Liv said. "They can shower back at the bunkhouse if they want to. It's more important to ensure they're clean for their trainers. When the trainers are done with them, they only need the worst of the muck cleaned off."

When the ponyboys were clean, they were unbound, ungagged, and sent behind the partition to dress and leave for the day.

"What do they do all afternoon? There weren't any guys in the bunkhouse yesterday when I got there."

Brian nodded. "Yeah, they're encouraged to do some service at the main house. Cleaning, washing dishes, cooking—whatever they like to do and are willing to do. They're paid and the money comes off their membership fee."

I nodded. It was brilliant, really.

"Most of them would engage in service as part of the submissive experience anyway, so to be paid for it is a bonus. And they get to do it in their street clothes, not plugged and harnessed, which might happen occasionally as a severe punishment for some violation of house rules or something. It's not unheard of here."

"Nope," Liv agreed. "If you ever see a ponyboy in full pony gear cleaning the main house, you know they did something very, very naughty. And they aren't paid for a punishment, obviously."

I felt my gut clench as I imagined it. What a debasement, to have to go over to the main house dressed as a fetish pony and spend your morning or afternoon scrubbing floors and cleaning bathrooms. These people were fucking sadistic. And brilliant.

"You hungry?" Liv asked me.

"Starving."

"There are sandwiches, salads and drinks in the fridge here for us every day," Liv said, beckoning me over. "Looks like tuna salad, chicken salad or ham and cheese today. What do you fancy?"

I took a tuna salad sandwich and a Coke and sat at the table after washing my hands at the sink.

"So," Brian asked as he unwrapped his ham and cheese. "What do you think so far?"

I took a bite of my sandwich and chewed, swallowing carefully. "I think I could get used to this."

"Better than looking after real horses?"

I shrugged. "Not better, exactly. Different, obviously. Very different. But...not unpleasant." I glanced at Liv.

"*Not unpleasant.*" She grinned. "Hmm. We'll put that on the brochure."

I smiled.

Brian chuckled. "I can't believe Mitchell didn't tell you what you were in for when he recommended us."

"He probably figured I wouldn't be brave enough to try it."

"But you are."

"I thought it would be a stupid move to go home and not even see what it was all about."

"And now you've seen it?"

I shrugged. "I can work with this. I could use a vacation I'm paid for."

"It's hardly a vacation. We work pretty hard."

I raised my eyebrows. "Have you ever worked in a stable with *real* horses?"

Liv and Brian both shook their heads.

"Then don't talk to me about work. So far, this place has been easy. And...way more fun. I could get used to it."

Brian nodded. "I hope you do. I'm not exactly thrilled to be leaving, but it's time for something else, and I can always come back."

Liv nodded, throwing her arm around my shoulders. "Exactly. And in the meantime, me and Jensen will keep everyone up to snuff, right?"

I popped the last bit of sandwich into my mouth and grinned. "Absolutely."

*

After lunch, we tidied up and prepared for the next shift.

"I'm going to give you Hunter," Liv said. "He's easy to manage. Luke's a fucking handful, even in here, so Brian can deal with him."

I blushed, recalling my interactions with Luke in the bunkhouse. "Sure."

"Oh damn, I forgot my water bottle at the house. Back in a flash," she said. "Brian's gone to get more lube." She laughed, glancing over her shoulder. "You'll hear lube mentioned a lot around here."

"I'm sure."

I was alone, standing awkwardly by the table when Luke came around the partition, completely naked, and walked to the end of the showers. He hesitated when he saw me, but quickly recovered and took the space under a shower head.

I couldn't help but stare. Luke with nothing on was transfixing. An image likely to appear in my dreams over and over again. My eager eyes devoured every inch of the blond man, examining the tight muscles of Luke's arms and the span of his shoulders, his narrow waist, his long, powerful legs and the ever-present tension I could almost see beneath the surface.

Luke lifted his head ever so slightly, and his eyes pierced mine with affront. Heat flushed my cheeks, but I couldn't look away. I remained pinioned by Luke's gaze until Hunter and Ben came into the room.

Luke returned his gaze to the floor and I felt...released? I also felt challenged. What the fuck was Luke's problem? He was naked and presenting himself to be treated like a piece of livestock, so did he not think I was going to get something out of that?

Fuck him.

I walked over to him, feeling more confident. Maybe in the bunkhouse I'd be Luke's bitch, but in the grooming barn, Luke had to obey *me*. My gaze wandered freely over his smooth muscles and I noticed his cock was half hard already.

"Arms up," I said, moving close and touching my finger to Luke's bicep. His head jerked up, and our gazes caught again. This time, Luke's eyes expressed surprise, then wariness.

I stared at him, saying nothing more, wondering if he would obey or laugh at me. For a moment, it was touch and go. Then his eyes softened, and he slowly raised his arms above his head as he licked his lips nervously.

Satisfied, I grabbed the hanging cuffs and buckled them around Luke's strong wrists. My hands may have lingered a second longer than they needed to, but I didn't think Luke noticed. He had turned his head away as if he couldn't bear to look at me.

I grabbed a clean ball gag from the table. The other ponyboys were behaving themselves—remaining silent and still and keeping their gazes on the floor. Feeling a surge of confidence, I moved close to Luke and lifted the ball gag up in front of him.

"Want this?" I asked as Luke's eyes flicked to me.

As we locked gazes, I opened my own mouth and popped the ball inside.

Luke's eyes widened, and he almost said something. Instead, he blinked and watched as I coated the ball with saliva, then slowly removed it from my mouth.

"Open," I said in a low voice.

Luke jerked against his cuffs as if trying to break free, pupils blown. But he opened his mouth and allowed me to put the wet ball between his teeth and buckle the gag behind his head. As I glanced down, I noticed his cock filling up quickly.

Well then. Now I had Luke bound and gagged and semi-hard. I glanced down at his cock again. My tongue came out to lick my lips as I met his gaze.

The way Luke looked at me, like he would take anything I wanted to give him, felt intoxicating.

Luke made a sound in his throat and pulled hard on his restraints, eyes wild and drool dripping from his gag. The other ponyboys shot surreptitious glances our way, shifting their feet but maintaining obedient postures.

I let my hand drop and gave a noise of chastisement as the door opened and Brian came in with the extra lube.

"Oh great, you're getting started. Hope he wasn't too hard to handle?"

I watched Luke close his eyes and shudder as I replied to Brian's question in casual tones.

"Nope. It's all good." I moved away from Luke and over to Ben, getting the other ponyboy to reach up.

"Excellent. Glad to see you're getting the hang of this."

Brian took care of Hunter's cuffs and ball gag while I finished with Ben. The work was becoming familiar to me, and I certainly had my fill of appreciating the male form in so many ways.

By the time we were done, Liv had returned. "I told Jensen we'd give him Hunter today. He's a little easier to manage than some others who shall remain nameless." She gave Luke a meaningful look.

But Luke had closed his eyes and tried to calm his breathing, so she shrugged and turned her attention to Brian, who said, "Yeah, I don't think Jensen has any problem handling Luke. But I'm sure Hunter will behave beautifully for him."

A whimper came from Luke, making Liv and Brian glance his way.

"Is he all right?" Liv asked. "He looks upset, and it's weird he's not kicking up a fuss."

"Let's enjoy it while it lasts," Brian muttered, picking up a loofah and moving toward Luke.

The afternoon grooming session ran similar to the morning one, and Luke behaved himself impeccably. I gave Hunter a vigorous rubdown, a thorough wash and kitted him out, then inserted the butt-plug tail. I tried not to watch Brian insert Luke's tail, but it was impossible to look away from the normally rebellious pony submitting to such debasement. Luke was stunning and ferocious when he dominated and lusciously seductive when he gave himself over. He didn't even realize it. But I did.

Whether I had thrown him for a loop earlier and put him off his game was anybody's guess. But looking at Luke in body harness, boots, and cock cage, with his goddamn pony tail in, made me go jellylike all over, except in one spot where I was stiff as an iron brand.

Chapter Eight

The afternoon passed quickly while we cleaned tack and polished boots. When the ponyboys returned, they submitted easily to a quick hose down.

"You'll notice none of them are wearing their cages," Brian said. "Which is great because they tend to be exhausted, obedient and pliable if they've been rewarded with an orgasm. But a reward is dependent on their behavior. Looks like even Luke was a good ponyboy today," he said, eyeing the man in question.

Although seeing Luke all dirty and spent was enough to make me want to rev him up again.

I expected a few words from the rebellious ponyboy once his gag was removed, maybe telling Liv and Brian what had occurred earlier or trying to provoke me into doing something else I shouldn't. But Luke was quiet as a mouse and simply disappeared behind the partition to get dressed.

I helped Liv and Brian wipe down the showers and rinse the soiled gear to clean properly the next morning. The ponyboys were dismissed earlier but my shift didn't end until four.

Brian had to give Adam a report on my progress back at the house, so he went with Liv. I dried my feet off, put on my socks and boots, and grabbed my hat, lifting it to my face to smell its familiar scent. As I inhaled the embedded dirt and dust from countless summers, a calm feeling drifted through me. I had handled everything the BCR had thrown at me. I might be a regular cowboy in a new world of kink, but I'd held up pretty well.

I put on my hat and strode down the dirt path toward the bunkhouse, wondering what other challenges awaited me.

When I wiped my boots on the rubber mat and entered the cabin, all the men stopped what they were doing to look at me. I shut the door behind me, ignoring them. I tossed my hat on the end of my bunk and sat, pulling off my boots.

I'm not sure what I'd expected but it wasn't this. I placed my boots neatly on the floor by my bunk and sat there, looking around at everyone silently. Luke was nowhere to be seen.

Finally, Callum walked over and extended his hand. I blinked in surprise but accepted the gesture. The tall man drew me up so we stood at eye level.

I cleared my throat. I had no idea what to say. "Look, I'm sorry if I—"

Callum grinned. "Don't be sorry. I enjoyed every minute of it."

I grimaced awkwardly. "Oh. Oh, good. I wasn't sure how things were going to be back here after...that."

Callum licked his lips as his eyes drilled into me, all kinds of intense. "Well...they can be any way you want them to be. I...uh...I'm pretty good at massages."

It took a second for me to recognize this as a proposition. I was surprised, although I had given this man a much-needed hand job earlier.

God, this place was such a mindfuck.

"Oh, yeah, thanks, but I was just going to take a quick shower."

"Okay," Callum nodded. "Sure."

I smiled. "Thanks though. Maybe another time."

Callum blushed. "Definitely. Let me know."

"I will," I said, digging a pair of clean briefs out of my bag, grabbing a towel, and heading for the bathroom, hoping with everything I had left to find it empty.

When I pushed the handle and swung the door inward, I gave the large room a quick scan. There was no sign of another occupant, so I let the door swing shut and went into a changing stall to divest myself of my soiled clothes. Once naked, I exited the stall and made a startled sound when I noticed Luke leaning against the closed door, staring at me with a satisfied look on his drop-dead-gorgeous face. He was in a pair of skimpy black boxer briefs, and his arms were folded over his chest.

My stomach lurched. *Jesus Christ.* Luke looked as if he had plans, and I could only imagine what those might be.

"Hey," I said, with a nervous smile I hoped might disarm him.

Luke's eyes travelled slowly down my naked body to my bare feet and back up to my reddening face. My nervous system followed his lust-filled gaze with a trail of goose pimples along its path. I shivered.

The blood rushed to my dick, making it rise and point directly toward the man giving me a heated, predatory look.

Before I could think of something to say, Luke strode forward and grabbed a metal chair from the changing area. He quickly tilted it and braced it snugly between the floor and the door handle, effectively preventing anyone outside the room from getting in.

"You going to take a shower?" Luke asked. "Or stand there gawking?"

Oh shit.

He waited there, the door braced shut, expecting me to put on a fucking show.

Goddamn it.

I summoned every ounce of acting ability I had and nonchalantly walked towards the shower farthest from Luke. My heart pounded, and I desperately wanted to see if he had followed or still stood by the door, but I didn't dare look. When I got there, I turned on the showerhead and ducked under the warm spray, welcoming the warmth and wetness on my sweaty skin, despite everything else. My heart pounded in my chest, my cock throbbed, and it took everything I had not to turn around.

I was reaching for the shampoo when Luke's hand came into view, grabbing the bottle off the shelf. "Hold out your hand, cowboy."

I froze, then did as Luke instructed, holding it out flat though it was shaking.

"What a good boy," Luke murmured, pouring shampoo into my palm. I stared at the white liquid, smelling summer sunshine and ripe fruit, then lifted my eyes to his and felt a jolt at the hunger in the blond man's gaze.

Luke nodded as if confirming the effect of his presence on the newest member of the BCR staff. "Well, what are you waiting for? Your hair is filthy."

"Fuck you," I said, feeling stirrings of anger now. What the hell was Luke's problem?

He raised his eyebrows. "Oh, I hope so. But first, I want to watch you wash your sexy hair, all right? I take it back, it's not filthy. But my imagination is."

I panted as I watched Luke's gaze drift down to my hard dick.

"Hmm. Looks like your imagination is as dirty as mine."

My chest rose and fell. "Fine. I need to wash it anyway. I mean, that's what I came in here for."

I hoped Luke didn't notice my fingers shaking as I lifted them to my wet hair, rubbing the pearly shampoo into the strands. He watched me, eyes electric with desire. Then he poured some body wash into his own hand.

I closed my eyes, not wanting to see what Luke would do now because I already thought I might explode with the tension.

Slippery, warm fingers wrapped around my erection.

My eyes snapped open. I gasped.

Luke lifted a finger to his lips while his other hand moved back and forth on my cock. "Keep washing your hair. Don't stop until I tell you it's time to rinse," he said, voice low.

I let out a shaky burst of air as I tried to obey, fingers trembling as I made stuttering sounds of intense pleasure. For a moment, I thought I might come and humiliate myself even further as he competently stroked me. Then, thankfully, Luke let go and moved to my testicles.

I grunted and closed my eyes, dick twitching in the empty air as he fondled me. I kept my hands in my hair, rubbing the shampoo into my scalp and wondering what he would do next. Hot water pounded my chest as I inhaled the fruity scent of body wash and the smell of wet cotton from Luke's soaked briefs.

His fingers moved from my testicles to snake over my hips until they cupped my ass. They glided, with the aid of the body wash, along my skin in the most teasing way, and I had to concentrate to keep my hands on my head. Once I regained some level of control, I risked opening my eyes.

The sight of Luke so close and the feel of him so near caused my breath to catch. He gazed at me with a crooked smile.

"Hi," he breathed, squeezing my ass.

I blinked. "H-hi."

My voice sounded low and breathy—my desire so obvious I wanted to sink to the floor and die of shame. But there was no hiding from Luke. And there was no hiding from whatever drew us together. It felt like a tractor beam pulling me in.

Luke's smile widened, and he squeezed my ass again, digging his fingers into the flesh. "You have some serious booty there, cowboy," Luke murmured. "You get that definition from doing grunt work on a real ranch?"

I nodded, unable to form a coherent answer as Luke's hands slid around my waist to my belly where his fingers toyed with my happy trail.

"Well, we'll have to try to keep you in good shape here, huh? Now you're dealing with the likes of us."

My arms grew tired from keeping them up, but I didn't dare disobey him. I'd stopped rubbing the shampoo in and stood stock-still as Luke trailed a long finger up my abdomen and ghosted it over my nipple.

I inhaled sharply, cock twitching so hard it brushed against his thigh.

"You like that?" Luke asked, pinching gently.

"Yeah." I gasped.

He glanced down at my twitching cock. "Oh, you really do."

While Luke teased my nipples, my hands dropped from my head and wrapped around his wrists, not to stop him but to hang on for dear life.

"Oh, cowboy, you shouldn't have done that," he murmured. "You know what cowboys get when they don't listen?"

Luke's seductive voice sent shivers through me, and the underlying threat made me moan.

"What?" I asked.

Luke grinned and stepped back. While I watched with wide eyes, he hooked his thumbs under the waistband of the boxer briefs and pushed them down his damp legs, kicking them off.

His sizeable cock bounced free as he wrapped long fingers around it and stroked slowly. "This. This is what they get. If they want it."

My mouth opened but couldn't form words. My gaze flicked from Luke's cock to his eyes, then back to his cock, *hallelujahs* going off in my head.

"I want it," I finally managed in a deep voice I didn't recognize.

A loud rattling startled us as someone tried the main door. Then came pounding and a pissed-off voice: "Who's in there? What's going on? You can't hog the showers!"

"Ignore him," Luke said, continuing to stroke himself and licking his lips as he regarded me hungrily.

"Who is it?" I asked.

"Does it matter?" he said, eyebrows raised.

I shrugged.

His lips curled in a sneer. "I'm gonna fuck you no matter who's out there trying to get in."

The statement hung in the air between us for several moments. I didn't argue.

"But first you need to rinse your hair."

I stared at Luke, having completely forgotten about my hair.

"Shit."

"Do it."

I swallowed hard, not wanting to take my eyes off Luke. Not only because Luke was so fucking hot—all wet and naked in the shower with me—but because I didn't want to be so vulnerable. But I took a deep breath, tipped my head back under the hot water, and carded my fingers through my wet hair, closing my eyes.

I didn't realize Luke had dropped to his knees until the man's hand wrapped around the base of my throbbing dick and a warm mouth engulfed me.

"Oh," I gasped, head falling forward, shampoo dripping down my face into my eyes. It stung and burned but Luke's mouth on my cock felt like heaven.

"What the hell is going on in there? Is that you, Luke?" someone yelled.

Luke pulled his mouth off me to shout, "Yes!" then dived back in.

I groaned way too loudly.

"Who's in there with you?"

Luke didn't answer. I gaped down at him as he worked my cock with a vicious intensity that threatened to milk me in one explosive burst. Right when I was about to shoot, he released me and licked his lips. "Tell them."

I didn't know what he meant at first. My brain had been scrambled by his powerful technique and getting so close. "What?"

"Tell them it's you."

"No!"

Luke's fingers slipped between my legs and squeezed my testicles, hard enough to make me squeal.

"Tell. Them."

I gasped with discomfort, trying to wipe the shampoo and water from my eyes and get myself together. I'd do anything to get Luke to let go.

"It's me!" I shouted out.

Luke squeezed harder.

"Ow. Fuck!"

"Your name, stupid. Tell them your name."

Oh God, the pain. Make it stop. "It's Jensen!"

Luke relaxed his grip, and I shuddered, leaning against the tiled wall.

"Why is the door braced shut?"

"It's Ben," Luke said quietly.

"I wanted some privacy," I replied loudly, voice betraying me by wobbling several octaves.

Luke gave me a thumbs up and dived back on my cock.

"Okay. Fine. But don't stay in there too long. Some of us want showers too."

I grabbed Luke's shoulders. "Stop. You have to stop, or I'm going to come," I whispered.

Luke pulled his mouth off me and stood, turning off the shower and grabbing a towel.

"Not before I get my cock into you." He threw the towel at me. "Here. Dry off. Go into the changing stall over there when you're done."

I stared at Luke. "Why?"

"Because I'm going to fuck you, cowboy. If you don't want me to, you'd better leave right now. I won't follow you."

I watched Luke dry himself off, wiping the towel over his junk and swiping it between his thighs.

Yeah, I wasn't going anywhere.

I walked slowly over to the stall Luke had indicated and stepped into it. I stared at the tiled wall and waited.

"Up on the bench, cowboy."

Instead of obeying, I turned to glance behind me.

Luke stood in the entrance to the stall, his eyes feasting on me as he stroked his erection.

"You can't tell me what to do," I said.

"Sure, I can. It's up to you whether or not you do what I say."

"If I don't?"

"Then I won't fuck you, and you can take your ready-to-bust nut to bed for a very long night."

He stepped forward and placed a hand on my shoulder. His gentle touch startled me after those harsh commands. He stroked softly over my shoulder and glided his hand down my back and over my ass, almost reverently.

His voice—low and private—conveyed all his intentions. "But if you do as you're told and kneel up on this bench," he murmured, gliding his fingers lightly along the top of my ass, "I will give you exactly what you need. What you want. You know it, and I know it."

I breathed hard, closing my eyes, loving the way he was touching me. He had me and he knew it. After a few moments, I lifted one knee and placed it on the bench, and then the other, balancing with my hands on the cold tiles of the wall. I swallowed hard. "Fine. Go ahead."

Luke inhaled sharply. "Oh, Christ, cowboy. I don't think I could stop now if I wanted to."

"You could. And you would if I stopped you."

"Fine. True. I'm not into straight-out rape," Luke murmured, his finger pressing between my buttocks and finding my hole. "Anyway, I want you to beg me."

I tried to laugh but it came out a moan. "I'm not gonna beg you. I have *some* dignity."

"Not from where I'm standing, and it's fucking glorious."

I gasped as Luke grabbed my buttocks and pulled them apart.

"God, you are so pretty here. Do all cowboys have such pretty pink holes? Or just you?"

I could only stutter and gasp, feeling incredibly vulnerable. "Dunno."

"Well, this hole is fucking beautiful. And I can't wait to fill it."

I nodded, desire pooling deep in my belly at the prospect of getting fucked by this upstart ponyboy. I had no problem obeying his orders when he stood behind me with an erection and a plan.

I felt a bit better being in the stall, but I'd still have to try to be quiet if I didn't want the entire bunkhouse to echo with my groans. Hopefully, Luke wouldn't make me scream.

He moved further into the stall and let the steel door swing shut. I heard the latch click, and my pounding heart went into overdrive as my cock throbbed. I pressed my forehead against the tiles, trying to stay calm as I heard the snap of a lid opening.

"Oh fuck, you have a gorgeous ass, cowboy. Totally wasted on the horses you used to look after."

I thought his comment so funny, I burst out a laugh that became a moan as I felt Luke's lips on my shoulder, and then his fingers trailing lube down the small of my back and into my crack.

Game on.

"Oh fuck," I moaned, closing my eyes and arching against his touch, pushing my ass out.

"Oh, holy fuck you are begging for it, aren't you?" Luke breathed, raw lust in his voice. "You want me to fuck you, cowboy? You want me to fuck your ass and make you come in my hand?"

I made a noise—a long drawn out moan—as I nodded frantically. "Yes. Please."

Luke chuckled, rubbing so much lube along my ass crack it dripped down to the bench. "I thought you weren't gonna beg?"

"S'not begging. It's being polite."

Luke laughed. "Well, you are a very polite cowboy, I'll give you that. Although, nothing I'm seeing right now looks very polite. And I hate to tell you, but I'm not polite at all. Although you're probably aware."

I groaned deep as Luke's finger pushed its way into me. My body almost let him in without thinking.

"Oh fuck, you're ready for me, aren't you, cowboy? Ready for a good strong fucking?"

"So ready." A desperate whisper. I wasn't even sure he heard it.

"I'll bet. Looking after the livestock here tends to have that effect. Imagine, getting fucked by the ponyboy you had in harness and tail this morning? Doesn't the idea just blow your fucking mind?" Luke said.

I swore, sweat rising on my skin as I waited for the bliss that was coming. Luke fingered me like a pro, and I hoped his skill was a sign.

"You got a condom?" I asked desperately, praying he did. I don't know why I hadn't thought of asking before now.

"All wrapped up and ready for you, cowboy. But here," Luke said, and pressed something wet, soft and cold against my lips. "You'd better bite down on these so you don't make too much noise, or we'll both get busted. Open."

I parted my teeth as Luke pressed his wet, balled-up boxer briefs between them, at the same time withdrawing his finger and sticking two into me.

I gasped, feeling like an itch I'd had forever was finally being scratched. He pumped them expertly, hitting the best spot as I garbled nonsense. "Oh my God, yes, oh God, yes, there." My words, muffled by the wet cotton, were barely intelligible.

"Easy, cowboy," he said. I could tell he was smiling, and it made me warm and shivery all over. But I was desperate to have him inside me.

I grunted, pushing against the wall, displaying myself for him.

A soft noise, such a vulnerable sound, came from him as I felt his cock where I needed it. Gently, so gently I wondered if this was real and not a goddamn dream, he pushed his cock inside me.

"Oh fucking Christ!" Luke hissed. "Jesus, cowboy, you feel amazing. So good."

I bit down hard on the wet cotton and pushed back, desperate for full penetration. As Luke slid home, he made the same noise and pressed his forehead to my back. We stilled, our harsh breaths the only thing breaking the silence.

"You okay?" Luke whispered, tongue coming out to lick at the sensitive lobe of my ear.

"Mmm, need it." I tried to enunciate clearly, which was difficult with a pair of briefs wedged in my mouth.

Luke chuckled. "I know you do, cowboy. I know it. I could see it when I made you come so fast yesterday."

Memories of being sucked off at my bunk filled my head as Luke started to move, and I was glad I had the cotton briefs in my mouth to muffle my sounds. The sheer depravity of getting fucked in the showers by a kinky ponyboy had me right on the edge already.

Luke's hands gripped my hips as he slid his dick almost out, then pushed back in, and I thought I might lose consciousness it felt so good.

It had been months since anyone had fucked me like this. And I'd never been fucked by anyone like Luke before. A man so connected to his own sexuality he was willing to wear a pony harness and a butt-plug tail for the perverted fun of it.

Now the memory of Luke in his pony gear filled my head, and I started to completely lose it. "Fuck me. Fuck me hard, ponyboy," I growled, not sure if Luke could even make out what I was saying.

"Oh hell, you kinky fuck," he moaned, speeding his movements and shoving me against the tiles with the force of it. "You like watching me in my harness all day and then getting fucked in the showers, don't you?"

I groaned and nodded, meeting Luke's thrusts and not sure how much more I could take before I blew my load, even without Luke's hand on me. And suddenly, it *was* on me.

He wrapped slippery fingers around my cock and stroked it so slowly I could have cried.

"Come for me, cowboy," he murmured in my ear.

Stars exploded behind my eyelids as the orgasm coiled in my balls and burst through my cock like a lightning bolt. I howled into Luke's shorts as I came hard, fluid splashing against the tile and dripping over Luke's hand.

"Jesus, Jesus," Luke swore. "Oh fuck."

Luke's thrusts became erratic before he stilled, forehead against my sweaty back as he achieved his own release. His soft, high-pitched moan was better than anything I had heard at the ranch so far. It made my wrung-out cock weep and my heart expand exponentially.

Tiny tremors continued to rock me as we stayed connected. I listened to the slowing of my heartbeat and enjoyed the intimacy of Luke's embrace. We shared no words, only a sense that what had occurred was only the beginning of something bigger than both of us. At least, that's how I felt, and I could only hope he felt it too.

"Whoa," Luke said finally. "You almost did me in." He grabbed the base of the condom with his fingers and pulled out.

I whimpered as the very full, tied-off condom landed on the bench beside me.

"Look what you did to me, cowboy," Luke said, sliding his arms around me and moving in close to embrace me from behind again. He nuzzled into my neck and up to my ear. "Look at the big load I dropped, just from being inside you." He kissed me tenderly, and I covered his hand with mine as he carefully took the cloth from my mouth with the other.

I licked my lips, then turned quickly and found Luke's mouth with my own, kissing him with passion and gratitude.

He responded in kind, holding me carefully so I wouldn't slide off the bench. After several breathless moments we pulled apart and gazed into each other's blown pupils.

"Well, fuck, cowboy," Luke said softly. "You are totally going to ruin my reputation."

I raised my eyebrows, wondering what he meant.

"My reputation for not giving a damn about anything."

Chapter Nine

Luke exited the shower room first, a towel wrapped around him, crumpled boxer briefs in hand. I figured he made his exit in such a way that he could deflect some of the attention we might have garnered.

"Where's Jensen?" Hunter asked. "You didn't leave him groveling on the bathroom floor, did you?"

Luke barked a laugh. "Jensen can take care of himself. Don't you fucking worry. It's a wonder I can still function."

Hearing him, I closed my eyes and felt my cheeks heat. Looked like Luke wasn't going to deflect anything. I should have known.

Now I had to go out there—I had to go out there with everyone knowing what had occurred between me and Luke. At least the mechanics of it. Nobody would understand the repercussions of what it meant between us.

I put on my clean boxer briefs and made sure I looked okay. At least I wasn't erect anymore. Luke had dealt with my desire on an expert level.

When I walked out into the bunkhouse, all eyes went to me, the silence louder than if they'd been talking.

"Sorry," I said. "Just wanted a little privacy."

There were some chuckles and murmured comments I couldn't make out. I walked quickly to my bunk and started to get dressed, cheeks burning with embarrassment.

"So Luke could get his dick wet, no doubt," Callum muttered loudly. "Why is Luke always the one to initiate the newbies?"

I froze. I glanced at Luke, getting dressed beside me. His forehead creased as he focused on his clothes and didn't meet my gaze.

Callum stood and came closer. "You know that, right? He fucks everyone. Doesn't make you special or anything."

Luke did up his pants and reached for a shirt from the top bunk. "What the fuck do you know, Callum?"

Callum laughed. "I know more than poor Jensen, who probably thinks you actually have emotions. I know you use people for your own kicks."

I kept my eyes on Luke, refusing to believe what had happened in the shower room was simply a random fuck. It had been so much more. Hadn't it? But then, what did I know? I was such a greenhorn in this place. It was entirely possible I'd been completely bamboozled.

Luke turned around slowly and gave Callum a look out of those hard blue eyes. "You don't know shit, Callum," he said, so softly I wasn't sure the other man heard him. "You keep your hands off him and your mouth shut, you hear me?" he said loudly so everyone in the bunkhouse heard him as he stared at Callum. "This cowboy's mine."

Luke pulled on his shirt, grabbed his Vans, and strode out of the bunkhouse, leaving a stunned silence behind him.

I stood motionless, fingers on the buttons of my clean shirt, eyes on the floor as I wondered what had happened.

Of all the things I'd expected Luke to say to Callum, *mine* was not one of them. It made me feel claimed. Maybe I hadn't imagined everything I'd felt in there. After a few seconds I forced my shaking fingers to finish buttoning; then I glanced around the room.

Men stared at me with disbelief and, possibly, admiration? Respect? I couldn't be sure, but I'd gained a different place among the group.

I stole a glance at Noah, who had been sitting quietly on his bunk through the entire exchange, and he looked gobsmacked.

"He's never done anything like that before," Noah said. "I think he really likes you."

I nodded, relief flooding through me.

Noah gestured in the direction of the other men. "Don't let them get to you. You're doing fine."

*

Later, at the main house, I sat at a table apart from the crowd, turning my hat over and over in my hands and wondering if I would ever fit in. I hadn't filled a plate because my stomach felt unsettled.

"Jensen."

I looked up to see Adam Marsland walking toward me.

"Hey."

"Just the man I wanted to see," Adam said, plopping down on the bench of the picnic table and placing his plate of food on the top.

"Oh?" I said, worried there was a problem.

Adam looked me over while he arranged his napkin. "How are you holding up?"

I felt a strange sense of pride in what I had accomplished so far. Strange because it seemed weird to be proud of sticking a butt plug into someone. I shrugged. "Fine. Good."

"It sounds like you're doing a great job. Liv and Brian can't say enough good things about you."

I blushed but I'd really needed the reassurance. "Thank you. That makes me feel like I'm on the right track."

"They also said you handle the ponyboys like a natural"

I blinked at Adam. "Well, I do have experience settling obstinate animals. And keeping them happy and healthy."

Adam grinned. "I'm, uh, glad you can translate that to fit our needs."

"It's not hard. Humans are still animals, right?"

Adam nodded. "They are." He stared at me. "What did you take in university, Jensen?"

"Uh, well, finance. But I minored in anthropology."

"Uh-huh. That's an interesting combination."

"Yes. Anyway, quite a few ancient civilizations created mythologies around half-human, half-animal creatures: Centaurs, mermaids, fauns."

Adam laughed. "Okay then. I guess I don't have to worry you're having a hard time with your duties." He forked some salad into his mouth and chewed. "How are things at the bunkhouse?"

The question was placed innocently enough. I hoped Adam hadn't heard about Luke's commandeering of the shower room.

"Good. I guess."

"You guess? Everyone treating you okay?"

I might have hesitated too long before I nodded.

"You sure? I know how young men can be around somebody new. A bit of teasing is par for the course, but if anyone steps out of line with you, please let me or one of the trainers know."

I smiled, covering my doubts. I didn't want Adam to know what had happened between me and Luke was making me question my decision to stay. Because if I was falling in deep with someone who only wanted a fresh piece of ass, I wasn't sure I'd recover.

"It's a lot to take in. But I'm getting along okay."

A paper plate with two hot dogs on it slipped onto the table under my nose. I looked up to see Luke plunk himself down on the bench opposite with a similarly adorned plate.

"Luke," Adam said.

"Adam."

"Nice of you to bring Jensen some supper."

"He's too skinny. Cowboy needs to eat." Luke gazed hard at me as warmth and relief radiated through me.

Adam laughed. He stood up, grabbing his plate. "I'll leave you to your dinner. I need to talk to Brian. Cheers."

Luke nodded and I said, "Okay."

I placed my hat on the table and smiled at Luke. "Thanks."

"I didn't know what you ate on your dogs, so I got you ketchup and mustard."

"Sounds perfect." I took a bite and chewed slowly, gazing across the table at him, remembering everything he'd made me feel.

"Fuck," Luke swore, licking his lips.

"What?"

"You even eat like a cowboy. You're fucking killing me."

I couldn't help laughing because now he was here I felt so much better. "This is how I eat. Sue me."

Luke shook his head. He leaned forward so he could say, in soft tones, "I don't want to sue you, cowboy. I want to see those lips around my cock for a change."

I almost choked. I coughed and wiped at my mouth with the back of my hand, blinking back tears.

He grinned. "Yep. That's how it's gonna go too. You know how big it is now, don't you?"

Catching my breath, I grabbed the bottle of water Luke had opened, tipped it back and drank a mouthful, watching him all the while, and remembering how big his cock felt inside me.

But I had to know.

"What's going on?" I asked.

Luke's expression changed. "Huh?"

"What do you want from me? I mean, beyond the obvious and what you've mentioned."

Luke stared at me. His eyes flicked over to my hat and back to me. He shrugged. "I like you," he said finally, so quietly I barely saw his lips move.

It was my turn to nod. "I like you too. But if it's only boning you're after, you picked the wrong cowboy."

Luke held my gaze as the statement hung in the air between us. Then he shook his head from side to side. He casually reached his arm across the table and played with the edge of my paper plate. "Oh no. You are, in every way, the very right cowboy, Jensen. You're mine. And I'm not fucking sharing you with any of them."

I picked up my hot dog, and took another bite, watching Luke. After several minutes during which our gazes held, I nodded silently.

"And you may have the upper hand in the grooming barn," Luke murmured, eyes moving to my hand wrapped around my hot dog, then back to my eyes. "But everywhere else you are my bitch. Understand?"

My cock stirred and I couldn't deny the ease with which I would accept that deal, at least temporarily.

"Fine."

Luke smiled, blushing now, and picked up his hot dog, ready to take a bite.

"For now," I said.

"Can I sit here, please? With you guys?" A hesitant voice said behind me. I glanced to my side and saw Noah standing with a plate and a Coke.

It was interesting my first instinct was to see if Luke would approve, rather than giving Noah permission right away. Luke winked and gave me a quick nod.

"Sure," I said.

Noah sat on the bench beside me and gazed across at Luke. I wasn't sure I'd ever seen Noah acknowledge Luke before, and for some reason I'd imagined Noah was intimidated by the handsome and oppositional ponyboy.

But Noah didn't look worried. And Luke gazed at Noah as if he'd expected him to show up.

"Hi Luke," Noah said softly. "How's your weiner taste?"

My eyes widened as I narrowly avoided choking again.

Luke chuckled. "Delicious. And don't you know it."

Noah blushed and squirmed on the bench, taking a delicate bite of his hot dog. He glanced at me. "Hi."

I swallowed. "Hi."

"Not as good as Jensen's weiner though," Luke muttered, grinning devilishly. "His is particularly edible and very juicy."

This time I did choke. I coughed and sputtered and managed to get the bread out of my windpipe. My eyes watered as I took a drink.

"Don't look so fucking shocked, cowboy," Luke said. "Noah and I have a long standing...friendship. If you're a good boy and make me happy, maybe you can be a part of our friendship too. But only if I allow it. Got it?" Luke's deep-blue eyes conveyed all the hidden meanings of his sentence very clearly, causing my cock to press harder against the denim of my jeans.

"S...so, I have to share you but you don't want me to fool around with anyone else?"

Luke inclined his head slightly. "Well, when you put it like that, it does seem unfair. But that's the deal. You only have to share me with Noah. And he's so fucking sweet I can't even imagine you being upset about him."

Luke was perceptive because I *wasn't* upset about it. I was intrigued. I turned to Noah who continued to eat his supper quietly.

"So, you and Luke, huh? I never would have guessed."

Noah shrugged and gave me a shy smile. "We keep it quiet. Luke doesn't want the other guys teasing me."

I turned slowly to stare at Luke, eyebrows raised. "But they can tease me?"

Luke shrugged, and licked his lips. "I figured you could handle it," he said to me. "And I really wanted to fuck you in the showers."

*

Lying in bed at the bunkhouse later, my mind whirled over everything that had happened over the past forty-eight hours. I wondered if I was the same person who had innocently driven to this hidden resort a day and a half ago. I didn't think I was.

Which wasn't a bad thing. I only felt irrevocably changed.

It had been years since I'd had any kind of purpose. I had a place here and I didn't feel invisible anymore.

My ass was sore from the adventure in the showers, but I liked that. It reminded me it was real and not a figment of my imagination. The entire experience with Luke had blown my mind. If it had only been some fun between two horny guys, I would have valued it.

But it had been more. Luke had wanted me, and still wanted me, all to himself to do with as he pleased. And the idea made me more excited than anything. Maybe I *was* the kinkiest of the entire bunch.

I gazed at the grey leather of my hat, hanging on a nail I'd hammered into the end of my bunk. The hat reminded me of who I had been and who I still, in some ways, was. I wondered who I would be a month from now.

Luke was asleep in the bunk above me, but a soft voice called out in the nearby darkness. "Jensen?"

Noah.

I turned my head and saw the shadow of Noah's form crouched beside my bunk.

"Yeah?"

"I don't like the rain."

My addled brain couldn't figure the statement out. It had started to rain as I had made my way back to the bunkhouse, and now the sounds were loud against the roof. But why was Noah telling me this?

"Okay?"

"Can I...can I come in with you? To snuggle. I don't want anything else, and Luke would be pissed. But I just..." The frustration in Noah's voice was heartbreaking. He sounded fearful and ashamed, angry at himself because he was reduced to begging. "I only want to snuggle. Until the storm is over. Then I'll go back to my bunk. I promise."

I stared at Noah for a long moment in the dark, but I found it impossible to refuse. Though I doubted I'd get much sleep sharing my narrow bunk with Noah, no matter how innocent it was supposed to be.

But maybe it was about time I exercised some self-control in this hedonistic space. I was perfectly able to be with someone in a platonic sense and might find Noah's presence comforting, if I could only keep the thoughts of how Noah looked in his fetish gear out of my head—at least for the time it took for the rain to stop and for Noah to go back to his own bed.

I lifted the blanket. "Sure. Come on."

"God, thank you." Noah slipped smoothly into the bed and pressed himself against my back, trembling as a crash of thunder sounded nearby. "I'd be nervous getting into bed with anybody else, even Luke, 'cause it'd end up being something else entirely." Noah said. "But I trust you, Jensen. I don't know why, but you strike me as a gentleman. Maybe it's the whole cowboy thing. I believe you'll be respectful of my boundaries."

My breath caught in my throat as Noah wrapped his arm around me and pulled close.

"Yep. I'm a gentleman cowboy, all right," I murmured, remembering getting plowed into a bench by the man sleeping peacefully in the top bunk. The guy who also had some kind of thing going with the young man now nestled snugly against me, both of whom would be completely under my care the next day at the grooming barn.

I drove those thoughts from my mind and closed my eyes, feeling every little tremor passing through Noah's body until I managed, somehow, to fall asleep.

Chapter Ten

When I woke the next morning, it was again to male voices talking and teasing. Noah's arm was still draped over me. The poor guy had fallen asleep finally and hadn't woken up in time to go back to his own bunk. And now we were both in for some teasing.

"Awe, how cute? Noah and Jensen all cuddly and cute together. Cowboy gets around."

I counted to three and opened my eyes, shifting so I could look at whoever had made the remark. It was Callum, of course.

Hunter gazed down at us and shrugged. "Better than Noah whimpering in his own bunk all night. Guy's terrified of storms. I'm sure Jensen was only providing some comfort. And I, for one, appreciate his kindness. I slept like a fucking log."

I was about to say something when Callum grinned and winked at me. "No worries, my friend. Any buddy of Noah's is a buddy of mine." He held out his hand. "Peace?"

I regarded the outstretched hand, then moved my own to meet it, trying not to wake Noah, who was still sleeping deeply, looking tousled and adorable beside me. "Peace."

We shook and Callum went back to his morning routine.

A head popped over the edge of the upper bunk.

"Good morning, cowboy," Luke said, voice rough with sleep. He didn't act surprised to see Noah in my bunk. He shook his head. "Guy is twenty-one and scared of thunderstorms. Thanks for looking after him. If he'd have crawled into my bed, we might have blown our cover. I don't know how you can resist such soft skin and his sweet mouth."

Resisting the man's charms had been difficult. My morning erection stirred from Noah's closeness. But I'd managed, and we'd both gotten a decent night's sleep.

"Noah," Luke barked, startling the younger man awake.

Noah blinked and sat up, looking around as if he remembered nothing from the night before. "What?"

"Get the fuck out of my cowboy's bunk. I know you weren't doing anything—you're not supposed to—but now you're awake, get lost."

Noah came to his senses. He pulled away from me and stood up shakily beside the bunk in his little red boxer briefs.

"But first, give Jensen a kiss on the cheek to thank him for being so nice," Luke ordered.

Noah blushed, then leaned down and pressed his soft lips to my stubbled cheek. "Thank you. I mean it," he said before tossing Luke a sheepish smile and moving off to find his toothbrush and washcloth.

I gazed up at Luke, who was still bent over the edge of the top bunk, watching me.

"Time to get up and face the morning, cowboy. Who knows what the day will bring?"

Who knew, indeed? The possibilities made my head spin.

*

Two weeks passed.

Somehow, I got used to the daily experience of intimately grooming these handsome men and to the ribbing and teasing going on daily in the bunkhouse. I became familiar with the techniques and the implements popular with this particular brand of role-play. And I adapted to doing nasty dirty things with Luke when we could snatch twenty minutes somewhere private. Things that made my heart beat faster and my cock weep more than ever before. He knew how to fuck; goddamn, did he ever. And he knew how to make me his bitch. I loved every minute.

My second week, I went on the night shift and learned how to keep the modern stables clean, how to disinfect the various stations, and how to clean spunk off a variety of surfaces. The feel of the job was different, but not bad. I continued to enjoy making things clean and tidy and neat.

I'd learned how to wash men and mop floors with the same purposeful intention, the distraction of caged cocks and hard muscles always there, but I got better at ignoring them. At least, I could ignore these things with some ponyboys. Both Luke and Noah continued to affect me to my very core, and I had to conceal my desire for the younger man on many occasions.

Because, so far, Luke hadn't repeated his suggestion of sharing Noah with me, and I didn't dare propose the idea. Even though, at night when I was alone in my bunk, the thought of being with Luke and Noah in the showers was pretty much all I could think about.

This place was doing a number on my inhibitions.

I'd finally had a heart-to-heart with Mitchell on my phone up at the house. After reaming him out about not preparing me for any of this, he apologized, but his reasons were what I'd suspected, and I knew he was right. I'd have never taken a chance on this place if I'd known what went on here.

*

When I got back to the grooming barn with Liv after working a week on the night shift, I felt more prepared for the routine of readying the ponyboys for their trainers. Adam had sent Connor to the bunkhouse with a couple pairs of cotton shorts in my size and a new pair of flip-flops, so I could dress more appropriately for the job. This would be Brian's final week at the ranch, and I wanted to prove I was more than ready to take over.

When Liv asked me to look after Noah's preparations, I felt my stomach do spontaneous somersaults as I walked over to the patient man waiting in the grooming stall. Noah looked like the subject of a questionable Renaissance painting, naked and golden, gazing at the floor obediently and awaiting instruction.

I cleared my throat, trying to ignore the surge of blood to my cock as my body registered this as the same man who clung to me on stormy nights and disturbed my sleep with impure thoughts. His smell had grown familiar now and tripped something in me, like a key fitting a lock.

"Arms up," I instructed.

Noah raised his delicately muscled arms, pale with a light dusting of dark blond hair, up to the cuffs I fastened around his willing wrists.

"Good boy."

I'd been told to be free with my praise in the grooming barn, because the trainers were sometimes stingy with theirs, and the positive reinforcement would encourage the ponyboys to be obedient and gentle. That was the goal anyway. The technique worked easily with Noah, who seemed in his natural state as a naked and pliant submissive.

Soon, I had the gag in place and the cock cage on. I tried to ignore the fact Noah watched my hands closely as I fastened the steel cage around his penis.

Picking up the loofah, I concentrated on giving Noah a thorough rub-down. He made delicate grunting sounds that went straight to my cock, but I tried to block them out. I didn't need my mind going anywhere close to where it wanted to go right now. I wanted to do my job.

As I worked, I caught glimpses of Noah's grey eyes regarding me with something approaching adoration, which gave me more satisfaction than I liked to admit. Lorraine hadn't requested Noah have his tail inserted this morning, which I found disappointing. *What the hell was I becoming?*

I found the task of thoroughly washing Noah incredibly affecting. After all the nights we'd spent cuddled together, I felt very protective of him and cherished the intimate act of caring for him this way.

Afterward, I dried him and fitted him into his collar and body harness. Stepping back to look over my charge, I was pleased and aroused with the result. As always, Noah looked gorgeous in his pony gear. But now I felt like I had a hand in creating the effect and in placing him into the submissive headspace he wanted, needed, to be in for the morning session.

I removed the gag and released the wrist cuffs, allowing Noah to bend and put on his boots. When the ponyboy had trouble with a knot in one of his laces, I instinctively stepped in.

I bent to my knees and took over the job of untangling the stubborn knot. When I'd succeeded, I glanced up to see Noah watching me with a similar look of adoration. I couldn't help smiling at the handsome ponyboy and doing up the laces of both boots, giving him a firm pat on the ankle when I was done.

"There you go."

"Thanks," Noah whispered. The ponyboys were supposed to be silent even after the gag was removed but I nodded and smiled at him.

I was surprised to find everyone's eyes on me when I stood and dusted my palms on my shorts. But they soon turned back to their tasks as if they hadn't been distracted by my spontaneous gesture.

The rest of the morning passed, with cleaning and maintenance tasks taking up the time. Liv and Brian chatted about Brian's upcoming departure, and I lost myself in the monotony of my routine.

Liv's radio crackled and a female voice said, "Liv, are you busy?"

Liv took the device off her belt and pressed the button. "Hey, Lorraine, what's up? Over."

The female trainer laughed. "Besides Noah's cock right now? Not much. But I want Jensen to see what happens when a ponyboy does everything he's asked to for his trainer. Over."

I closed my eyes, feeling a surge of desire as I realized what Lorraine's words meant. Liv replied, and I heard the smile in her voice. "Copy that. I'll send him your way."

"Cheers, love."

"Ten-four," Liv replied, putting the radio away. "Jensen, you've been summoned. Lorraine and Noah are in the arena. She's been teaching him some new moves for a show this weekend. But she implied he's getting his reward for good behavior." She exchanged a look with Brian.

I nodded. "Okay. Do I need to bring anything?"

Liv shook her head. "Nope, just your pretty self," she said, winking. "But don't forget your hat. I'm pretty sure Noah would want you to wear it."

I felt the blush rise to my cheeks but grabbed my cowboy hat off the hook by the door and exited to the sounds of Brian's chuckles and a suggestive whistle.

As I made my way along the dusty path toward the arena my eye was caught by motion in the pasture as I heard Kamal's yell and the crack of his bullwhip. For a second, I was distracted from my objective and walked up to the fence to get a closer look.

Kamal, in jeans and a button-down shirt, looked every inch the pony master, wielding his whip. He was running Trey and Callum around the outdoor ring. Michael stood leaning up against the fence on the other side, watching the ponyboys run in the dirt.

They were tired, their steps faltering as they tried to keep pace. Being a ponyboy at the BCR was physically challenging despite being the answer to a submissive's fantasies. It was easy to see how they kept in such good shape. Kamal saw me watching and gave a little salute before yelling another order at his charges.

I tore my eyes away from the fenced yard and made for the arena where Lorraine must have Noah on his own, which fact only somewhat lessened my apprehension.

My vision took some time to adjust to the dimness as the door shut behind me. Some movement and the sound of a low voice to the left drew me forward.

A tall, brown-skinned woman with black hair in a long braid, wearing jeans and a button-down shirt, like the other trainers, and Blundstone boots, spoke softly in Noah's ear as the blindfolded ponyboy leaned in an awkward position beside her.

The ring in Noah's leather collar was attached by rope to a high ring in a hitching post near the wall. He was bent forward, boots planted several feet behind him, his torso supported by two evenly spaced wooden bars reminiscent of an oxer—a kind of device usually used for horse jumping. As I got closer, I was correct in my assessment. The double poles kept Noah, whose arms were restrained behind his back in the leather cuffs, from falling forward. One bar supported him at his pelvis and the other at his chest. The fact Noah's trainer had him splayed out over a horse jump in a vulnerable position made my mouth go dry and my dick start to swell. The oxer was an ingenious form of debasement that played right into the role-play element of a human pony ranch.

Noah's cock had swollen as much as possible in the restrictive steel cage. Moisture oozed from the tip as Noah whimpered in some distress. Lorraine heard my approach and turned from her charge, smiling and extending her hand. "Hi. I'm Lorraine."

I tried to collect myself as I shook her strong hand and noticed the glint of a delicate gold stud in her pretty nose.

"Jensen," I said. "You wanted me?"

Lorraine turned back to Noah and stroked her hand along his pale flank. "Noah wanted you. You are his reward for everything he did for me this morning." She gave Noah's buttock a sharp slap, eliciting a moan. "At least, you're an integral part of what I'm going to do with him."

I blinked in surprise. "I don't understand."

Lorraine smiled. "I asked him what he wanted. Most of what he told me was fairly standard, but he said he wanted you to watch. And he's been such a good boy today I decided to indulge him."

She smoothed her hand along Noah's skin where the flesh looked pink and tender from, presumably, at least a few other spanks.

"Um, okay. Where do you want me to stand?" I asked, voice a trifle shaky.

"On the other side of him, there. I've got a stool for you. You'll have a good view of everything."

I nodded and made my way around the naked ponyboy. I saw Noah incline his head slightly toward me, the black cloth of his blindfold preventing him from seeing. Without thinking to ask for permission, my hand came out to cup Noah's stubbled chin gently in my palm. "I'm here," I said softly and then let go, glancing at Lorraine.

She raised her eyebrows and said, "That's fine, but don't touch him again without my permission. He's my property in this arena and, therefore, my responsibility."

I nodded. "Of course. I'm sorry." I would be learning the shifting dynamics in this place for some time.

But Lorraine smiled warmly. "Don't be. It's procedure. I may well ask for your assistance at some point." She raised an eyebrow at me. "Would you be okay with helping me?"

Would I be okay with—?

My mouth opened, then closed again, then opened. "Uh. Yeah. Okay." I got up onto the tall stool, resting my feet in their blue flip-flops on the rungs. My shorts stretched tight over my erection, and I had to adjust myself.

The possibilities of what might happen made me dizzy, and very, very horny. If I touched Noah under Lorraine's supervision, would Luke have a problem with my actions? Then again, Luke would never know...unless Noah told him.

To me at least, what happened in the grooming barn or arena under the direction of the trainers was not connected to the goings-on in the bunkhouse. In the bunkhouse, everyone was their own agent. In other areas of the BCR, the ponyboys and I myself, to a degree, were guided by established procedures. Procedures I was slowly beginning to fully understand.

"Okay, first things first, Buttercup," Lorraine said to Noah. "Let's get this off."

Her delicate hands went to the cage on Noah's engorged cock, deftly releasing the clasp and removing the device as Noah moaned and squirmed.

"Don't you dare come yet, you little devil. Or you'll miss out on the fun I'm going to give you. And your buddy Jensen will have walked all the way out here for nothing."

I wanted to argue because watching Noah come from Lorraine's hands removing his cock cage would have been worth all the awkward conversations I'd had at the BCR so far, but I didn't dare say anything. Plus, she had a point. I was so ready to see what she had in store for him. And from what she'd said earlier, his reward would all be things he'd expressly requested.

"I'll give you a few moments to collect yourself and get used to having your cock out. As you know, you'll need more self-control to stave off your orgasm without the cage on. And I don't want you to come until I give you permission." She glanced at me. "Standard procedure."

I nodded. *Okey dokie then.*

I watched, fascinated, as Noah's unrestrained prick swelled fully. A bead of pre-come gathered at the tip, then dripped over the sensitive frenulum, making Noah shudder. But he maintained control. Barely.

Lorraine smoothed her hand over Noah's plump backside as she spoke to him in soft tones. "Good boy. You were so good for me this morning. Obedient and enthusiastic, giving me everything as always. I can't wait to show you off this weekend. You gonna win me a blue ribbon again?"

Noah only whimpered and nodded.

Lorraine grinned. "You looked stunning today. You have the perfect combination of athleticism and submission for this, Noah. You were made to be a ponyboy."

I felt my chest swell with pride for Noah at Lorraine's sincere and heartfelt words. Noah had been nothing but kind to me since my arrival at the BCR, and I could only hope the best for him.

"Too bad you can't see your cowboy friend here. He looks so pleased for you, and he's wearing his hat and everything."

Noah turned toward me, making a frantic sound. The bars creaked in protest.

"Maybe I'll let you see him a bit later. For now, I need you blindfolded, so you can concentrate on what I'm doing."

Noah whimpered and shook his head, for all the world like a pissed-off pony. I couldn't help but laugh.

"Right?" Lorraine said with a grin. "He's a good little pony."

Then Noah made a neighing sound, and the unexpected utterance rocketed through me, making me feel strange and ashamed. I squirmed on my seat, wondering why such a sound from a sexy man goofing around should make me so uncomfortable.

Lorraine must have read my expression. "Takes some getting used to," she said, petting Noah tenderly on his buttocks and down the backs of his thighs. "But there is nothing wrong about going into your head and being what you want to be, no matter how weird it might seem to someone else. Some people are uncomfortable with animal role-play because they feel it's a step away from bestiality. But none of these guys, or any of the staff here, want anything to do sexually with a real animal. The idea is absurd."

I could see the truth of this. I'd spent years looking after real horses and not once had the thought crossed my mind. Interspecies sexual interaction was a pretty hard limit for me and for most people, thank God. But I couldn't deny there was something extremely exciting about the ponyboys at the BCR. Whether it was their willingness to indulge a kink that pushed the envelope of acceptability or the freedom with which they entertained a part of their psyche others might shy from, I wasn't sure.

"Pony play, or any type of pet play, is about accessing the primal brain where thoughts of anything but the present moment are superfluous. Animals don't have jobs to stress about or friend and family dynamics to fret over. The animal brain is a very simple headspace to be in. Am I fed? Am I horny? Am I well-cared for? Am I loved? Can I come?" She pinched Noah on the butt cheek, making him gasp. "And the answer is no, not yet, in case you were wondering, my sweet."

Noah huffed and shifted, his cock jutting, balls heavy and tight behind.

"Who needs meditation and anti-anxiety pills when you can be a pony for a day?" I offered. "Or six weeks."

"Exactly," Lorraine said, gazing at me with respect. "Have we converted you so quickly?"

"I think so. I haven't seen anything I can object to so far."

Lorraine nodded. "Okay. Well, I might test you this morning. But remember, everything I do to Noah he has expressly requested. And he has a safeword he can use if anything is too much or he changes his mind."

"Okay." I said. "What is it?"

"Hmm?"

"What's his safeword?"

Lorraine grinned again and tousled Noah's hair. "Tell him your safeword, Buttercup."

"Saddle," Noah murmured, voice husky.

"Nice," I commented.

"Now," said Lorraine. "We'd better get started. Noah wants some satisfaction before he's sent back to the grooming barn. Right, sweetheart?"

"Yes, please," Noah croaked.

"So polite," Lorraine commented, giving Noah a hard slap on the rear again. The sound made me jump. "They aren't all like this. One, in particular, likes to give his trainer a run for his money."

"Luke," I said.

"Hmm, how did you know?"

"A hunch."

She slapped Noah hard on the ass again a couple of times, the sound echoing in the large arena. Noah moaned and shifted his feet.

"He really likes my bare hand on him, but it's starting to sting, so I'm switching to the crop," she said, picking up a braided leather riding crop from a small bench. She held the implement up for me to see. "Hence the name of the ranch. Most of them enjoy crops, so the name makes sense."

Oh, hell yes, I thought before I could help myself. I wasn't a rider, so I'd never even held one, much less used a crop for its intended purpose. In fact, I'd seen them in the tack rooms of barns I'd worked in, and I can't say I didn't think of the sexual connotations back then. It was only a tool. But the implement would save Lorraine's hand and presumably give Noah the sensation he craved.

Lorraine stepped back. "I'm going to warm you up now."

She tapped Noah's pink skin with the tip of the crop, gradually increasing the speed and intensity. Noah shuddered and gasped, trying to stay still under the onslaught, his cock leaking with need.

The sounds of leather on skin filled the space and I tried not to squirm as I watched with wide eyes. Noah loved every minute of Lorraine's attention, even as the strikes became more forceful and closer together. Lorraine moved around so she could access different parts of Noah's body. First his buttocks, and then his thighs, then his shoulders and chest.

Noah breathed heavily and whimpered, gasping as a particularly hard flurry of strikes descended on him. Becoming more and more excited, he shifted against the bars and humped the air.

"Easy there. As much as it might thrill Jensen to see you come hands-free from this, I won't allow it. Collect yourself. I'll give you a moment."

Noah sighed as Lorraine snapped on a pair of black nytril gloves and picked up something else from the bench.

The item in question was a large black dildo, realistic, with bulging veins and a definitive head.

She held the object up for me to see. "For your information, each ponyboy has his own collection of toys, exclusive for use on him, for hygiene purposes. In case you were wondering." She winked, passing me some gloves and a bottle of lube. "You can do the honors. Coat the thing well."

I couldn't help a small laugh while I put the gloves on over trembling fingers.

"What?" Lorraine asked with a smile.

"Is that the motto here?"

"Quite."

I squirted some lube into my hand and began to coat the toy, finding my desire growing while I handled the imitation cock and watched Noah shift from side to side with anticipation.

When I was done, I handed the dildo back to Lorraine. I rubbed my gloved hands together, slippery now, and wondered what to do about cleaning them. "May I please have a towel?" I asked, seeing one on the bench.

Lorraine smiled, rubbing the tip of the dildo along Noah's crack in a teasing way. "Shame to waste all that lube."

I blinked, wondering what she meant. Noah whined and pushed his ass out as if he wanted the dildo and he wanted it now.

"If you want, you can stroke him while I play with his ass." She said those words so sweetly, as if she were asking me if I wanted wine with my dinner. Her deep brown eyes evinced intelligence and warmth beneath her thick lashes as she looked at me.

"You mean, his cock?" I breathed, hardly able to get the words out.

Lorraine's laughter echoed off the wooden walls. "Yes, Jensen, his cock. I'm sure he'd be happy if you did." But she gave Noah's ass a slap with her free hand. "But don't you dare come. Not till I say you can."

Noah moaned and shook his head again, grunting as Lorraine fingered him briefly, then pushed the head of the dildo into him.

"Good boy. I know you can take this."

Lorraine slowly pushed the black dildo into the obedient ponyboy as Noah groaned deep in his chest. My thighs trembled as I moved closer, reaching out to wrap my gloved hand around his arching prick.

Noah cried out, and I stilled my grip, not wanting to push him over the brink when he'd been expressly forbidden to orgasm.

"Oh, yes, you like his touch, don't you. You like having a cowboy's hand around your cock," Lorraine crooned, and I marveled at her ability to dominate in a way both caring and cruel at once. "Well, go on," she said to me. "I'll let you know if I think it's too much for him."

I nodded, tightening my grip and starting to stroke slowly.

Noah made another sound low in his throat and licked his lips, hands fisting and un-fisting behind his back, the sight of his desperation maddeningly arousing to me. I shifted my feet and tried to concentrate on my task. My tan cotton shorts felt tight, and I knew Lorraine wouldn't miss that.

"Looks like your cowboy is enjoying himself," she murmured, twisting and gently thrusting the toy in Noah's ass. "Are you okay?"

"Yeah, I'm okay," I breathed, eyes fastened on Noah as he moaned, "Yes. Fuck, yes."

Lorraine laughed softly. "Well, I was asking Noah, but I'm glad you're surviving this, Jensen. So far."

Noah made a desperate sound.

"Jensen, stop. Let go of him," she said, stilling her own movements.

I did. Noah shuddered, and he almost lost the battle. With an extraordinary amount of will, he was able to hold off.

"Good boy. You are amazing." Lorraine held the dildo deep and still while Noah worked to collect himself. "Your cowboy is turning out to be a skilled hand at looking after ponyboys, isn't he, Noah?"

Noah moaned and shook his head violently from side to side.

Lorraine laughed and gently began to move the toy again. "Oh, he is. I bet he can get you off while I fuck you with this big rubber cock. You want to come, Buttercup? You want to come all over Jensen's pretty hand?"

Oh, Jesus Christ. I want you to. I want you to come all over my hand, you sexy-ass pony.

Noah thrust hard into my grip, his entire body trembling with barely restrained desire. He panted and whimpered as Lorraine continued to fuck him with the dildo.

"Say you want to come. And then I'll let you."

Noah's words were quiet yet desperate. "I want to come on Jensen's hand. I want to come on Jensen's hand. Please!"

"Jensen's *pretty* hand," Lorraine corrected.

"His pretty hand. His pretty hand. Please let me come on Jensen's pretty hand. Please."

"Okay, Noah. You can come now."

I kept my strokes firm even as I felt Noah's movements quicken. Noah yelled as Lorraine thrust the toy deeply and twisted gently. His cock pulsed in my hand, shooting white fluid over my knuckles as he shook and cried out. His whole body shuddered for several seconds as the intense orgasm took him.

He lay there, spent and wracked with aftershocks while Lorraine helped me tidy up. Finally, we helped him stand while Lorraine removed the blindfold.

"Have a look at your cowboy, Noah."

Noah blinked his beautiful grey eyes in the dim light, gazing at me as though I was the answer to his prayers.

"Doesn't he look hot with the hat and the hard-on in his shorts? I think he liked watching you."

Noah breathed deeply, trying to recover, his eyes dancing over me. But he shook his head.

"He's not my cowboy. He's Luke's. He's Luke's cowboy," Noah panted. "I only borrowed him." He turned to Lorraine. "Don't tell Luke, okay? Please?"

Lorraine looked confused, then smiled. "Of course not. Why would I tell Luke?"

Noah gazed at her with the adoration of a sub for its mistress and bowed his head. "Thank you."

Lorraine nodded. "Good work, today, Noah. As usual." She slapped his bare behind, making him jump. "You put on quite a show."

Indeed. A show I wouldn't forget any time soon.

Chapter Eleven

Lorraine handed Noah's lead rope to me. "Here. Take him to the grooming barn. Give my little Buttercup a good hose down. I worked him hard this morning."

"Okay. Sure." Any remaining doubts about my willingness to perform these duties had left me at the warm gush of Noah's pleasure over my gloved hand.

Lorraine flashed me a smile and laid her small hand on my arm. "You did great. I'm so glad to meet you. See you at supper tonight."

I nodded and tipped my hat. "Great to meet you, Lorraine."

Once again, I was trying to walk with a pretty substantial hard-on, at least beginning to subside, although images of what I had witnessed kept threatening to reignite my desire. And the knowledge I had sweet, submissive Noah on the end of a lead rope didn't help.

Noah cleared his throat. "Can I talk? Or do you want me to be quiet?"

I glanced back at him. "You can talk. I like the sound of your voice."

"Oh," he said, sounding surprised and pleased. "And, uh, did you like...what you saw...in there?" Noah's voice had gone so quiet I had to stop walking to make sure I heard him. A hot breeze blew the hair off his sweaty forehead.

I grinned and lifted my hat from my head, pressing the brim to my heart. "I've never seen anything...so goddamn hot...in my fucking life."

Noah blushed and grinned, the dimples in his freckled cheeks going deep. "Really?"

I laughed, replacing my hat and shrugging. "Maybe I've lived a sheltered life up to this point," I admitted. "But you looked so...I mean, you still look so...damn pretty in your gear and I...I'm glad you found a place to explore this side of yourself. The pony play is so much a part of you. I can't imagine it being buried and never seen."

Noah stared at me, eyes wide and blinking like a stunned colt.

"I mean, you're fucking beautiful," I stated. Because he was.

Noah moved forward and nuzzled his face into my shoulder, knocking my hat into the dust. But I didn't care. I turned toward him, and when Noah's lips found mine, the kiss felt unavoidable and inescapable.

I enjoyed the gentle press of Noah's lips on mine, trying not to think about Luke and his "rules," then pulled away and grabbed my hat off the ground, dusting the brim against my thigh. "Now, come on. I need to get you clean or Lorraine will have my hide."

In the grooming barn, I removed Noah's leather gear and hosed him down, using a soft cloth and soap on his sated penis and testicles. This was above and beyond what was expected but I felt moved to perform this intimate task and neither of the others made any objection.

And Noah's sweet smile as he moved around the partition was reward enough.

*

In the afternoon when the other ponyboys presented themselves for grooming, I tried to keep my eyes off Luke. I didn't want Luke's overwhelming presence to eclipse the memory from this morning.

But the endeavor was hopeless. Once I caught sight of Luke's tanned body, head bowed, wrists clasped at his back, I was overtaken, once again, by the obstinate man's very presence. And when Luke peeked up at me and winked, then gazed down again so quickly none of the other stable hands noticed, I felt a bolt shoot from my eyes to my cock.

This place was legit going to kill me.

Liv assigned me to Hunter again, thank God, but he was beside Luke and each time my eyes glanced over they went to Luke's cock in the restraining cage, the cock I'd had inside me, again, the previous evening.

Luke had climbed down from his bunk in the dark of night and woken me. We'd snuck into the showers, and he'd fucked me right against the wall this time, under the warm water, slippery and slick. This time he'd brought a pair of clean socks, rolled in a ball, for me to bite on, to muffle my noises while he pounded me hard and expertly until we'd both come at the same time. Then he'd turned me around and kissed me hard before sending me to back to bed.

Seeing Luke restrained was a crazy rush. Because the man was usually so full of aggressive, assertive force, being privy to this side of him proved a complete mindfuck.

There was no denying Luke was here of his own free will. That he, like the other ponyboys, paid the BCR for the experience of being treated this way. But submission went against his natural inclinations so much his presence here puzzled me.

His presence also made me crazy. I tried to keep my eyes off Luke and on Hunter, who was as attractive in a different way but didn't affect me at all. I must be getting used to all the naked flesh on display at the ranch. Or at least, used to some of the ponyboys.

Fortunately, Luke didn't put up any sort of fight in the grooming barn, and I wasn't called out to assist a handler. As much as I was curious to see Kamal deal with Luke, I was a little scared of the intimidating trainer. I spent my time cleaning tack and washing the shower stalls and doing other manual labor until the ponyboys returned.

While Hunter and Ben relaxed under our attentions, Luke became restless. He shook Brian off and growled.

"Liv, give me a hand, would you? He's being an ass."

Liv glanced their way but she was in the middle of removing Ben's complicated arm bands. I, on the other hand, had already removed Hunter's and had also fastened his wrists above his head. I was getting used to my duties.

"Jensen then. Come here and hold him, would you?"

I moved over to where Brian was grappling with a twisting and turning Luke. "What the fuck is wrong with you? You want a paddling? Hmm?" Brian asked, frustrated.

I moved forward and took Luke forcefully by the shoulders, gripping him hard and keeping him still so Brian could unbuckle the bands.

"Shh, settle down, big boy," I murmured, pinning Luke with a forceful gaze. *There you go, I'm in charge here.* "Let him get these off you."

Luke stilled and glared at me as if he wanted to break free. I raised my eyebrows and tilted my head, tightening my grip slightly. We both dropped our eyes to his raging erection.

"I think I know what's causing the problem," I smirked, gesturing with my chin to Brian who followed my gaze.

"Well, probably, but I can't attend to both at the same time. And I don't know if I'm so inclined to attend to his dick with the goddamn attitude he's giving me. If you can get him to ask for a hand job politely, I'll think about it."

My gaze drifted back to Luke's, still steely and obstinate, but now conflicted. He had heard what Brian said. But I still had an impossible task before me.

"You heard him, Luke. Do you want a hand job or not?" I said.

"Fuck off, cowboy."

"Not until you behave yourself. I'm helping Brian." I said.

"I can't...even think. He fucking rode me ragged." Luke spat onto the floor of the grooming bar. "Didn't finish me."

"Who, Kamal?" I asked.

"Who the fuck else?"

Brian finished with Luke's bands and stretched his arms up, fastening them to the wrist cuffs. "Why didn't he finish you, Luke? Weren't you behaving?"

"Bastard's got it in for me, I tell you. I've asked Adam to switch me to one of the others."

Brian laughed. "I'm pretty sure none of the others want you, Luke. You're a goddamn hazard to yourself and everyone else."

"*Fuck. You.*" Luke hissed, staring at Brian.

"Hey, I'm gone after today. So, you can curse at me all you want. Jensen's the one who'll have to deal with you."

Luke turned toward me as I finished removing his harness and collar, leaving the man completely, gloriously, naked.

"You want me to..." I asked, pointing at Luke's standing prick.

"What the fuck do you think, cowboy?" Luke said, but the vehemence of his tone was more modulated.

Still. I raised my eyebrows, not moving, staring him down. "I'm supposed to get you to ask politely. Want to surprise me, or are we going to leave you alone and spray you down?"

Luke worried his lips, obviously struggling with what he wanted and what he had to do to get it. He glanced at Brian who ignored him, picking up the pieces of Luke's gear and taking them to the pile.

"Ask me nicely, Luke, and I'll look after you," I promised, taking a step and leaning in close. "Maybe you can help me out later." I said softly, so the others wouldn't hear.

Luke cleared his throat, cheeks flushing. His voice was a desperate whisper. "Please get me off, cowboy. I'm begging you. I can't think of anything but fucking your sweet ass in the shower, and it's making me fucking crazy." Luke's blue eyes flashed up at me. "If we were in the bunkhouse right now I'd flip you over your bunk and fuck you in front of all of them. Let them see how good we fit together." His chest rose and fell with deep, ragged breaths, and his prick twitched with eagerness.

"See," I said, hands trembling. "How easy was that?" I could picture him doing exactly what he'd described.

Luke's lip curled up and he yanked at his bindings as I turned to Liv. "Can you throw me the lube?"

"Sure. Gonna give him some relief?"

"He's earned a bit of relief."

Brian shrugged. "I don't know if I'd go that far. But whatever. He does settle for you. Good luck with him."

"Could I have some gloves, too, please?" I asked Liv.

Liv grinned and passed me a pair. "Here you go, cowboy."

Luke watched with wide eyes as I drew the gloves on and coated both hands with lube. He pulled at his wrist cuffs again, making the chain rattle loudly.

"Stop. One more outburst and I'm done," I said. "Behave or I'll take my hands off you. You choose."

Luke considered the question, then nodded.

"Good boy," I said, pleased he'd given in.

I wrapped my right hand around him, giving his cock a few rough pulls. Luke groaned and closed his eyes, grimacing as if my strokes were painful. I moved my hand down over Luke's testicles, teasing the skin behind them, eliciting a high-pitched whine. The fingers of my gloved left hand slid between his ass cheeks, sliding and searching for that most vulnerable spot. When I found his anus, I pressed a fingertip against the yielding flesh.

Luke's mouth dropped open, and he gasped as my finger slowly breached him. "Fuck! Oh fuck."

Liv, Brian and the other ponyboys watched as I fucked Luke's ass with my finger and stroked his cock, spiraling Luke's need into a desperate frenzy in a matter of moments.

I added a second finger, then twisted my palm over the tip of Luke's cock and back down, repeating the move two more times.

Luke cried out and jerked, spurting over my hand. I continued to pump him with my fingers as I milked him until Luke sagged in his bindings and whimpered, "You win. You fucking win, cowboy."

I peeled off the gloves and hosed off the sweat and come from Luke's pale skin. I didn't speak again, but when I released Luke from his wrist cuffs, I gave him a quick slap on his ass as he moved toward the partition.

He froze, and I wondered if he would turn back and curse me. I almost hoped he would. But he only took a deep breath and continued walking.

I didn't feel at all victorious. I was hard and aching in my shorts, for the second goddamn time in a day, and I had no idea if I'd get any relief anytime soon. If Luke was mad about what had happened, hours might go by before the man looked at me or spoke to me again.

And I wasn't going anywhere near Noah outside of the barns.

*

I didn't have a chance to worry about it.

As I walked alone past the arena on my way to the bunkhouse, the door creaked open, startling me. A hand shot out and grabbed my wrist, pulling me inside the dimly lit building.

My heart hit the top of my head as it jumped a mile. Someone pushed me against the wall roughly.

"It's me." Luke's voice sounded shaky and raw as he pressed himself against me, lips on my neck, teeth nipping at my ear.

The relief at knowing my attacker didn't make my heart pound any less. Relief and something else. My cock, which had finally settled after forty-five minutes of end-of-day drudgery, sprang back up like an eager spaniel, hungry for its master's touch.

"What are you doing?" I stuttered, placing my hands on his chest and pushing. He was strong and didn't budge which made me hornier.

Luke grinned against my skin, scraping teeth over my Adam's apple as he grabbed my hair and pulled my head back.

"Showing you who's boss," he panted.

"Okay, okay. I know," I said. "I wouldn't want you to be any other way."

"You like this? You like me like this?" he asked.

I swallowed the groan trying to leave my throat. "I love it."

"But you like me all tied up, too, don't you? At your mercy?" His voice shook.

"Yes."

There was a pause during which he licked a trail from my Adams apple to my ear. Then he spoke, "Well, aren't we a couple of confused fuckers?"

"I'd say, versatile." I struggled for breath as Luke pressed into me.

"I want to take care of you," Luke breathed, hand sliding down to press against my prick, now hard as a rock in my shorts.

"God, you must be exhausted. You don't have to…" I protested, secretly dying to have Luke's mouth on me again.

Luke had already popped the button and zipper by the time I finished speaking. "Oh, I want to, cowboy. I owe you one."

I shook my head, pushing gently on Luke's shoulders. "You don't owe me."

"You want to keep arguing? Or you want me to suck you off? I know you've probably been hard all day. Who wouldn't be?"

I sighed, dropping my arms. "Fine. Okay. You're right." I watched as Luke sank to his knees and slipped his hand inside my shorts, pulling my cock out. "I've been hard all day."

"So, I'm gonna take care of you, and then we'll go to the bunkhouse. And then we'll have a nap. And then we'll go to the bonfire."

I gasped as Luke's tongue traced a path along my dick. "I keep...hearing about a...bonfire."

Luke kissed and tongued all along the length of me as he spoke. "The party's a yearly thing. Canada Day is on Sunday, but we'll be too tired from our weekend. So, we're having the bonfire tonight."

I nodded, not really caring about anything but Luke's mouth on my cock.

"Everyone goes," Luke said, tonguing my tight balls and flicking toward the other place, only for a second, enough to make me gasp. "You'll have fun. They make us play games."

"What?" I gasped. "Games?"

Luke laughed. "Well, normal games. Like volleyball. Anything so they can watch us prance around half-naked, right?"

"Oh. Okay. Only the ponyboys?"

"Anyone who wants to. Sometimes the trainers or the stable hands join in."

"Oh." I closed my eyes and moaned as Luke finally took my cock inside his warm mouth. "Shit, Luke, this won't take long."

Luke didn't reply, but kept working my dick, gripping tight at the base and sucking like a champ. All the memories from my busy and arousing day returned to me as I cried out and spilled in Luke's mouth.

"Fuck, oh fuck, oh God," I cried, thrusting into his wet heat, coming so hard I felt my legs trembling. If not for the wood wall behind me, I might have collapsed.

Luke released me, wiping his mouth with the back of his hand, and stood, dragging his body along mine. He tucked my cock back in my shorts and zipped me, gazing into my unfocused eyes as he did.

"Good cowboy," he said, with a wicked grin as he cupped my chin and kissed me hard on the mouth.

My lips parted eagerly. I let him take what he wanted, my tongue exploring his mouth, tasting myself there. He controlled the kiss at first; then he became soft and tender, surprising me. I responded in kind as warmth blossomed in my belly.

When Luke pulled away, he covered his confusion with a joke. "You're the king of hand jobs, but I'm the queen of oral."

I grinned, still breathless from the kiss. "Sure."

I hoped he wouldn't find out about the other hand job I'd given today. "You know, I don't always, uh, orgasm so fast."

Luke raised his eyebrows.

"I mean, I have some control. Usually." I felt the heat in my cheeks.

"Cowboy, anyone with half a nut who was new to this place would've spilled in his pants by now," Luke said gently. His look conveyed affection and respect. I found myself drowning in the unexpected kindness.

Then he pulled away, his hands making sure my clothes were tidy. He cracked the arena door, checking our surroundings. "The coast is clear," he said, then pushed the door wide. "Come on."

I followed him out, fear we'd be discovered a small flutter in my throat. Luke shut the door carefully behind us, making sure nobody had seen us exit the barn. Then he started walking along the dusty path, glancing behind to make sure I was following him.

"Fuck," Luke said, shaking his head like something annoyed him.

"What?"

"You in that goddamn hat. It's gonna be the end of me."

I blushed, adjusting my hat so the brim sat farther back, and smiled.

*

All eyes were on us when we opened the bunkhouse door and entered together.

"Where the hell were you guys? The bonfire's tonight, you know," Ben commented. Everyone was getting ready. Except for Noah, who lounged on his bunk dressed in a clean shirt and a pair of red shorts, reading. He glanced at us, then returned to his book.

"I know, Ben. We were enjoying the weather." Luke commented, stripping to his boxers and collapsing on my bunk. "Fuck, I'm wrecked."

I didn't know what to do. I was beat as well, but should I climb up and use Luke's bunk? Or was this an invitation? If so, to what?

"Jensen," Luke murmured, reaching his hand out in a beckoning gesture. "Strip and get in here with me."

I glanced around at the other ponyboys, who looked as shocked as I was. I looked quickly at Noah who kept reading, a pink blush on his cheeks. Then I slowly removed my shirt and shorts until I was in my boxer briefs as well and got into my bunk behind Luke, curling around him in the coolness of the air-conditioned room. He was warm and smelled amazing, and I felt my prick jerk at his back.

"Down boy," he whispered, and I smiled against his shoulder.

After a few moments and some hushed comments, the other ponyboys went back to what they'd been doing.

Chapter Twelve

I woke to a warm hand on my cheek. I looked up to see Noah gazing down at me.

"You better wake him up. They want us at the main house early for the barbecue, and then there'll be games and prizes," Noah said with a smile.

Jensen nodded. "Okay. Thanks."

Our eyes held for several moments as we shared the knowledge of our earlier intimacy. Then Noah smiled. "See you later."

"Yeah."

After Noah left, I gently pushed at Luke, who had wrapped himself around me at some point, in an effort to rouse him. "Wake up. We have to go."

Luke mumbled under his breath. I was pretty sure I heard a curse.

"Hey, we have to go," I repeated.

In one movement, Luke turned and pushed me onto my back, looming over me in the late afternoon light. He held my wrists in his hands and regarded me with a half-lidded gaze as my entire body went on alert.

My eyes widened, but I kept still.

"Did you sleep?"

"Yes."

"Good," Luke murmured, eyes raking down my body. "'Cause I've got plans for later."

My dick swelled, pushing up at Luke, whose own erection pushed back.

"I think everyone's gone to the main house," I said, licking my lips and staring at his naked shoulders and chest. "We could...do something now."

Luke grinned at me. "You," he said, poking me with his index finger, "are a naughty little cowboy."

I smiled. "Not so little."

Luke laughed, then pushed off me and stood up, gesturing at my groin. "Not little at all. No. But we need to get going." He looked for his shirt and found the item on the foot of my bunk.

I couldn't hide my disappointment. "It would only take a minute," I argued. Because suddenly, I wanted Luke so badly, I could taste my desire.

"Oh no, it wouldn't. The next time I have you the whole thing is going to take a long, long time because I am going to enjoy every inch of you, cowboy. Now, do as you're told. And wear something nice. We're going to a party."

*

We walked to the main house together, a companionable distance apart, trading occasional glances. I felt the urge to reach for Luke's hand, but I squashed the compunction, not at all confident he'd want me to.

I liked Luke. Liked his bravado and his obstinance though he was a little immature. I liked the way he looked at me as if he owned every inch of my body and he could take what he wanted whenever he wanted. As if he'd never desired anything more than to have my cock in his mouth or my ass in his hands. I liked the play of power between us—the way I was in charge in the grooming barn, but Luke was in charge everywhere else.

His control made me feel safe in a strange way. I knew what the rules were. I'd happily play by the rules if I got to keep this job and enjoy some physical release as well. The emotional connection was a bonus if it wasn't all my imagination and it existed at all.

Then there was Noah.

Noah was a whole different challenge. I still wasn't sure if I was allowed to desire Noah. I wasn't sure if wanting Noah was within the rules Luke had drawn up. But I couldn't deny I did desire Noah, in ways different to how I felt about Luke.

Because Noah was the opposite of Luke. Noah was shy and polite, where Luke was brash and rude. Noah thought about things before he said them, whereas Luke opened his mouth and said whatever came to mind. And Noah slid effortlessly into his role as a submissive ponyboy, whereas Luke would fight his submission at every turn, even though Luke, like Noah, had consented to everything.

Luke was a puzzle and a predicament needing to be worked out. And I had time.

The main house was buzzing with activity. All the grills were going, and the delicious smells of barbecued steak and shrimp filled the summer air. Everyone had dressed a little more glam than usual.

Liv had on a purple dress and some tan wedges that elongated her slim legs. Kamal wore slim, checkered pants, which emphasized the muscles of his thick legs and the bulge in his crotch, with a light-blue cotton short-sleeved shirt and grey fedora. He looked classy and elegant. Lorraine totally rocked a burgundy sari with a pair of wrap sandals, and she'd dotted a red spot in the center of her forehead. I found it difficult to place this as the same woman who'd teased and tormented Noah in the arena. Adam and Michael, the other trainer I'd had some brief contact with, were dressed more casually in khaki shorts and golf shirts, and Hiro, the only trainer I'd not been formally introduced to, had on tight black, short chinos and a form-fitting, salmon button-down emphasizing his slim, muscular build.

At Luke's urging, I had borrowed a pair of ankle-length tan chinos, but wore my own light-blue button-down with rolled-up sleeves, and my Blundstone boots. And my hat. Luke had placed it gently atop my head and given me a look indicating he would brook no argument.

I looked okay, but not as stylish as most. I'd have to ask Adam if I could have an afternoon off to go shopping in town. The expectations of my current position had taken me by surprise. *Wasn't that the world's most valid understatement.*

Luke looked delectable in his black chino shorts with the hems rolled up a couple of times, a grey button-down short-sleeve shirt and white sneakers.

And Noah.

God, when I caught sight of Noah, my stomach flipped. He wore snug navy shorts with large pink irises all over them topped by a white short-sleeved button-down, with a pair of navy boaters. He looked like a college kid at a coed barbecue. Remembering him in the pony-play gear bent over two jump bars and getting his ass swatted with a riding crop, I felt a bit faint.

Noah stood by the food table, holding a paper plate. His brow wrinkled and he worked his lower lip, like he couldn't decide what to eat and the effort of the decision was killing him. I'd already observed it sometimes took him massive amounts of courage to make simple decisions. No wonder he was so comfortable playing pony when the expectations were explicitly laid out for him.

Luke walked over and gently took the plate from Noah, spooning some potato salad, and then coleslaw, then grabbing a pickle and a piece of steak. He passed the plate back to him and said, "If you're a good boy, I'll let you choose your own dessert."

Noah's relief was evident. He took the plate and said, "Thanks. Can I sit with you?"

Luke nodded. "Of course, you can. You and Jensen both."

Noah peered at me, cheeks coloring and eyebrows squeezing together. "Okay. Sure," he said with attempted nonchalance.

Luke looked at Noah like he'd grown a second head. "Uh, yeah, good try, ponyboy. I know you have the major hots for my cowboy, so there isn't much use in pretending you don't want to eat your supper beside him." His gaze flicked between Noah and me. "I also know the feeling is mutual." He gestured to me. "Come on. Get a plate and let's find a table."

I stared at him, wondering if somehow Luke knew what had happened in the arena this morning. But he couldn't know. Maybe I simply wasn't as good at hiding my feelings as I thought.

I loaded a paper plate, starving after my busy day and anticipating a delicious meal and interesting event. So far, the evening had already surprised me.

As Noah, Luke, and I made our way to an unoccupied table at the edge of the gathering, I noticed the other ponyboys watching with interest. I was more than aware

Callum had a physical interest in me, but I had no idea what drew the interest of the other men. What was the big deal?

But maybe they weren't interested in me at all.

Luke had said he and Noah kept their relationship under the radar. But here they were eating together and hanging out with me, who everybody knew had something going on with Luke. They were probably wondering what was going on between the three of us.

So was I.

We ate in silence, exchanging glances, more focused on eating than anything. Music played loudly and the sounds of other conversations filled the silence of the evening. When Noah had finished everything on his plate, Luke whispered, "Good boy," across the table, making Noah blush and glance at me. I couldn't help smiling at the obvious pleasure he got from Luke's praise.

"You want dessert, sweetheart?" Luke asked. "Jensen, take him to the food table and let him pick something. Or help him pick something if he can't decide. And bring me one of whatever he chooses."

Noah and I stood. We walked together to the small dessert table. As we gazed over the myriad of offerings, someone nudged my arm.

"The apple pie is excellent."

I glanced over to see Ben standing beside me, gesturing to the severely decimated pie in the center of the table.

"Thanks," I said, "But Noah's picking for us."

Noah looked like he suddenly couldn't take the pressure. "No, you choose, Jensen. Luke likes chocolate."

I blinked. "You don't have to pick something chocolate because Luke likes chocolate."

Noah shuffled his feet and glanced shyly at Ben, who watched him closely. "I guess not. But he wanted me to pick something he'd like."

I glanced back at Luke, who was picking at his coleslaw and not paying any attention to us.

"Did he? Well, let's get two of those chocolate tarts and whatever you want. Do you want to try the pie?"

"The pie is awesome," Ben said. "The berry cobbler's nice too."

"I, uh, I'll try the apple pie, I guess," Noah said.

"Good choice, Buttercup. Uh, Noah." Ben cleared his throat, scrambling. "Sorry. I shouldn't have called you that," he said, embarrassed.

Noah shrugged and gave Ben a sweet look. "No problem. I like my nickname."

"Buttercup suits you," I said.

Noah looked like he would melt under the dessert table. He didn't know what to say.

"Why are you two hanging out with Luke anyway? I heard he put up a big fuss in the grooming barn and you took the piss out of him. Not sure why you want to expose yourself to more of his rudeness."

Noah's expression changed as he took in what Ben had said. "He's a decent guy under the surface. He struggles because—never mind."

"Pardon? You got some inside info on our rebel without a cause?" Ben asked, not unkindly, but with an innocent curiosity.

"No," Noah said so quickly his obfuscation was obvious.

"Let's get some pie. I've got the chocolate," I said.

Ben turned to me. "Jensen, are you playing volleyball with us later?"

I glanced from Noah to Ben. "Uh, sure. If you need someone."

Ben grinned. "We can always use a strong body." He looked me up and down and winked. "You'll do."

I found myself laughing. "Okay. I'll do my best."

When we got back to the table, Luke had finished and sat there twirling his plastic fork.

"What did Ben want?"

"He invited me to play on his volleyball team later," I said. "We got you a chocolate tart." I put one of the rich desserts in front of Luke. "Noah said you'd like it."

"Noah was right. But you didn't follow my instructions."

I blinked at Luke. "Huh?"

"You were supposed to bring me one of whatever Noah was having. I see Noah is having the apple pie."

I smiled, unsure. "Are you serious? I brought you a tart. A chocolate tart."

"You didn't do as you were told, cowboy. You think I wasn't going to notice?" The disapproval in Luke's casual tone went straight to my dick. Don't ask me why.

It was ridiculous for Luke to be upset about something so trivial, of course. But while part of me wanted to argue with him, a larger part of me wanted to play this game.

What would he do about this perceived disobedience? And would I like it?

"No."

"So, you knew I'd notice and call you on it?"

"Maybe." I hadn't considered him challenging me, but I wanted to find out what he would do. Because I wasn't actually scared of anything Luke might think up. I was excited. And, *oh look at that,* hard.

Luke smiled and picked up the fork I had placed beside the small dessert plate. He stared at me as he began to eat the chocolate tart, slowly and deliberately. I went from mild curiosity to intense desire in an instant.

The way Luke slid the chocolate-covered fork into his mouth, using his tongue to tease the silky goodness off the plastic, was enough to make me worry I'd mess my pants. When he slid the utensil back out, slowly, staring at me as his lips sucked the final bit off, my mouth opened and I sighed helplessly.

Noah watched us, too intrigued to start his dessert. He held his fork in his motionless hand, eyes glancing from Luke to me and back again.

"Eat your pie, sweetheart," Luke told Noah, keeping his eyes on me. "You didn't do anything wrong."

Noah relaxed and took a forkful of the pie to his lips.

"Neither did I," I said, voice barely there as my dick throbbed.

"Oh, cowboy. I'll always be the judge of that."

*

By the time I'd finished dessert my cock had calmed down. Maybe Luke had seen how the fork had affected me because he put the utensil down and popped the rest of the tart in his mouth, chewing perfunctorily and ignoring me. I clasped the edge of the picnic table until my pulse returned to normal and I could think clearly.

Which happened as Adam stood to make an announcement.

"Happy early Canada Day, everyone! We're all very lucky to live in such a beautiful country. In a moment we're going to ask for some volunteers to play a few games of volleyball. There will be prizes, and not only for the winning team. We'll be awarding prizes to recognize effort, gamesmanship, creativity, chutzpah, and of course, Best Chest. So, work it, boys. And girls, if any of you want to participate."

"Yikes, I better go change," Liv said, getting up and running into the house. "I'm on your team, Ben!"

Adam continued, "After the prizes are handed out, we'll head out to the far pasture for a gigantic bonfire, the likes of which you've never seen before."

Whoops and hollers resounded.

"Performances begin at one pm tomorrow in the first corral. Which gives you a little time to sleep in and get your act together. If you're a ponyboy in the first performance, you might want to keep your drinking under control. Either way, I'm expecting top performances tomorrow for our weekend guests. Don't disappoint them. *Or* me."

Adam stepped aside as Ben grinned and started to gather his group together. The team consisted of him, Liv, Callum, Trey, Brian, and myself.

The other team was made up of Hunter, Luke, Noah, Aiden, and Kamal.

Liv returned from the main house in pink bike shorts and a bikini top. The men took off their shirts and shoes to shouts and whistles from the crowd. Feeling self-conscious, I did the same.

"I'll hold your hat, cowboy," Lorraine said, picking it up off the table and putting it on. She looked adorable, like a kooky Bollywood star. I grinned and winked, moving off to join the team.

As I did, I noticed a small group of strangers in fancy clothes hovering beside the main house by the fence separating the stables and pastures from the path to the resort. Most of them held glasses of wine and must have wandered down after their fancy meal to have a look at the 'livestock'.

Callum winked at me as he found a spot for himself in front of the net. "Ready to show your stuff, cowboy? We know you're good at giving hand jobs. You got any other talents?"

I blushed. "I can throw a mean spike," I said. "Just wait."

"I bet you're pretty good with those lips too," Callum said. "But I guess I should ask Luke."

"Knock it off, Callum," Ben said. "We're here to play ball, not to talk about our cocks."

"Speak for yourself," Callum muttered, but the remark was his last as the game started.

*

We played four games, and I found myself thoroughly enjoying the activity. It wasn't a hardship to play volleyball surrounded by gorgeous, half-naked men and one really cute woman, who were all a little buzzed and intent on letting loose for the evening.

We won the first two games, then got trounced in the third and fourth. A tiebreaker was announced, and Luke's team won by a margin.

Luke behaved himself, in general, except for the occasional curse or insult thrown at another player. But never Noah. Noah, he encouraged and helped since the guy looked completely out of his comfort zone. I could see Luke was holding in his obstinate tendencies in order to put up a good show of sportsmanship and not ruin the pleasant evening.

In the end, Luke's team won the grand prize, which was a trip into town next week for lunch. Ben won the award for gamesmanship, me for effort/participation, and Kamal for Best Chest, which made everyone groan because, apparently, he won this award every year. I was not surprised. The man was built.

Kamal put his arm around Luke as we walked off the field and commented on his lack of rebelliousness during the game. "You played well, Luke. I told you if you focus on your performance and not everything you don't like, you'll be a star."

Luke shrugged Kamal's arm off and said, "I did it for Noah."

Kamal let him go and gave me a resigned look. "That man is his own worst enemy."

I nodded, watching Luke head over to the cooler and grab a beer. "Why does he come here if he hates the place so much?"

"He doesn't hate the ranch," Kamal said. "He needs the BCR. And he loves the place so much he has to pretend he hates it." He shrugged. "He's complicated. Luke's got some issues. But being here helps him work them out. Even if it doesn't seem like being here is helping him, it is."

I wasn't sure I believed Kamal, but I nodded.

"He's a good guy, Jensen. He's had...a rough time. It's a wonder he can function at all."

"What do you mean?"

Kamal shook his head. "You'll have to get him to tell you. Might help too. But don't push him. Wait until he's ready."

"Okay."

"I can see he's gotten attached to you right out of the gate. Don't let him scare you."

"He doesn't. I like him," I said.

Kamal smiled. "Good. He's not as tough as he pretends. Cheers."

I watched Kamal of the 'Best Chest' walk away and felt someone put my hat back on my head. I turned to Lorraine.

"Thanks."

"No problem. You play pretty good for a greenhorn. But then, that's been the general consensus here." She grinned and winked. "Feels like you're one of us. See you at the bonfire."

I let the feeling of acceptance wash over me. I could barely remember my life before arriving at the BCR. I was glad I'd already found a place here.

Chapter Thirteen

I fixed my hat more comfortably on my head and picked up my shirt from the bench. I was so hot and sweaty I didn't put it on.

"Fuck! You look hot, cowboy," Luke said into my ear, wrapping an arm around my waist and tickling my belly with his long fingers.

I smiled and rested my hand on Luke's arm. "I am hot. Sweaty, I mean."

"I know exactly what you need," Luke winked.

"Uh, well, I don't think we can sneak into the arena right now. Maybe the bunkhouse?" I said as I watched the rest of the group make for the far pasture.

Luke snorted. "Not what I mean. Surprisingly, but no." He picked up his shirt from the grass, swept the fabric under each arm, and then tossed it back to the ground.

He looked so good, standing there in the fading light, half naked. I licked my lips as my cock started to fill again.

Luke pulled away from my intense gaze and pointed to where Noah sat on the steps of the main house, which had been entirely abandoned now everyone was on their way to the bonfire. Even the curious onlookers had returned to whatever the resort offered on a Friday evening.

Noah had put his shirt back on, but his flushed cheeks and messed-up hair made him as delectable as Luke.

"Grab a beer and follow me," Luke said as he walked over to Noah and whispered in his ear. Noah laughed and shook his head. Luke said something else, and Noah looked at me, something hungry in his gaze. They spoke together briefly; then Noah stood.

"Aren't we going to the bonfire?" I asked, gesturing with my beer towards the others. They were far in the distance.

Luke shook his head. "Nah. Too much smoke and socializing for my taste. Plus, the mosquitos are awful."

"Then, what?"

Luke gestured to the back door of the main house. "So, Adam has the best room in this place. And I asked if we could use his huge soaker tub while everyone was at the bonfire."

I could already feel the clean water on my sweaty skin as Luke spoke. "He said yes?"

Luke nodded. "As long as we tidy up when we're done. You want to?"

"Sure. All—" I glanced at Noah. "—three of us?"

"Sure. Why not? You got a problem with Noah?"

I glanced at Noah, but he wouldn't meet my gaze. "Not at all."

"Good. Come on."

Luke pushed the door open as we followed him inside.

The house was shadowy and dark, with only some emergency lights coming from empty offices.

"Are you sure Connor isn't in here catching up on some work?" Noah asked Luke.

"No, I saw him with the others heading to the pasture," Luke said. "Nobody's here. Only the three of us."

Noah hesitated as Luke started up the stairs to the second floor. "Adam really said you could use his room?"

"I think he wanted Jensen to be impressed by the size of his...bathtub," Luke smirked. "That cowboy's got everyone trying to impress him."

I shrugged. "I'm not sure why. I'm nobody. Just a guy looking for a decent job."

Noah came up the stairs behind me as I trailed Luke closely.

"Looking hot as fuck in your cowboy hat and sliding into the kink like nobody's business. Yeah, you're nothin'." Luke laughed.

"I have no idea what I'm doing," I said.

Luke stopped in the upstairs hallway and turned to face me. "I call bullshit. You've got everyone by the balls the way you are in the grooming barn. And *out* of the barn? You're like this wide-eyed innocent at every turn but you're up for anything. And I'm taking control now. 'Cause if someone doesn't, you're gonna burn out in another week. These guys will make mincemeat of you."

"Oh, come on," I said. "That's ridiculous. I can handle them."

Luke raised his brows. "Oh, really? Well, we're never gonna know because you're mine and nobody else gets to mess with you." He glanced behind me. "Except maybe him. If he's a good boy and you want him to."

We walked farther down the hall before I said, in a shaky voice, "I have no issue with Noah messing with me."

When we got to the last door on the left, Luke turned the handle and pushed slowly. He flicked on a light.

"*Shangri La*," he said, beckoning us in past him. "This is the sitting room. Bathroom's through the bedroom."

I glanced at Luke as I walked past him. "Why are you so intimate with Adam's room?"

Luke grinned. "He's my therapist. We have a little chat once a week. This is a lot more comfortable than his office downstairs."

My chin dropped. "Your therapist? He's your...therapist?" I looked at Noah, who nodded.

"While I'm here. I have a different one in Ottawa, but they know each other. My therapist in Ottawa recommended I try this place and see Adam for a bit."

"Adam's a registered psychotherapist," Noah said softly. "He's here for any of us if we need him."

I was speechless.

"What?" Luke asked.

"A registered psychotherapist running a pony-play ranch?"

"Why does that seem strange to you? You don't think pony play has psychological benefits?"

I blushed. "I...never really thought about the psychological benefits of pony play. I mean, I never thought about it until I started working here."

"Yeah? Well join the rest of the kink-phobic population," Luke said. "I'd been experimenting with kink in the city, but not safely. I ran into some bad shit. My therapist said Adam could help me explore my needs in a safer way."

Wow. That was...interesting. "I'm not kink-phobic," I protested.

Luke flicked on the light in the en-suite bathroom.

"Holy fucking shit," I said.

The room was huge, with a giant oval whirlpool tub at one end and a double shower at the other. A large marble vanity with two sinks stretched between them.

"I told you the bathroom was nice."

"The bathroom's...amazing. It's almost as big as my apartment in Ottawa."

Luke raised his eyebrows. "The bathroom or the tub?"

"Very funny. The bathroom."

Luke turned on the taps for the soaker tub, checking the water temperature. When he was satisfied, he dried his hands on his shorts and opened a cupboard in the vanity, taking out a large bottle. He checked the label and made a face. "I told him to stop getting this flowery shit. But I guess he likes flowers."

Luke tipped the bottle over the tub. "Bubble bath. We might as well go the extra mile."

"How often do you use his tub?" I asked, finding it strange for Luke to be so familiar with Adam's room.

"Only when he lets me. Baths help me relax. Don't narrow your eyes at me, cowboy. There's nothing going on between me and Adam. That would be super inappropriate, and I don't even think he's good-looking. Plus, he kind of feels like my dad most of the time." Luke made a face. "And, uh, gross."

"Who sounds kink-phobic now?" I said with a grin.

"Har har. If Daddy kink is your thing, sure, go after Adam."

"You're way hotter than Adam," I said, mouth going dry as Luke pushed his shorts and boxer briefs down.

"Good to hear. Noah, strip. You, too, cowboy. Everything but your hat."

I tried to keep my eyes off Noah as he meticulously removed his clothes but couldn't quite manage. I kept peeking surreptitiously until Luke said, "Go ahead and watch him. He doesn't mind. Do you, Noah?"

Noah blushed but shook his head with a shy smile. "No."

"He likes having people watch him. Right?"

Noah nodded, glancing at me.

"You looking forward to your performance tomorrow, Noah?" Luke asked.

"God, yes." Naked, now, Noah stepped into the tub and sank to his chest. "Oh, that feels so good."

Luke stepped into the tub next, sinking down beside Noah, and said, "Get in here, cowboy."

I shucked my shorts and boxers, then steadied my hat with one hand as I stepped carefully into the tub, trying to ignore my half hard cock and aching muscles. I hadn't played sports in a very long time.

As I sank into the bath, my hand cupping my junk, the water enveloping me, I couldn't contain a moan of sheer, sensual pleasure. "Oh my God, so good."

Luke grinned and moved to the side so we each had ample space to relax. "I knew you'd like this."

I grinned beatifically at him and leaned my head back, nudging my hat forward so the darned thing would stay perched on my head.

"Fuck," Luke swore. "That hat will be the end of me."

"You said that before."

"Only 'cause every time I see you in it, I want to fuck you and suck you all kinds of ways." He glanced at Noah, who licked his lips, then back at me. "Again. And again and again. I had no idea I had a thing for cowboys till you showed up."

I smiled dreamily, pleased with the attention. "Yeah? Well, I had no idea I'd get off so hard seeing men dressed like ponies with fucking butt-plug tails and cock cages. Go figure."

Luke and Noah laughed.

"Well," Luke said. "Don't we make a kinky threesome." He dipped his head back to wet his hair. "You ever try group sex, cowboy?"

"What?"

"A threesome." Luke's tongue lingered on his top lip as he waited for my answer.

I shrugged. "No." I glanced at Noah, whose eyes had gotten wider. "Not yet."

"Figures," Luke muttered.

God, what was his problem? Why did he have to be such an asshole? An asshole who made me hard every time he looked at me. "Why do you think I'm so innocent, anyway?"

"Because Connor said you almost came in your pants when Adam showed you the photos in the album."

I remembered my reaction to the picture in the album. Luke had a point.

"I'm not innocent," I said. "I'm not naive. You think I haven't done some things?"

Luke raised his eyebrows. "What things?"

"I spanked a guy over my lap once," I said. "He liked it."

"I bet he fucking liked it," Luke said, winking. He played with the bubbles, then spoke without looking up. "You ever been spanked over someone's lap?"

I blushed. "No," I said, a little too quickly.

"'Cause I'll spank you over my lap whenever you want a good hiding, cowboy. Or whenever I think you need one."

I squirmed, feeling my cock thicken.

"Luke gives really good spankings," Noah said softly, glancing at Luke, then at me.

"I bet he fucking does," I said, breathless all of a sudden.

Luke grinned, like he wanted to show me right then.

I cleared my throat. "Anyway, I'm not some stupid virgin. I've fucked lots of guys."

Luke's eyes narrowed. "Fucked them? Or been fucked?"

"Both."

Luke nodded. "I like your style."

I tipped my hat and gave Luke a smoldering grin. "I thought that was established."

Luke didn't say anything. Then he lifted his chin. "Noah?"

"Yeah?" Noah was breathless from watching the exchange.

"I want you to do something for me."

"Okay."

"I want you to go over there and sit on Jensen's lap. I think he might have something for you."

Noah looked at me with dark eyes and licked his lips. "Okay."

I sat up straighter, cock hardening more at the look in Noah's eyes and the tone of playfulness in Luke's. My hat started to fall but I righted it.

"You're getting better at following instructions," Luke nodded, eyeing me. "Almost as good as Noah."

Noah moved in close to me, face a mix of desire and uncertainty. He glanced back at Luke.

"Go on. Jensen won't mind. Will you, Jensen?" Luke asked, voice hoarse.

I didn't look away from Noah, who inched closer.

"I've never heard you say my name before." At least, I didn't think so.

"Huh. Really?"

"Yeah."

"You like the sound of it?"

"Well, it's my name, so, yeah. But I like when you call me "cowboy" too," I said, feeling heat in my cheeks.

Noah chose that moment to slip one arm behind my neck and climb onto my lap. I gasped as his hip brushed against my hard-on, and he gave me a sweet, hungry smile.

"Hello, beautiful," I said, wrapping my arms around him and pulling him close. Noah felt heavenly in my arms, warm and slippery, and I knew Luke had no issue with it. That Luke had, in fact, demanded this intimacy.

Noah hid his head in my neck, soft tongue coming out to lick and taste.

"Oh, Jesus," I said.

"He's sweet like honey, that one. He'll kill you with his charm," Luke said, voice low and deep.

I didn't doubt Luke's assertion. Noah was killing me now. My cock ached with want but my heart melted in my chest.

"I want to kiss you," Noah whispered in my ear. "Ask Luke if I can."

I moaned as my eyes flitted to Luke. His arm moved as he stroked himself underwater, heavy-lidded eyes on us.

I wasn't sure I could actually speak. I cleared my throat. "Noah wants me to ask you something."

Luke's gaze locked on Noah. "What, sweetheart? What do you want?"

Noah turned his head to gaze at Luke. "I want to kiss him. Can I kiss him?"

"Oh fuck, yeah. Your sweet lips will blow his head off. Go on."

Noah puffed out a laugh and ran his left hand to cup my jaw, turning my face. He gazed into my eyes, conveying such genuine affection and desire I couldn't help but lean forward and press my lips against his. He gasped and opened his mouth, sliding against me with eagerness as we sank into a tender, exploring kiss.

"Oh God, you two look amazing," Luke moaned. "Fucking perfect. My cowboy and his pony. I'm gonna come watching you."

I glanced his way. Luke's mouth was open, his eyes half lidded as he watched us, arm moving slowly and evenly. I moved my hand down Noah's body until I found his full cock.

"Oh God," Noah moaned. "Oh God."

"What's he doing?" Luke panted.

"He's touching me." Noah sighed.

"Where?" Luke asked on a small moan.

"You know where."

Luke laughed and I smiled.

"Is your prick hard, Noah?" Luke asked.

"Yes."

"Do you like Jensen touching your dick?" he added.

"Yes." Noah closed his eyes. A loud groan came out of his mouth as he thrust into my grasp.

"Do you like the feel of Noah's cock, Jensen?"

I hissed. "God, yes. He's so sweet and hard, and I want to make him come. Like I did this morning."

I froze suddenly and so did Noah.

"Shit," Noah breathed.

God, I was an idiot.

"Uh," I muttered. "Um..."

"What?" Luke said. "What did you say?"

"Nothing," I murmured. "I want to make him come."

"Don't you dare. Not till I say so."

"Lorraine made him help," Noah said, turning to face Luke. "In the arena today."

Luke blinked. "Fuck, really?"

Noah nodded.

"Help, how?"

"He..." Noah started.

"No, I want Jensen to tell me."

I moved my hand gently on Noah's swollen cock, remembering. "She got me to jerk him off while she pushed a dildo in and out of his ass."

"Oh hell," Luke groaned. "Fuck."

"Yeah. It was fucking hot," I admitted. "He came all over my hand. I wondered if you'd be mad."

"I'm not mad," Luke said. "I'm fucking jealous. You lucky fuck."

I gave Luke a sheepish smile as I stroked Noah.

"Now stop talking, and kiss my boy again. Make him crazy. He's wanted to kiss you since you got here."

I turned my head to find Noah's mouth again. We dove eagerly into the kiss, a deep, openmouthed communion of tongues and souls.

Noah rose up, hands on my shoulders, so he could kiss me while I stroked him. I lost myself in the experience, the press of Noah's slippery body, and the sounds of Luke's arm pistoning in the water.

"Oh fuck, oh fuck," Luke panted. The water splashed as his hand sped up. "Oh God, gonna come, gonna come," he moaned. We turned as one to see Luke, eyes closed, mouth open as his body jerked with release. He groaned, then whimpered as the pleasure began to fade.

"Great. Now there's jizz in the water," I said.

Luke grunted and sighed. "Huh. You're lucky I don't make you drink it." He stood up, a bit shaky, water and bubbles sloshing off him. "Time to get out anyway. I want you on Adam's bed after you dry each other off. I'll be waiting."

"On his *bed*?" I said. "Did he say we could use his bed?"

"No questions, cowboy. Go."

I looked at Noah as Luke grabbed a towel and padded out of the bathroom. Noah shrugged. "We better do what he wants."

"Or what?"

"Or he might change his mind about letting you touch me."

I felt my dick twitch. Yeah, I wasn't going to risk Luke changing his mind. "Okay. Come on then. Out you get."

Noah stepped out of the tub and waited while I did the same.

"Come here," I said, picking up a towel and wrapping him in the terrycloth material. I wiped him roughly, then used the towel on myself. "Go on. I'll be there in a minute."

I took a moment to breathe, using the towel to dry myself and wondering if I was getting in over my head with them. They had an interesting relationship, and I wasn't sure if it was wise for me to intrude. They appeared to want me to. And I couldn't resist even though resisting might be the smart thing to do.

When I walked into the bedroom, I was not prepared to see Noah on his hands and knees over a dry towel, facing Luke, who sat against the headboard, legs crossed.

"Now, you are going to prove to me you know your way around the male body, cowboy. Specifically, Noah's body."

No problem there.

I nodded smartly, once, then glanced at the closed bedroom door. "How much time do we have? I mean, Adam could come back any minute."

"Nah. He'll be at least another hour. We've got some time."

"You sure?"

"I'm sure."

I took a deep breath. "Okay."

"Now. Noah here is a strange animal. He doesn't particularly like to get fucked."

"Luke..." Noah murmured.

"Although, he might make an exception for you, cowboy."

"But...but I saw Lorraine using the toy...and he definitely liked that."

"A toy is different," Noah said quietly. "That's when I'm a pony. And it's a toy. Not a guy's...dick."

"Okay," I said. "You don't have to explain. You don't want me to fuck you."

Noah moaned with frustration. "Not with your cock. But you can use your fingers or...or your tongue."

"Oh," I said. "God, yes. Not a problem."

I met Luke's gaze over Noah's back. He nodded. "Go ahead then."

"Can I at least take my hat off?" I asked.

"Sure," Luke said. "If I can wear it."

"Here." I took the hat off and threw it to Luke, who caught it and put it on.

Noah moaned again. "Oh, Jesus Christ. Come on. Please."

Luke laughed and touched his finger to Noah's lips. "Shh. Patience, sweetheart."

"But I've been patient. I've been waiting all this time."

"Shh," I said, getting onto the bed behind him. I stroked his smooth buttock, sliding my thumb down his crack, teasing.

"Now give him a smack," Luke said.

I glanced up. "Yeah?"

"Noah?" Luke asked.

"Yeah. Spank me. Then lick me. Please, Jensen." Noah's body quivered in anticipation as I smoothed the skin again and brought my hand down hard, making him gasp. I slapped him two more times, then dug my thumbs into his crack and pulled his cheeks apart to reveal the wrinkled pink flesh between.

Noah's lips parted as he whined with eagerness.

"So pretty," I crooned. "You are so pretty here." He smelled like flowers from the bubble bath. I leaned forward and touched my tongue to his clean skin.

"Fuck!" Noah cried out, dropping to his elbows in front of Luke, cheek resting on Luke's calf.

Pleased with this response, I grinned and pressed the flat of my tongue against him, pressing firmly and undulating slowly.

"God yes," Noah whimpered.

I felt like I would go mad from the sounds Noah made. I pressed my cock against the mattress as I tongued him with skills I hadn't rolled out in a very long time. Luckily, eating out a guy was like riding a bike. You never forgot once you'd learned.

After a little while, Noah began to squirm and beg for more, and Luke had to clamp down on his shoulders to keep him still for me.

"Okay, I guess you pass. Pretty obvious you've done this before," Luke admitted. "Now fuck him with your fingers." A small bottle of lube landed beside my knee.

I teased Noah for a few more seconds, then grabbed the lube and squeezed some out at the top of his crack, letting the cool liquid run down to his hole and taint.

"Oh God, that looks hot. So shiny and slippery," I breathed.

Noah groaned and widened his legs. He reached underneath himself and grabbed his dick, giving it a pull.

"No, no, not allowed, sweetheart. Hands off. Only Jensen or I can touch your dick."

Noah made a sound of protest but let go, moving his hands back beside his head.

"Good boy. You are such a good boy. Jensen's going to finger fuck your ass, then he's going to make you come when I say. Okay?"

Noah nodded. "Okay. Okay."

Smoothing lube over Noah's hole, I eased the tip of a finger inside, listening to his quick breaths. It didn't take long to work the digit all the way in. He trusted I wouldn't hurt him.

"Okay?" I asked.

"Feels so good," Noah moaned.

"He's been waiting a long time for this," Luke said.

"I only got here two weeks ago," I reminded him.

Luke shrugged. "Okay, he's been waiting for two weeks then. He's wanted those fingers since he saw you the first time."

"He told you?"

"He didn't have to. I can tell what he's thinking most of the time."

I looked up. "And me?"

"What?"

"Can you tell what I'm thinking?"

Luke grinned. "I hope you're thinking what I'm thinking."

"Which is?"

"After you get Noah off, I can tear your sweet ass up again?" Luke said, licking his lip and tipping the cowboy hat. "With this hat on and screaming yee-haw as I pound you into Adam's mattress?"

"Oh fuck," I said. "Sure. I mean, I am now."

I pushed a second finger into Noah's ass, making the man cry out and push back against my hand.

"Reach under and feel how hard he is, cowboy. Boy's dripping all over his towel."

I slid my other hand past Noah's tight balls and along his shaft, which was very wet at the tip.

"Oh God, Noah, you do like this."

Noah gasped. "Do you? Do you like fingering me?"

"Oh fuck, I love fingering you. I love doing this for you." I played with the wet tip of Noah's cock while I pushed my fingers deeper. "I love your ass."

Noah moaned with desperation as I teased him. "Oh God, I need to come. I need to come so bad. Can I, Luke? Please!"

I peered at Luke who simply raised his eyebrows.

Pulling my fingers slowly out, I swiveled and slid underneath Noah, on my back. When I was in the right position, I slipped the two fingers back inside and pushed him forward so his cock slid into my open mouth.

"Oh!" Noah said, "God...fuck..."

"Yes!" Luke swore, holding tightly to Noah. "Yes. Suck him off. Milk his cock, cowboy."

Noah and I moaned as he thrust into my willing mouth.

"Jesus Christ," Luke swore. "You're as dirty as I am."

I wanted to agree but couldn't say anything with Noah's cock down my throat. Soon Noah gave a high-pitched cry and climaxed, his ass clenching around my fingers, cock pulsing streams of jizz that escaped my mouth and dribbled down my chin, even as I tried to swallow the stuff.

Noah barely kept from falling on top of me. His body quivered with aftershocks and I didn't release his cock until his orgasm was well and truly over. When I finally let my lips slide from his softening cock and after I pulled my fingers from him, Noah slid down the bed and collapsed into my embrace, nuzzling and kissing my face and neck.

"Thank you, thank you," Noah murmured. "You are so sweet."

I laughed. "I don't feel very sweet right now." I pressed my hard cock against Noah's belly, making a small whimper. "I feel so horny now. You have no idea what you do to me. Both of you," I tilted my head back to glance at Luke, who was crazed with his own lust.

"I can suck you," Noah said, lifting up.

"I've got a better idea," Luke said. "Turn over."

Of course, Luke had a better idea.

Noah quickly rolled over on the bed, dick shiny with saliva and semen.

"On your hands and knees, cowboy. Time to get mounted like the pony you want to be." Luke said, voice harsh. "Noah's going to suck your cock while I fuck you."

I wasn't sure if I liked the pony analogy or not, but I didn't much care right then. I got into position over Noah, smiling down at him as he licked his lips and opened his mouth. Luke's fingers slicked the lube onto me then pushed inside as Noah guided my cock between his lips.

The sensation was overwhelming, even more so when, after very little preparation, Luke pressed his condom covered erection against my hole and the tip slid inside without much problem.

I gasped, squeezing my eyes shut at the mild burn as Luke's cock pushed into me. "Oh my God," I moaned as all sorts of hidden nerve endings did a happy dance. "Oh God, Luke. Fuck."

"I think I know why you like this hat, Jensen. I feel ten feet tall and three feet deep in your ass right now."

"Jesus!"

"Whoa, cowboy. Don't you come yet, you hear? You wait for me."

"Oh Christ. I don't know if I can. Not with Noah's mouth on my...oh God, oh fuck, hurry up, will you?" My voice rasped and wavered.

"So demanding. Not quite domesticated are you? But I will make you into an obedient little pony if it kills me. And it might." Luke's words broke with gasps and little sounds of desperation. He moved hard, fucking me with intention as I struggled to obey, although my body silently screamed with tension needing to be released.

Finally, Luke grunted and stilled, pressed flush against me, cock deep as it could go. His hands gripped my hips as he gasped, jerking minutely as he came. "Oh, yes, yes, yes," he moaned, waiting until he'd emptied before saying, "Come now. Come in Noah's mouth."

And I did, without any other warning. My mouth in an O as my throat made no sounds when the orgasm ripped through me. My ass clenched around Luke's cock, still deep inside me, as my cock exploded down Noah's throat.

Finally, I heard my own loud cry as the pleasure took me, accompanied by the sounds of footsteps and a door opening.

"What the *fucking hell* is *this*?"

Chapter Fourteen

I froze, gasping with the aftershocks of my orgasm as Luke pulled roughly out and Noah scrambled from underneath me, knocking me onto my belly.

Adam's angry voice made me dizzy and sick.

"*Three* of you? On my *bed*? What in the ever-loving *fuck*?"

I tried to speak. Nothing. My mouth flapped mutely.

"Jensen?"

"I'm sorry," I managed. "He said you knew. He told us it was okay with you." This assertion sounded lame and unlikely to my ears now.

"Luke," Adam said, his voice quieter but more threatening. "Put some fucking clothes on and explain yourself."

I heard a sniffling sound and looked up to see Noah huddled against the headboard. I forgot my own nudity and crawled over to embrace the man, covering him and holding him.

"It's okay. It's not your fault," I said.

"No, this isn't Noah's fault. And I'm sure this isn't your fault either, Jensen. I'm sure I know *exactly* whose fault this is."

I saw Luke pulling his shorts on lazily, not hastily like I would in his place, facing the wrath of this older and bigger man.

"For fuck's sake, Luke. Are you trying to get thrown out of this place?"

"Your bedroom?"

"No, the BCR, you idiot. Are you testing me or something?"

"Fuck no. I wanted some action, and this was the best place to get some. You do realize there are only single beds at the bunkhouse? And I'm sick of fucking in the showers."

Adam stared at Luke for a moment like he wanted to kill him. Then he took a deep breath and turned to Noah and me. "I'm going downstairs. Get dressed and come down. I need to talk to both of you."

"What about me?" Luke asked.

"You stay right the fuck here until I come back. And if I come back to you jerking off all over my pillow, I will kick you off this ranch."

"No worries. The condom was pretty fucking full. I'm done for a while."

"Oh, you are done for a long while, Luke. Do you know what Kamal is going to say when I tell him?"

For the first time, Luke looked worried.

Adam nodded. "He's going to rub his hands together with glee and say "Oh goody," and you know it.

"Fuck," Luke said.

"Downstairs," Adam said to Noah and me. "I'll give you five minutes but not a second longer."

He left, closing the door and heading briskly down the hall.

"He'll calm down," Luke muttered. "He's jealous."

"He's not jealous. He's furious," I said, pulling on my pants. "I can't believe you lied to me. I can't believe you lied to him." I nodded to Noah, who was sniffling back his tears as he dressed with trembling hands.

"God, you're so naive," Luke said. "I can't believe you trusted me."

I glared at him. "Why wouldn't I trust you? Except for this escapade, you've been nothing but nice to me."

"You have a weird concept of nice, cowboy."

I nodded, stepping forward and snatching my hat off Luke's head. "Maybe so. But I was really starting to like you, Luke. I mean, *really* starting to like you. And now you've gone and fucked it up."

Luke nodded. "Yeah, well, fucking things up is what I do. Get used to it."

He seemed so disappointed in himself, but I didn't care.

"Fuck you." I reached out a hand for Noah. "Come on."

Noah took my hand easily and followed me out the door, not looking back.

*

I felt sick as I led Noah down the lighted stairs to Adam's office where Adam stood waiting. He gestured us inside and shut the door.

"Sit down. We need to talk about what happened."

Noah sat quickly and I took the remaining chair, removing my hat.

"I'm so sorry, Adam. Luke said he'd cleared the whole thing with you, but I should have known he was lying," I said, feeling terrible. Noah looked like he might start crying again. The anger I felt toward Luke was building, made worse by the situation he'd put Noah in.

Adam stared at me as I worried the brim of my hat with my fingers. He smiled, placing his hands into a triangle, elbows on the desk. His voice, when he spoke, was calm.

"Jensen. You've only been here a few weeks."

"Still. I should have realized." I felt like an idiot to have fallen for Luke's lie.

"I don't blame you," Adam said. "Luke is very...persuasive."

Adam turned to Noah. "And I don't blame you either, Noah. Your behavior in the bunkhouse and the stables is exemplary, and I realize Luke has a deep influence on you."

"What are you going to do?" Noah asked. "You're not going to kick him out... Please, don't kick him off the ranch."

Adam shook his head. "I don't really believe leaving would be the best thing for Luke, Noah. Don't worry."

Much of the tension drained from Noah and he slumped in his chair. "Okay."

"But I do have to punish him. You know that."

Noah nodded. "Yeah."

"Did you think for even one minute he might have been lying? You know I don't lend out my room on a regular basis. Or ever?"

Noah nodded. "I wondered. But he reassured me he had asked you, and you'd said we could use your room. I did feel weird about being there, at first."

"But Luke was pulling you along, and you're interested in Jensen, aren't you?"

Noah glanced at me and blushed. "Yes."

"Honestly, if you three weren't all over my stuff I'd be happy you're all getting along in such an...intimate way. I want you to understand I don't have a problem with the three of you being together like that. I have a problem with you all being in my room. On my sheets." He eyed them meaningfully. "And in my bathtub?"

We nodded.

"Uh-huh. I should have had a regular tub put in. It wouldn't have been so tempting."

I swallowed. "You have a really nice bathtub, Sir."

Adam nodded, resigned. "Did he use my bubble bath too?"

"Yeah," Noah said.

Suddenly, Adam laughed. He collapsed against the back of his chair and let the tension out, laughing softly. "God, I am going to kill him one of these days. Or haul him over my lap and spank the shit out of him. Except he'd probably enjoy a spanking. Anyway, I'm sure Kamal will start polishing the wood paddle when I tell him what Luke did this time."

"This time?" I said.

"Ah, Jensen, you may have become aware Luke is our resident troublemaker. He's been in hot water before." Adam gave them a weak smile. "But never in my bathtub. This is a first."

I smiled, trying to see the humor.

"Look, Luke has some problems. Which I'm not at liberty to share with either of you, in detail. You'll have to ask him if you want to know. But these are things not easy for him to share."

"Is he okay? I mean, I know he has to be punished, but do you think he'll be all right?"

Adam nodded. "He craves punishment. That's why he pulls this shit. He wants to be held accountable. He wants to learn to behave. I thought we were making some headway. Because if he doesn't learn to hold himself accountable, he'll always get into trouble."

"Oh."

"He didn't have a real authority figure for most of his childhood. Whether this stems from a lack of parenting, or the trauma he's been through, I'm not sure. Maybe both. I do know being here is keeping him safe, for now. I've still got a few weeks to get through to him, so when he does go back out there, hopefully he'll have better coping mechanisms."

I glanced at Noah, then looked at Adam. "I still don't really understand why a pony-play ranch is a good place for Luke if he's so messed up."

"Jensen, we're all messed up. None of us are perfectly adjusted. I certainly don't believe the BCR is the place for everyone who's struggling. But Luke was getting into some kinky stuff with people who weren't practicing safely. He likes kink; he likes role-play. He likes power play and discipline. A lot. And, I figured, at least if he can explore his needs here in a safely managed environment with trained staff who have lots of experience with healthy kink, it'll be helpful to him. At the very least, it lets him know a penchant for stuff like this is nothing to be ashamed of and gives him an idea of what to look for in a play partner. Or partners." He winked.

I nodded and put my hat back on. "That makes sense."

"I'm glad you think so. This ranch means a lot to me. I'm very lucky to be employed here."

I smiled. "I mean, I feel grateful too. Everything I've seen here, even though unusual and, frankly, mind-blowing, has been...mutually enjoyable and respectful."

"Consent is the backbone of the ranch. We do a lot of crazy things here, but everything is either requested or agreed to in advance. Every one of our ponyboys fills out an information sheet with things they want to do and things they don't want to do. So, even if they *are* being punished—" He gestured at the ceiling. "—like your priapic friend up there is going to be, the technique will involve activities he's agreed to. And he can always use his safeword. Always. Some of our trainers, Kamal, in particular, can be very creative within those boundaries. Which is why he scares Luke a little. Maybe a lot. But deep down, Luke gets off on his discipline. I don't think he'd get the same things out of, say, Lorraine, he gets from Kamal."

"I like Lorraine," Noah said softly, and Adam smiled.

"I know you do. And I know she can be as merciless as Kamal in some ways. Right?"

Noah blushed and the corner of his mouth twitched. "Right."

"But where her techniques are perfect for you, Noah, I think you will agree Luke needs something a little more...forceful. Threatening? Even if the consequence is threatening in a pretend way?"

"Yeah," Noah agreed.

Adam leaned forward. "And Jensen. How are you adapting to the requirements of your position?"

I squirmed, my freshly fucked ass a little sore. "Well, up until this incident, I thought I was adapting pretty well."

"I'm assuming everything was consensual between the three of you?"

"Oh yeah," I said. "Except for him telling us he had your blessing to use the room."

"Yeah, that was a cheap trick. But, otherwise, he didn't cross any boundaries with either of you, did he?"

We both said no.

"We were having a great time," I admitted, feeling the rush of blood to my cheeks. "Until you showed up. Honestly."

Adam grinned. "Well, I have been accused of ruining a good party before. But it's part of the job." He stood, extending his hand. "Anyway, I'd better get back there. God knows what I'll find if I wait much longer."

I shook his hand. "Thanks. I mean, for not being mad at me or Noah."

Noah shook Adam's hand, a little more at ease. "Yeah. Thanks."

"Well, I can't blame either of you for agreeing to a soak and a three-way, can I? The fact my room was involved was Luke's fault, and he will be dealt with."

*

The ranch was dark by the time we returned to the bunkhouse. We heard shouting from the far pasture, and singing, and in the distance, the bright flames of the bonfire shot up into the night.

"Adam must have come back early for some reason," I said. "Just our luck."

Noah nodded, falling onto his bunk and staring up at the bottom of the upper mattress. "I can't believe Luke lied to me. To us."

"Yeah, well he did. I'm not too thrilled about being hoodwinked either."

"I hate him a little for lying." Noah said. "And I don't like the feeling."

"Then don't hate him. Hating him is probably what he wants us to do. I've known people like him before," I said.

Noah turned his head. "Really?"

I nodded. "People who sabotage their relationships because they don't think they're worthy of anyone, deep down. The world makes more sense when things are consistent with what they're used to than if they were to strive for a changed outcome."

"Wow. Makes sense."

"Sure." I hesitated for a moment. "My brother was a bit like Luke." I stripped to my boxer briefs and got under the covers in my bunk.

"Really? Is he better now?" Noah asked.

"Nah. He's in jail. For armed robbery."

"Oh my God. Jesus. That's terrible." Noah sat up.

"He got in with the wrong crowd, drugs, all that stuff. We tried to help him but...we couldn't," I admitted. "And I'm not implying Luke is anywhere near as bad. But the attitude strikes me as the same. The sense people expect you to be bad so you simply fulfill their expectations."

I didn't want to examine what Luke's similarity to my brother meant about my feelings for him.

Noah nodded. "Right."

"So, if you really want to help Luke, don't fulfill those expectations. Don't hate him. Keep loving him if that's what you think you feel. Don't let him sabotage your affection."

Noah huffed and nodded. "Can I sleep in your bunk again tonight?"

I groaned. "Jesus Christ, Noah. You mean I have to figure out how to sleep with a hard-on again?"

He stood up and walked over to my bunk, peeling off his shirt and tossing it onto his bed. My eyes flew to his pale skin and dark nipples. I dropped an arm over my face. "Noah. You're killing me."

I heard him chuckle and the rustling of more clothes coming off.

"What are you doing?"

"Getting naked."

I peeked out from under my arm. Yep, he was naked. And beautiful. And standing right next to me.

"Why?"

"Because the others won't be back for a while, and I want to snuggle."

"Noah, if you come under the sheets with me, I won't be able to keep my hands off you." I figured honesty was important at this point.

"If I come under the sheets with you, consider that as permission to put your hands on me."

I blinked, staring at him as my mouth went dry.

His hand drifted down to his erect cock and he stroked it idly as he smiled. "Would be a good way to get Luke back. He's the one who lit the fire between us."

"Interesting perspective." I pulled back the covers. But as Noah climbed in beside me, I said, "Although I don't know if that's entirely true. He definitely stoked the flame, but I was already feeling the burn."

I breathed deeply as Noah settled under the sheets with me, my heart beating rapidly, my cock hardening more. His hair smelled like the bubble bath we'd used in Adam's huge tub and my mind went back there, to the unfolding intimacy and sudden pleasure before anything else had happened.

The heat from his body touching mine felt suddenly scorching. I felt his lips on my chin; then his mouth found mine. I gasped into the kiss as it became something wild and desperate. Noah rose up over me as my neck stretched to keep my mouth on his. He smiled and pulled back.

"I want to try something," he said.

"You can try anything," I panted. "Anything you want."

His fingers went to the waistband of my briefs, and he pulled them down my legs. I helped him get them off, then pulled him down on top of me again, guiding his face to mine so I could kiss him again. Our tongues tangled eagerly, the flames jumping between us.

"Oh God, you feel so good," Noah sighed, rubbing his cock against my hip. "I could do this all night."

I smiled against his lips. "Fine with me. At least until the others get back." I shifted my hips so our cocks rubbed together.

Noah groaned. "Oh God, Jensen. Do that again."

I did. We both made strangled noises of pleasure. I snaked a hand down and wrapped our cocks with my fingers as we pushed against each other.

"Feels good. So good," Noah sighed.

I swallowed thickly. "You want to try to come like this? Can you?"

He groaned again and nodded. "Can you?"

"Try and stop me."

"Why would I?"

I spread some of the moisture from my glans over us to help us slide together, and soon I felt Noah shudder and the wet heat of his release spill over me.

"Oh fuck," I groaned, coming right after him, clutching him close with my other hand as we trembled together. "Oh God, fuck..."

He peppered kisses along my chin and neck as we came down from the intense pleasure we'd made together until our heartbeats slowed and we caught our breath.

I slid my clean hand up the side of his head, twining my fingers into his hair and guiding his mouth to mine again. This time our kisses were sweet and unhurried as the spunk of our combined release cooled on our skin.

Finally, I pulled back and gazed into his unguarded eyes. "Do you think we have time for a shower?"

The grin lit up his face. "Yeah. My turn to clean you off, cowboy." He looked so cute trying to channel Luke's particular brand of insolence.

I smiled, barely recalling how this night had almost been ruined by Luke's deception.

Chapter Fifteen

The sounds of showers running and men talking pulled me from a deep sleep the following morning. Noah was wrapped around me, but we'd put clean boxer briefs on after our shower, in deference to sharing a bunkhouse with so many other men.

"Where's Luke?" Ben asked when he saw my eyes open.

"He's not in his bunk?" I asked groggily.

"Nope. We didn't see any of you three at the bonfire. Figured you were all getting your rocks off together back here. But Luke wasn't here when we got back, and he isn't here now."

Brian poked his head out of the bathroom, a toothbrush in his hand. "He's at the main house."

"What? Since when does he get to sleep at the main house?" Callum shouted.

"Since he got in deep shit for misusing Adam's bedroom," Brian explained. "Adam's keeping him at the house under watch for the day. Dude is in for some major punishments. And, uh, interesting times with Kamal, I'm sure."

"Fuck. Kamal is going to be all over him," Ben muttered.

"Yep."

"Poor Luke," Trey commented.

"Or, lucky Luke?" Callum said wistfully. "I'd give anything to have Kamal twist my balls and make me cry."

Brian laughed. "I'll let Adam know."

"On second thought..."

"You big chicken," Ben said.

"I heard he's big on paddles. I hate paddles."

"So does Luke," Trey offered. "Or so he says."

"Shit," Callum muttered.

"Yeah," Brian coughed, ducking back into the bathroom.

Callum sauntered over to my bunk, staring down at Noah who had woken up and now blinked sleepily up at him.

"So, what, may I ask, was Luke using Adam's room for? No doubt he tricked you into a nefarious rendezvous. I'm surprised you're not all under house arrest."

"We didn't do anything wrong," I stated. "Luke said Adam had given him the okay to use his room."

At least three of the other men started laughing.

"And you believed him? Jesus, you're dumber than I thought, cowboy," Callum scoffed.

"Don't call me *cowboy*," I said, pushing out from under Noah and standing up. I was slightly shorter than Callum, but I made the taller man step back.

Callum shrugged. "Why the fuck not? Everyone else does." He grabbed my hat off the hook and waved it in the air. "Yee-haw!"

"Callum," Ben said. "Knock it off."

"I'm not your cowboy, Callum. I'm your fucking stable hand. I jacked your fucking cock my first day on the job." I grabbed my hat back and put it on. I probably looked ridiculous, since I only had boxer briefs on, but I really didn't give a damn.

Callum shrugged. "That's an important part of your job, right? Jacking ponyboys when they're all hard and eager? Next time you can suck me off."

Brian had come back into the room. "Hey, Callum. Jerking your sorry dick is not a part of the job. That's voluntary. He didn't have to give you any help. He did it because he's a nice guy and could tell you needed some relief."

Callum ignored Brian and stepped closer. "You know what I need right now, cowboy?" Callum said, crowding me against the bunk.

"Fuck off."

"Since Luke's up at the house for a few days, maybe you can sit on my cock sometime."

"I'd rather get paddled by Kamal," I said through clenched teeth.

Callum grinned. "Pretty sure he'd beat you. I heard him talking about you the other day. Said you had a sweet ass, made for a paddle."

Noah spoke up from behind me. "Shut up, Callum."

"What did you say?" Callum looked past me to Noah with a scornful expression. "You think we don't know? You think we haven't seen you with Luke's cock in your mouth? You want a nice cock in your mouth, you come and see me, Buttercup."

And that was my limit. The anger made me feel twice my size. My fist shot out and caught Callum square in the jaw, knocking him backwards into Noah's empty bunk.

He bounced off the ladder, then fell to the floor, cursing and clutching his face. "What the *fuck*?"

But I was on top of him, ready to hit him with everything I had. All the stress, all the confusion, all the repressed desire coming out to shut the big bully up.

"Jensen," Noah interjected. "Stop."

By then, Brian had grabbed my arms and was holding me back. "Knock it off, Jensen. Stop now, and I won't tell Adam you attacked him twice. Once, Adam will understand, especially if we back you up. Twice? He won't be so forgiving."

I shook my head, hat falling and my too-long hair flying in my face. "Let me go. I won't go after him. He can fuck the hell off and leave me alone. Or I'll hit him again." I bent to pick up my hat and glared at the prostrate man. "Got it, Callum?"

Callum nodded, checking to see if his jaw was in one piece. "Fine. Don't come near me. Not in the grooming barn either."

"Not a problem. I'm going to the house right now to quit this job."

They all stared at me.

Brian said, "What?"

"I'm done. I'm done with this crazy place. You guys are all fucking nuts," I said, pulling on my pants. "Except for him." I glanced at Noah, feeling a small tinge of regret. But leaving was the only thing that made sense.

Noah sat on the edge of my bunk, hugging himself with his bare arms. "Jensen, don't. Don't quit."

But I was done. I'd had it.

I pulled a T-shirt on and grabbed my bag and my hat. I sat beside Noah and leaned over, giving him an openmouthed kiss that he returned with desperation. But I pulled back. "You're the best thing about this place," I said. "But I don't belong here. I'm only gonna end up causing trouble."

I stood, tipping my hat to the others. "So long," I muttered and walked out the door, letting it swing shut behind me.

The sun shone bright in the morning sky as I trudged along the dirt trail. I couldn't help but feel disappointed and sad to have to leave. But Luke was in a lot of trouble and Callum might have a broken jaw because of me. This was all too much.

As I walked quickly, duffel bag slung over my shoulder, I heard footsteps behind me. I assumed Noah had followed me so girded myself to say goodbye again.

But Brian's voice sounded behind me instead.

"Hey, wait up, Jensen. Slow down."

"No," I shook my head and kept walking. "I've got to go."

"I know you feel that way, but you're here to replace me, and I've already made plans. I'm expected at the University of Toronto next week. I can't stay." He was breathing hard since he'd had to run to catch up with me.

"Neither can I."

Brian examined my profile as we walked and remained silent for a few moments, gathering his thoughts. I doubted anything he could say would make me reconsider.

"Look, I know the BCR is a lot to take in," Brian said. "My first week here was insane. And *I knew* what I was getting into. I can't imagine being unprepared for any of this."

I gave him a look that said you have no idea what I've been through.

"But you've done amazingly well. If you're blaming yourself for what Luke got you into last night, you're full of shit. That mess was Luke's fault. Adam knows it. Noah knows it. Hell, even Luke knows he's to blame."

"I should have known Luke was bullshitting us. I'm not a stupid guy, Brian." I shook my head. "Not usually.

This place," I looked up at the wide-open sky, gestured toward the stables and corrals. "This place makes my dick happy, but the BCR confuses the shit out of the rest of me."

Brian nodded. "I know. You're right. What if I said you'd get used to the place eventually?"

"I don't know if I want to."

"Yeah, okay." He was quiet for a bit. Then he said, "You know, leaving is killing me."

I eyed him. "Really? Then why are you?"

"Because the opportunity came up, and I should probably continue my education. I might not be able to do this for the rest of my life even if grooming ponyboys is my fucking dream job."

"Grooming ponyboys is your dream job?"

"Sure. Are you fucking kidding me? I get to live here, in this beautiful place, surrounded by intelligent people and kinking the fuck out on a daily basis? This is heaven." He shook his head. "You know, Jensen, not everyone gets an opportunity like this. You better be sure you want to pass it up."

"I'm sure," I said quietly. "I thought I could do the job. I thought I'd fit in here. But I don't. I just don't."

We trudged on quietly. We were almost at the house when I heard my name.

"That's Noah," Brian said. "I'm going back. There's a show to get ready for today. A show you're going to miss, which is a goddamn shame."

And he was gone.

I kept walking. I'd almost reached the back door to the main house when I felt a warm hand on my shoulder.

"Jensen, wait."

I stopped but didn't turn. I was breathing hard from the pace I'd kept and so was Noah.

"Look at me."

I closed my eyes and turned, opening them to see Noah standing there in his boxer briefs and an open shirt, his runners untied, looking like a fucking angel. "I'm looking."

"Please don't go."

"I have to."

"No, you don't."

"Noah, all this shit is happening because of me."

Noah shook his head quickly from side to side. "No, this shit is happening because of Luke. And Callum. If Luke knew you were planning to leave, he'd be devastated."

I narrowed my eyes, trying to see if Noah really thought so or only figured such a dubious supposition would make me stay. "No, he wouldn't."

"Okay, so I can't prove how much he cares. But I'm pretty sure. And, anyway, *I* don't want you to leave."

"I know. But I can't stay. This job is too hard. Everything's too hard. My cock, most of the time, and figuring things out, and fitting in so I'm not messing everyone up. I'm done."

Noah nodded, blinking hard. He held something out to me. "Fine. Here, take this. My phone number and address. I'm here until the end of August; then I go home. Please, call me. I don't want this to be the end for us."

I gazed down at the crumpled piece of paper and then back at Noah. "Noah, I—"

"Take it."

I nodded. I put the paper in my pocket and turned to go into the house. I didn't look behind me as I let the door swing closed.

The big house was empty and silent. Connor wasn't at his desk, but I found Adam in his office. He looked up from his computer, raised his eyebrows and started to stand.

"Jensen. What can I do for you?"

"I'm leaving." I didn't have the patience for niceties.

He froze, then completed standing and crossed his arms in front of his chest. "Pardon?"

"I'm taking off. I can't stay here. I'm going to need my phone, please."

"I don't understand. You're not worried about last night, are you? I told you: you aren't to blame for anything."

I nodded. "I know, but I feel at least partly responsible." I glanced down the hall and then back at Adam. "And I, uh, I punched Callum in the face."

"You what?" Adam said.

I made my voice louder. "I punched Callum. He's bleeding, and I might have broken his jaw. I don't know."

Adam stared at me. He put a hand to his forehead and grimaced. "Jesus. What did he do?"

"He's been bullying me since Luke and I started getting together. He's jealous or something. I don't know. And he was being mean to Noah, and I couldn't take it anymore." My cheeks heated with shame. "I'm sorry. I hope he's okay."

Adam nodded slowly. "I do too. But Callum's had something coming for a while. From *someone*. He can't keep his damn mouth shut, and he's got the maturity of a ten-year-old." Adam scratched his forehead. "Let me contact Adrian. Don't go anywhere yet. I need to do some damage control before we get sued up the ass."

Adam went into his office as I waited outside the door.

After a few minutes he came out. "Adrian says Callum's fine. His nose isn't broken as far as he can see."

"I still have to leave, Adam."

"Fine. But you'll have to come back if Callum presses charges. I doubt he will but I wish you would reconsider and stay."

I didn't think Callum would press charges either. I mean, it was a punch for God's sake.

"I don't think so. I don't think I can fit in here."

"Jensen, you're already fitting in here."

We stared at each other.

Adam must have seen the determination in my eyes. He took a small key from his pocket and walked to Connor's desk. He unlocked the drawer where the phones were kept and grabbed one out, removing the piece of tape with my name written on it before passing it to me.

He sighed. "You're going to upset two of my favorite men by leaving right now."

I nodded curtly. "I'm sorry about Noah. I don't think Luke cares about anything other than my ass, frankly," I said. "Bye. Thanks anyway." I held my hand out for Adam to shake.

He took my hand between two of his, and I appreciated the genuine warmth in his gaze, mingled with what was probably regret. "Best of luck."

"Thanks."

He released me.

I chewed my lip. "For what it's worth, I think this place is amazing. The BCR just...isn't right for me."

"Okay," Adam said, distracted.

I nodded and hefted my duffel bag, then walked out the front door to the parking lot.

Now I was actually leaving, I felt shaky and subdued. But I knew I was making the right decision. If I stayed, things would only get worse. I'd make bigger mistakes. I'd have my heart ripped out of my chest by either Noah or Luke.

Leaving was the safest option, for everyone.

I unlocked my light-blue sedan and threw the bag in the back seat, then got in the driver's side. The car smelled stale and old, like my life had been before I'd found myself here. But it also smelled familiar. After I closed the door, I sat there with the windows rolled down, gathering my thoughts.

This was the right thing to do. I'd go home, look for an *actual* stable-hand job with real horses, where I wouldn't be risking anything at all.

After a few minutes a calm descended over me, and I was ready to drive. I put the key in the ignition. The engine came to life as the passenger door opened with a rusty creak.

"Not so fast, cowboy," Luke said as he plopped himself into my car and grinned at me as my chin dropped in shock. He shut the door and there were two of us in my stinky car.

"What the fuck are you doing here?" I gasped, gaze flying over the snug pair of pineapple-print boxer briefs, Docs, and leather collar he was wearing.

"Stopping you from being stupid."

I was transfixed by the ridiculous briefs. "What the fuck are you wearing?"

"What Kamal put me in at six this morning." Luke glanced down at his shorts. "Guy has a fruit fetish or something. You should see my ass. He paddled me so hard I can barely sit."

"You're sitting now."

"Yeah, and it's killing me, so thanks."

"You can leave," I said although something inside me had burst into life when Luke had appeared.

"Not gonna happen. Not unless you come back."

I sighed, turning off the ignition so I wouldn't pollute the atmosphere while I talked some sense to Luke. Some part of me thrilled to his presence, but the feeling came too late. I'd made my decision.

"I'm not coming back," I said, trying to be firm and soft all at once.

Luke shook his head and gave me a questioning look. "Why?"

"Because I have to leave." I couldn't put the fact of my departure more plainly.

"*Why*?"

Luke's obstinacy began to piss me off. I pulled my right hand off the steering wheel, then slammed my palm back down, making a satisfying *thunk*. "Because I don't fit in here."

"Bull. Shit," Luke said, narrowing his eyes. "You're fucking terrified of how well you *do* fit in here."

I stared straight ahead, at the big house full of clean offices and handsome, intelligent Adam and, somewhere, stern Kamal, waiting for Luke to return to his punishment. "No, I'm not. That's not—"

Luke shrugged. He looked away and started playing with the scratched and broken door on the glove compartment. "Adam said you punched Callum in the face."

"Yeah."

Luke laughed, a genuine, amused sound making me feel somewhat vindicated. "I don't see any problem. I see

Callum getting what he fucking deserved. Maybe he won't be such a douche now—if they don't kick him out."

"They're kicking him out?" I said, startled at this new information. I turned to face Luke, and he met my gaze with a serious expression.

"Adam's not sure how to deal with him," he said.

Wow. I had not anticipated my actions would have caused this much trouble. "Shit! I didn't mean for any of this to happen. They don't need to kick him out if I'm *leaving*."

Luke gave me a scornful look. "Oh? So, he can keep being an asshole to Noah and the others? Nice of you."

"That's not what I mean."

"You've got to be pretty self-centred to believe all of this is because of you."

"I'm not self-centred!" I mean, I didn't think I was self-centred. But maybe blaming myself for everything was a little narcissistic.

"Oh no? Did you ever think maybe Callum is an ass hat?" Luke said with total seriousness.

"Well...yeah."

He turned back to examining the broken glove compartment door. "And maybe I'm a fucking lunatic who can't do anything right? Including showing the guy I like he's more than a hot piece of ass to me?"

I stared at Luke's profile, noticing the telltale blush on his smooth-shaven cheeks, not sure I had actually processed his words correctly. Not daring to hope they were true.

"What?"

Luke gave a silent chuckle, then glanced my way with suddenly shy eyes. "Do I need to lay my feelings out for you? I like you, okay? I really fucking like you, Jensen, but the only way I've been able to show you is by...being physical...y'know? Very stupid and immature, I know. But you need to know there's more, at least on my side. In case that changes your mind about leaving, or anything. Which it probably doesn't."

I narrowed my eyes. "Did Adam send you out here?"

Luke met my gaze. "He told me you were leaving, and I might want to consider coming clean about my feelings for you."

His feelings for me?

"But how would he know?"

"Fuck, Jensen, he's my therapist. He knows everything."

I suddenly realized Luke was using my name and not his nickname for me. And I liked the sound of those familiar syllables in his mouth. I was becoming distracted by his almost naked state and his mysterious love of suffering at the hands of Kamal's ingenious tortures.

As if reading my mind, he drifted his fingers over his chest to his left nipple. He made a face. "Bastard clamped my nipples. I fucking hate that." Luke frowned, then smiled. "Except I kind of love it too. Go figure."

I stared at him, sitting there in his pineapple boxer briefs and leather collar, and I couldn't help smiling a tiny bit.

Luke saw my smile and gave me a full-on, shit-eating grin in return—so very Luke my heart ached. "Ah, there it is. There's my happy cowboy."

"Fuck." I swore because what the fuck was I going to do now?

"Well, not in here. Maybe in the shower later?" Luke said, waggling his eyebrows. "If I can stop being a wack job for a day?"

I raised my eyebrows. "Do you think that's possible? And how come all of our assignations involve water?"

Luke winked. "I like my cowboy's clean and fresh. And as to the other thing, I'll try if you'll stay."

I sighed, sagging in my seat. Everything had been clear when I'd gotten into my car. Now I wasn't so sure. Part of me was still tempted to close the book on all this, even after Luke's emotional confession. Abandoning the ranch would be the safe choice, and I could go back to living a boring, regular life. "I don't know..."

"Noah is crying in Adam's office right now," Luke said.

And I pictured poor Noah being devastated and taking the blame for my leaving.

"Fuck."

Luke played his fingers over the door to the glove compartment. "Do you know the last time I asked for anyone to—" He swallowed hard. "—to stay for me?"

My eyes widened. I shook my head. "No."

"Never. I've never asked anyone to stay because I liked them so much I couldn't bear to be left behind."

And all my arguments crumbled in a moment.

Without another word, Luke deftly climbed over the gear shift and straddled me, pressing his lips to mine in a tender, open-mouthed kiss that did crazy things to my heart, not to mention other parts of me.

Luke's lips felt gentler than I remembered, less forceful, as if I was something delicate and precious. I appreciated his tenderness. I smoothed my hands gently over the soft cotton fabric covering his ass as we kissed gently, exploring the new perspective we'd gained from his confession. I welcomed his exploring tongue, less insistent and more inquisitive now than ever before. I pushed back and chased the tip into his mouth, running mine over his palate softly, telling him silently how I felt about him. Running my hand down his ribs along the slight dip of his waist as I slipped my fingers under the waistband of those ridiculous briefs, cupping the curve of his ass while he let out the softest whimper and a hiss of pain.

"Holy shit. I can feel the heat and there's some raised lines here. Jesus. Kamal is an animal," I gasped against Luke's lips.

Luke hissed, pushing his mouth against me a little harder, his fingers coming up to caress my stubbled jaw. "I'll let you kiss my wounds better if you want, when they finally release me from my punishment."

"Promise?"

"Promise," he said, pulling back and placing three soft kisses on my smiling lips. "Come on. Noah has to perform today. And I have to suffer more of Kamal's devious tortures." He didn't sound too upset.

We got out of the car. Half a lifetime had passed as I opened the back door and grabbed my duffel bag. I followed Luke to the door, unable to stop my eyes locking on his ass in those snug shorts.

Suddenly, Luke stopped in front of me, causing me to halt. He thrust his hip out and hooked a thumb in the waistband of his boxer briefs, glancing behind him. "Wanna see?"

I licked my lips and nodded.

Luke pushed the briefs down, exposing his ass cheek.

"Je—sus," I commented, bending down to get a closer look.

The usually pale skin of Luke's ass shone a deep red with three raised white stripes running diagonally from hip to crack. "Yeah. I won't be borrowing Adam's room again anytime soon."

"Shit. I guess not." I shook my head. If those marks were on my ass, I'm pretty sure I'd be crying and trying not to move.

Luke pulled his shorts carefully back up. "I guess I got what I deserved. But those marks hurt like fuck. Still. Looks pretty killer. And I think Kamal enjoyed making me whimper and sob. So, y'know."

Adam was standing outside his office comforting Noah when we went into the main office.

"Thank God," Adam said. "He's got him, Noah. Luke's brought him back."

Noah lifted his head from Adam's shoulder and stared at me. I watched the emotion in his eyes turn from relief to sudden, outright hostility in moments. Then he disengaged himself gently from Adam, turned, and walked out the back door.

"Ah fuck," I said, dropping my bag.

I heard footsteps before Kamal appeared at the bottom of the staircase and approached us. Dressed in jeans and a black T-shirt, he held a braided black riding crop in one hand. I glanced at Luke in time to see his eye twitch as his gaze locked on the weapon.

"The drama's over?" Kamal said gruffly, giving me a friendly nod. "I can have my pineapple boy back?"

"Fuck you, Kamal," Luke said. "You're such a weirdo."

Kamal looked Luke over and licked his lips. "Oh, dear, the language. Upstairs, now. You have some floor scrubbing on your list before I strap you back to the bench and do more unspeakable things to you." He jerked the crop against his leg making a sharp slap echo through the hall.

Luke shuddered as his cock twitched in his tight shorts. "Fine. Love you too, Kamal." He threw me a tight smile as he walked past Kamal and clumped up the stairs.

Kamal chuckled and raised his eyebrows. "You sure you want to stay? He's not going to be domesticated anytime soon."

I nodded. "I promised. And I've got some ideas."

Kamal nodded. "I bet you do. You know, Jensen, from what I've heard so far, you might be a candidate for trainer someday."

"I was thinking the same thing," Adam said with a sly grin.

I held my hands up, shaking my head. "Stable hand is all I can handle at the moment," I said. "And now I need to go grovel for a certain person's forgiveness."

Adam raised his eyebrows and looked at his watch. "Yeah, well, hurry up. You both need to be in the grooming barn in twenty minutes. We have a show to put on. A show I'm relieved you'll get to see."

Chapter Sixteen

"Noah. Noah, wait," I said as I caught up to the shorter man walking swiftly toward the grooming barn. "I'm sorry."

Noah turned, giving me a furious look.

"I'm really sorry," I said, moving forward as if to embrace him.

"Don't. Don't touch me right now," he said, holding up his hand.

I stopped, gazing with guilty frustration at the man I'd hurt with my thoughtless behaviour. I didn't know what else to say.

Noah breathed carefully for several moments and let his hand drop. Then he spoke in a barely audible voice. "Wait until I'm in there. Ask Liv if you can get me ready today. Okay?"

I nodded, relieved. "Okay."

"Then you can touch me."

"Okay."

"And Jensen?" He said more loudly, while not meeting my gaze.

"Yeah?"

"If you ever pull something like that again, I don't know if I'll be able to forgive you." Noah blinked back tears. "I know we've only known each other a few weeks, but I fell hard for you. And Luke...I've never seen Luke want something so bad."

"Okay," I said. "I'm sorry."

Noah turned and opened the door to the grooming barn, stepping inside as it shut behind him.

*

Having been permitted this intimacy with the man whose heart I'd stomped on and spat out earlier, I put everything I had into preparing Noah for the show. Noah was sweet and fragile, and I'd treated him terribly.

I scrubbed him down and washed him clean, dressed him in the prettiest of show-pony gear, including a butt-plug tail and a leather bridle with stand-up leather pony ears, and a steel bit sitting between his teeth.

The last item gave me pause because, although the bridle looked incredible on him, I could only imagine how uncomfortable the bit must be. But when I placed the piece of metal into Noah's open mouth, he flicked his tongue out and licked my fingers, winking as if to put me at ease. I smiled and winked back, relieved to know I had restored his faith in me.

The final piece was an elaborate black-and-gold face mask, like the masquerade pieces seen at Mardi Gras parades, with two fine gold ribbons hanging down from each corner and silver sparkles and sequins sprinkled over the surface.

As I finished and stepped back to make sure everything was in place, I couldn't help a startled curse escaping my slack lips.

"Holy shit," I said, looking Noah over from his leather ears, face mask, and bridle to the collar and body harness, to his semi-erect cock in the metal cage, to his shiny Doc Marten boots.

"He is one sexy, motherfucking ponyboy," Liv said, gazing with admiration at Noah and putting her arm over my shoulders. "Wait until you see him in the ring. If you haven't fallen completely in love with him yet, you will then. Trust me."

"I think it's already too late for me," I commented softly, winking at Noah, which made him blush and shake his head with a *neigh*.

Liv laughed as my heart dissolved into mushy pieces.

*

I had time after the performing ponyboys were ready and warming up with their trainers to return to the bunkhouse for a shower and change into something more appropriate for the afternoon show.

The off-duty ponyboys lounged about the bunkhouse, reading or watching TV. Callum sat at the top of the ladder to the loft, long legs hanging over the edge, reading a mystery novel. He looked up when I came in.

I felt the heat of shame in my cheeks. "How's your jaw?" I asked. "I'm sorry I hit you."

"It's fine. Only a big fucking bruise. You didn't hit me so hard."

The sight of the mottled skin of his face made me sick to my stomach, knowing I'd caused his injury.

"Uh-huh."

"Peace?" he said, eyebrows lifted in a cautious query.

I nodded. "Peace. But please keep your mouth shut unless you're saying something nice. Or at least funny."

Callum grinned. "Deal."

I pulled some clothes out of my duffel bag and laid them on my bunk. I had no idea what to wear to a human pony show.

"Those dark jeans will do," Callum said. "You want to borrow a shirt? I have an extra white button-down I've ironed."

"Okay. Thanks."

"Might be a bit big on you," he said, climbing down the ladder with the shirt.

"I'll manage. You're not much bigger."

"Whatever you want to tell yourself," he said. He ran a hand through his short dark hair, looking sheepish. "Look, I'm glad you stayed. If you'd left because of me, I would have felt terrible. And been shunned by everyone." He held out his hand to me.

I stared at it. "It wasn't only because of you."

"I know. Still. We all like you, Jensen. Even me. I just have a weird way of showing you."

I took his hand and shook it once, and then let go. Turning my back to him I pulled off the T-shirt I was wearing and put his white shirt on. When I'd finished, I turned around and tucked the tails into my jeans.

"Nice. Sets off your bedroom eyes."

"Callum..." I groaned, rolling my eyes. When was he going to give up trying to seduce me?

"Kidding, kidding. Looks nice. Now let's get going. They'll be starting soon."

*

The sun was covered by wispy clouds as we walked to the large arena near the main house where the weekend shows were held. The air was warm but not as humid as usual. Several people were already seated on the padded bleachers.

There were men and women, some persons of no obvious gender, and a wide range of ages. Some of them wore jeans and nice shirts, others were attired in fancier outfits. A few of the women looked as though they were attending a real horse show, with cocktail dresses and fancy hats. There were also several attendees in leather fetish gear.

"Wow," I said.

"Yep. We have a packed house as usual," Trey said, fixing his shirt collar. All eyes were on us as we made our way to a special viewing area at the side of the fence where folding chairs had been set up.

"Do they know who we are?" I said quietly.

"Oh yeah. They know we're the off-duty ponyboys. They probably think you're one. Anyway, they know we're young, hot, and kinky as fuck. What's not to stare at?"

"Good point," I said.

Callum led me to where the other off-duty ponyboys, as well as Brian, Adrian and Liv stood at the nearside fence where we would have a good view of the proceedings.

I located Adam in his black tux, looking dashing and debonair, with young Connor beside him, similarly attired. I wondered if Noah's trainer, Lorraine, would wear a sari or something more suitable for handling a beautiful ponyboy in the ring.

The clouds passed by and the sun shone high in the sky as the time approached when the show was scheduled to begin. A light breeze cooled the back of my neck and brought the scent of summer grasses to my nostrils. As I lifted my hat to brush the damp hair from my forehead, I saw the three trainers walk out of the indoor arena and approach Adam with their ponyboys.

Michael came first, leading Ben by reins attached to his bridle, decorated with a braid of blue tassels down his back instead of Noah's gold. Michael wore a pair of white chinos with a black button-down shirt and a red bow tie, and clean black Blundstone boots. Next came Hiro leading Hunter who had red tassels down his back. Hiro wore black dress pants and a black button-down shirt with a vest but no tie. He had on dress shoes instead of boots.

Then Lorraine came in leading Noah by the reins. Lorraine, as always, looked stunning, in a black leather miniskirt split up the side, shiny black Doc Marten boots with red roses embroidered on them, and a lacy black blouse with drape sleeves. Her long black braid was coiled at the nape of her neck into a neat chignon. Her brown skin shone in the sun and the silver of the stud in her right nostril glinted. But not even her beauty could compete with Noah, who walked obediently behind her in his leather pony gear, proud as a peacock, almost preening. The normally shy and introverted man became something else as he marched proudly toward the outdoor arena.

A surge of pride filled me as well, for I had prepared him and knew what a kind and sweet man he was. At this moment I was so glad Luke had found me before I'd thrown all of this away in a state of fear and guilt.

Besides wearing the decorative leather attire, the ponyboys were bound in the habitual leather forearm cuffs, which made their chests puff out attractively.

Adam stepped into the arena while the trainers kept their charges at the gate. He lifted the red megaphone with *BCR Ranch* emblazoned on the side and spoke to the gathered groups.

"Welcome to the annual Canada Day weekend Pony Show at the Braided Crop Ranch! We are proud to present our highly talented and well-trained ponyboys for your viewing pleasure. Please, no photography of any kind during the show. Opportunities will be available later for paid photos with the ponyboy of your choosing. We also sell a variety of professional photos of our handsome and athletic livestock in our gift shop at the resort."

"Now, may I present to you, Mr. Michael Doherty and his ponyboy, Bubbles. Bubbles hails from Toronto, Ontario, is twenty-seven years old, six feet, two inches tall and weighs 205 pounds. He's a lot to handle, but Michael enjoys a challenge!"

I joined the others in clapping as Michael led Ben, aka Bubbles, around the ring to show off his accoutrements. Ben grinned and winked at the guests, nodding his head and shaking his tassels as he moved gracefully across the arena.

"Next, we have Mr. Hiro Sahndu with his ponyboy, Hurricane. Hurricane is from New York, New York, and is twenty-five years of age, six feet tall, and 198 pounds. I think you will agree Hurricane is a fine addition to our stables!"

Another round of applause greeted them as Hunter/Hurricane pranced into the ring, almost pulling Hiro off his feet before the small man jerked his reins and got him under control. The performance was all an act as Callum's eye-roll indicated to Jensen. "They do this every time. It's like Laurel and Hardy."

But I wasn't really listening. I watched, fascinated, as Adam introduced the remaining team.

"And finally, we have the stunning Ms. Lorraine Louis and her breathtaking ponyboy, Buttercup. Buttercup hails from Ottawa, Ontario, is twenty-one years old, five feet ten inches tall, and weighs 157 pounds. Buttercup is a veteran performer at the BCR and one of our most talented and enthusiastic ponyboys!"

Noah walked proudly behind Lorraine like he'd been born to be a ponyboy. His muscles rippled with fluid and graceful movements as he unconsciously monopolized the attention of the audience.

To my surprise, there were more ponies and trainers emerging from the stables. But these ponies looked different from ours.

"Where did they come from?" I said, in some degree of shock.

Brian laughed. "From our sister ranch across the lake. Adam likes to present a variety of ponies at the shows. Sometimes our ponyboys perform at their ranch. The variety makes the shows more inclusive and exciting."

"Sure," I nodded, transfixed on the arena as Adam introduced the three ponygirls and their trainers. They wore tight corsets which pushed their bare, breasts up and out, with ties at the back to restrict their arms. They wore leather bit bridles with pony ears and face masks, butt-plug tails and leather crotch harnesses, with only straps to hide their sex. The ponygirls also wore high leather boots up to their knees with steel buckles, but the boots were not heeled, making it easier for them to perform their routines. I wondered why no attempt had been made to have them look like hooves and asked Brian.

"Adam doesn't believe in the fancier trappings of pony-play ponies. He thinks they add unnecessary discomfort and a man or woman in leather fetish gear is as pony-like as one in a full body suit and horse head. He wants to emphasize the human aspect of pony play while still indulging the imagination of the participant. The bridle with ears and the butt-plug tail is all our ponyboys and girls need to get into the headspace. He feels like trying to have them look like real horses is useless when their humanity is what we celebrate here. He wants them to look like men and women who are playing at being ponies, for the fun and freedom of it. Which is exactly what they are."

"Some people get off on the more animalistic costumes, but here we keep things simple. Also, full body horse costumes would be very hot to wear." Brian nodded at the ring. "Now they'll take them out the gate and bring them back pulling the carts."

"Holy shit. Really?" I asked.

Callum nudged my shoulder. "Oh yeah. Now the fun begins. I wish I was in there today. They got beautiful weather and a good crowd."

Brian was right. The ponies and trainers paraded out of the ring, and Adam spent a few moments speaking to the mandate of the BCR Ranch and its sister ranch and what their goals were—essentially to provide a positive place for kink expression in a beautiful setting with opportunities for members to indulge their voyeuristic pleasures when they stayed at the resort. The monthly pony shows were a hugely anticipated part of the resort experience and what made this ranch different and unique.

"And now, for your viewing pleasure, the ponyboys and girls will take their trainers around the ring in some beautiful carts!" Adam announced.

Buttercup entered the ring first, pulling a small sulky with Lorraine perched daintily in the seat, holding long reins attached to Noah's bit. Seeing the handsome man I'd wounded earlier in such a position, dignified and debased at the same time, gave me a fluttery feeling in my chest and a very tight feeling in my pants. Noah looked like another creature entirely. Not a horse, but a prince or an ancient God. Something otherworldly with his leather pony ears, gold mask, and other accoutrements. An Egyptian hieroglyph come to life.

I watched the entire show with an ever-increasing need to gather Noah into my arms and tell him how beautiful he looked in his gear. I wanted to admit how much I was beginning to feel for him and how fascinated I was by Luke and by Luke and Noah's relationship.

I watched the ponyboys and girls show off their strength and agility by running obstacle courses and races. Their trainers ordered them to walk and run and trot in front of the guest judges so they could be assessed for any number of qualities.

"What, exactly, are they being judged on?" I asked.

Brian shrugged. "Energy, enthusiasm, grace, comportment, obedience, and their overall look, I guess. Also, on the ability of the trainer and pony to work as a cohesive team. At least, I think those are the categories. Those are things the trainers emphasize when the ponyboys are learning." He smiled. "I think your boy's got this in the bag."

I blushed. "My boy?"

"Oh, come on, Jensen. Noah's head over heels for you. The way he came after you today..." Brian shook his head. "Don't hurt him again, okay?"

I felt the heat in my cheeks as I watched Noah outshine the other young men and women in the show ring. "God, Brian, how could I? I can barely breathe, watching him."

"He's pretty special. I'm glad you got to see him perform."

"Me too," I said, feeling nauseous at the thought I'd almost missed this. This most secret, yet public part of Noah's personality.

By the time things were beginning to wrap up and the contestants were assembling for the distribution of ribbons, four o'clock was approaching. The contestants were streaked with dirt and sweat, chests heaving from exertion.

One ponyboy in particular looked completely exhausted but held his head in his gold mask proudly, gazing right at me.

"Incredible, isn't he?" A familiar voice said.

I turned, surprised to see Luke leaning on the rail beside me, dressed in jeans and chucks and a green button-down short-sleeve shirt.

My face split into a grin to see him there. "God, yes. He's meant for this. They're all great but there's something about Noah."

Luke gave me a slow smile. "I'm glad we agree."

I looked him up and down, wondering if he still had on the pineapple briefs or his own boring blue ones. "So, Kamal turned you loose?"

Luke grinned. "Kind of."

Hmm. "How's your ass?" I couldn't help asking.

"Sore as hell. But some of Kamal's methods aren't so straightforward."

"What do you mean?"

Luke took my hand and pressed the palm against the front of his jeans. There was something hard there, but metal, not flesh.

My chin dropped. "Did he *cage* you? Outside of the stables?"

Luke laughed and nodded, more amused than annoyed.

"How long are you locked up?"

He shrugged. "Until Kamal decides I've learned my lesson, I guess. I don't really want to think about it."

I licked my lips. "I want to see your cock in that thing when we get back to the bunkhouse."

He raised his eyebrows. "Sure. Does my annoying predicament turn you on? The thought I can't come or get really hard right now?"

"Uh, yeah. Those damn cages turn me on in the fucking stables."

Luke grinned lazily. "Well, isn't that interesting. I was right."

"How?"

"You're as fucking kinky as the rest of us."

We watched as the ribbons were presented and Noah won the top prize—a blue ribbon for comportment and presentation as well as overall performance.

"That's our boy," Luke said, looking so pleased I could have kissed him. Especially since he'd included me in his comment. I'd been so worried I didn't have a place here when I had the best spot after all.

*

For thirty minutes after the show, the ponyboys and girls had to patiently pose for photos with anyone who paid for them. Noah, with the blue ribbon attached to his bridle, was in high demand.

Luke and I watched as he spoke calmly and respectfully to people, answering questions and talking about the experience of being a ponyboy at the BCR. A few times he caught my eye and sent me a shining smile, reassuring both Luke and me he was still having a wonderful time.

"You'd better get him to the grooming barn. He's gonna crash soon, and he's in desperate need of a hose down," Luke said. "Take good care of him, okay? He's giving us everything he has today. Mainly to impress you."

I nodded, blushing. "Yeah, well, mission accomplished."

"Good. You should be fucking impressed. That man there is a keeper. And so are you." Luke took my hand and pulled me forward, giving me a quick kiss on the lips. "Now go. Take care of our boy before I have to slap your pretty ass. I'm serious, y'know. About taking you over my knee."

I blinked at the look in his blue eyes. "I can hardly think of any place I'd rather be."

I let my gaze linger on him before I took off for the grooming barn.

*

By the time Noah and the others returned to the grooming barn they looked shattered. The ponygirls and their trainers had used the showers first and were on their way back to the other ranch. Brian, Liv, and I gave the place a good hose down before we brought our ponyboys inside.

The first thing I did was remove Noah's bridle, sliding the metal bit—wet with his saliva—out of his mouth and kissing him where the device had left red marks at the corners of his lips.

"Noah, you looked incredible out there!"

Noah gazed at me with tired blue eyes and a slow smile. "Really? You liked the show?"

"God, Noah. You don't realize how utterly beautiful you are. I mean, you're a good-looking guy in shorts and a shirt, but hell, put you in full show-pony gear, and you are blowing my fucking mind."

Noah looked pleased. He stood still as I removed his gold mask and wiped his face with a warm cloth. He let me take tender care of him, stripping him of his gear and revealing him in his vulnerable nakedness as I did. His cock swelled as much as possible in the restricting cage and fluid had leaked onto the glistening metal.

Noah caught me looking. He peered down at himself and back at me. "I always get horny out there. Something about the—" He licked his lips, which were dry and looked sore from the stretch of the bridle. "—submission and objectification. I guess."

I nodded, carefully unfastening the wet cage and pulling it off.

Noah hissed and closed his eyes as his cock filled with blood and lifted from his thighs. "Oh God," Noah moaned. "Feels so good to have the cage off..."

I nodded. "Looks pretty fucking good too. Do you want me to jerk you off right now? Or wait until later when I can take care of you better?"

"I can wait," Noah said breathlessly. "Waiting will be torture. But I like torture."

"Kinky boy," I said, kissing him on the cheek. "Beautiful kinky boy."

"God, you're..."

"Hmm?" I said, turning the hose on and making sure the water was warm enough.

"I really like you, Jensen," Noah murmured. "Please don't go anywhere. At least until my six weeks is up."

"I won't. I promise."

Chapter Seventeen

The barbecue at the main house was a cheerful event after such a successful show. The performing ponyboys became the subjects of much praise, admiration, and envy.

But there would be another show on Sunday afternoon featuring Trey, Callum, and Ben. Ben would perform twice since he'd been needed to fill in for Luke. Part of Luke's punishment was not being allowed to perform, and it was hitting him hard.

"It's killing me not having a chance to be out there," Luke admitted to me. "I may be a bit of a show-off."

"No kidding?" I laughed. "I'd have never guessed."

"Asshole," he said, but pulled me close and ruffled my hair. He was really trying to be nice to me, I could tell. I appreciated the effort. Now he'd confessed his true feelings, I didn't mind his habitual attitude of barely restrained disdain. Because I enjoyed being his whipping boy, more than I wanted to admit.

He was right. I *was* as kinky as the rest of them.

I overheard Noah discussed frequently. Generally excellent in the ring, he'd been particularly impressive in the show today. I hadn't been the only one to notice.

Adam made a point to congratulate Noah in front of Luke.

"Noah, I'm glad you were able to rise above the emotional toll last night's and this morning's events must have taken on you."

"Thanks," Noah said, glancing at me and Luke. "Performing was just what I needed."

Adam grinned and nodded. "Kind of like saying 'Fuck you, guys, I'm fabulous. So, stop jerking me around and bow down at my feet'?"

Noah blushed. "Kind of."

"There will be some kneeling at Noah's feet. Don't you worry, Adam," Luke said, grinning lasciviously.

Adam laughed. "I'm sure. Because kneeling is probably much more comfortable than sitting on a paddled ass right now, right Luke?"

Luke took an aggressive bite of his burger and spoke with his mouth full. "Fuck you, Adam. You knew Kamal was gonna take this punishment and run, didn't you?"

Adam placed his hands on the table, leaned down and stared Luke in the eyes. "I told Kamal to make you very, very uncomfortable. If that involves a paddle to the ass and a metal cage on your presumptuous cock, then so be it."

They stared at each other, the oppositional energy palpable at the table. Then Luke shook his head and actually laughed. A genuine expression of amusement at his own expense. Adam smiled.

"Yes, Daddy. I'll be a good boy now," Luke said, winking at me.

"Excellent," Adam returned, straightening up and putting one hand on Noah's shoulder, the other on mine. "Good luck, guys. He's all yours. At least until he reports to the main house for more of Kamal's punishments tomorrow."

"Ah fuck," Luke groaned.

"Did he say how long you have to wear the cage?" Adam asked.

Luke laid his head on the table and closed his eyes. "No."

Adam grinned. "Good. I'll have to give him a raise."

Luke lifted his hand and gave Adam the finger, without lifting his head.

But Adam laughed. "Have a great evening, boys. By the way, I had the cleaning crew give the old shed on the back property a little bit of a spruce up, in case you're ever on the lookout for a bit of privacy. There's a clean mattress in there now."

Now Luke did look up, eyebrows lifted in surprise.

Adam continued, "I haven't told anyone else. Can you keep it a secret?" He looked doubtful. "I'm giving you the opportunity to surprise me. And now there is absolutely no reason for you to break into my room."

Luke tilted his head. "Well, except for the amazing bath—"

Adam held up his hand. "If you ever put your bare ass in my bathtub again, Luke, I will tell Kamal to pull out all the stops. I'm not fucking kidding."

Luke shook his head. "Seriously, thanks for the shed thing. You've made my evening a much more enjoyable prospect."

"No problem. And keep your fucking mouth shut. Or you guys will have to draw up a schedule because everyone in the damn bunkhouse will want to use the shed."

"Understood."

"Noah?" Adam said.

"Yeah?" Noah asked, having trouble drawing his eyes away from Luke at the moment.

"Congratulations again. You were the pride of the BCR today. Good work."

Noah's smile at Adam's praise was worth every single thing I had gone through so far.

"Thank you."

With that, Adam left them.

Luke stood, pointing at the food left on our plates. "Okay, boys. Finish eating because we're going on a little adventure walk tonight."

*

The shed Adam had referred to was a dilapidated structure on the edge of the farthest pasture. Far from the bunkhouse and past the location of the annual bonfire, the small building sat on the edge of the woods at the end of a faint trail in the grass.

We took turns showering and then surreptitiously left the bunkhouse after dark, claiming to be stargazing or some fucking shit. I figured the other guys knew we were off to fuck in the woods but didn't realize we had an actual, more comfortable, destination. We used Luke's flashlight to find our way.

Adam had not lied.

Although the shed appeared sketchy from the outside, the inside looked quite comfortable with clean wood floors, a small table and, yes, a mattress bigger than expected, covered with clean sheets and blankets. Against the opposite wall was a worn love seat with flat and faded cushions.

There were no windows, which suited our purposes well. There were two oil lanterns on hooks by the bed and a book of matches on the table. Once they were lit, the little cabin felt cozy and comfortable.

"I can't believe Adam did this for us," Luke said. "You should have seen the place a few weeks ago. I won't lie.

I've fucked guys here before. But it was pretty gross, and I'd honestly given this place up in favor of blocking the shower door for ten minutes."

"Ten minutes?" I said, eyebrow raised, trying not to think about who Luke might have fucked here.

"Well, I took my time with you, cowboy. Because who wouldn't?" He looked me up and down.

"Sweet talker," I said, blushing.

"Yeah? That's all the sweet-talking you're gonna get tonight." He sat down on the love seat and patted his lap. "You get your sweet ass over here, cowboy. I believe I promised you a spanking."

Noah had plopped down cross-legged on the mattress. He watched us with a small smile.

"Takes a pretty big set of balls for someone in a cock cage to assume the dominant role," I said, smirking. "I know enough about kink to know that. You should be on your knees for *us*."

Luke grinned. "Maybe later. Right now, I need to release some aggression and anger from being under Kamal's sadistic hands all day. And a promise is a promise."

I glanced at Noah, who shrugged. "You'll like it," he said.

"Why don't you spank him?" I asked Luke, suddenly nervous.

"Because I want to spank you right now. Maybe I'll spank him later. If my hand isn't too sore." He gave me a mischievous look.

"Fuck."

"Over my lap, cowboy. Now." Luke sat back against the cushions of the loveseat, eyes sparking with energy and excitement.

"Fine. You want me naked?" I asked, figuring I might as well get all in at this point.

"Not yet. Keep the briefs on. But for God's sake, take off the fucking hat. My dick is sobbing in this cage right now."

I laughed, taking off the hat and tossing it to Noah, who placed it on the bed beside him.

"Fine. God, you are dramatic."

"Just wait."

I pulled off my shirt and shorts, toed off my flip-flops, and walked the three steps to Luke. "How am I supposed to do this?"

Luke reached up, grabbed my wrist and pulled me down. I fell gracelessly on top of his lap, my other arm arresting my fall on the couch cushion, one foot still on the floor, with my other leg bent on the love seat.

"That's how," Luke murmured, softly since we were now intimately entwined.

"Shit," I whispered. My thigh had bumped the hard steel on Luke's cock. "Is that a cage on your cock, or are you glad to see me?" I quipped, trying to distract him from my vulnerable state.

Luke chuckled. "Well, both really. This is one situation where I can actually say this might hurt me more than it hurts you." He squirmed, trying to get comfortable under my weight.

"Sorry." But I wasn't sorry.

"Not your fault. But this is turning me the fuck on which is making the cage really uncomfortable," Luke said. "Par for the course, I guess. Maybe I can tell Kamal about this tomorrow, and he'll go easy on me since I'm basically punishing the fuck out of myself right now."

"I'm not sure why you're insisting on this since you can't even come," I commented.

"Oh, I'll be able to come. Don't you worry. My orgasm won't be as epic as usual, but..."

I had no idea what Luke meant, but Noah laughed softly. And that made me curious to find out. I was about to ask when he grabbed the waistband of my boxer briefs and pulled them down.

"Oh fuck yeah," Luke breathed, fingers gliding softly over my ass. "Come to Daddy."

I couldn't stop the small sound I made as my eyes closed with the unexpected jolt of pleasure and my cock jerked against Luke's thigh.

"Oh? Like a little age play, do you?" Luke said. I couldn't see his grin but I could fucking hear it.

My eyes flew open. "No."

Then Luke spanked me, hard, on one cheek.

"Ow!" I yelled.

"Don't. Lie." Luke said. "Did you like that word I used?"

"Yes," I whispered. "Fuck, I liked it. Why? Why did I like it?"

Luke laughed and spanked me again.

"Ow. Jesus!"

"Because you're a naughty little boy. You know you are." His voice had become silky smooth and seductive as he stroked the tips of his fingers over the screaming skin of my ass in a most arousing way.

I heard a gasp and looked over to where Noah sat watching with heavy-lidded eyes, one hand down his pants.

Luke followed my gaze. "Speaking of naughty little boys, Noah."

Noah moaned as his hand moved beneath his clothes. "Huh?"

"Yeah, I'm talking to you," Luke said, now rubbing his hand more firmly over my smarting cheek. "How many spanks should I give this naughty cowboy?"

Noah didn't answer right away so I pleaded for mercy with desperate eyes. "Noah, come on. Go easy on me. I'm not used to this."

Luke continued. "He almost took off on both of us this morning, remember? I think he needs to understand the pain he caused."

Noah smiled and nodded.

My ass clenched, which Luke did not miss.

"Oh, he's scared. But his cock's hard too," Luke told Noah. "How many?"

Noah thought for a moment as he continued to masturbate. "Ten."

"Okay," Luke said. "Ten to start. Sure."

"Ah, shit," I moaned. "My ass hurts."

"Good. Your gorgeous ass is hurting me too. My cock is so confused right now. This is turning me on so much but every time I try to get hard, the cage hurts, and I get soft again. Your safeword is *pony*. Ready?"

I wasn't ready at all. "No!"

"One," Luke said, bringing his hand down hard.

The pain cut through me again and throbbed in concentric circles through my brain. I'd never been spanked as a kid. This was both worse and better than I'd imagined. There was pain, for sure, but as it echoed through my body and warmed every part of me, my cock took notice and jerked its approval. But this made me feel vulnerable and confused. I scrambled to escape. But Luke bent my arm against my back, keeping me there. "Oh no, you don't."

"Please! I'll suck Noah off! I'll let you piss on me! Whatever!"

"Tempting. But no. Two."

"Ow! Shit, Luke!" I whimpered.

"Three."

"Oh God!" The humiliation was worse than the pain now. My cock was obviously on board with what was happening, and I felt like a puppet on Luke's lap. He must know what this was doing to me. His control over my body was complete.

"Four."

"I can't believe you're—"

"Five."

"Fuck!"

"Six."

I stopped talking. It was impossible to make words when your ass was literally on fire and your cock ready to explode for some unknown reason. I groaned through the next four spanks, closing my eyes and praying for the ordeal to be over and also for the humiliating discipline to go on forever. My cock pressed wetly against Luke's thigh. Kink was damn confusing.

"Okay, enough for you, cowboy. Any more and you'll be sobbing or coming or both and that's not what I'm going for. At least, not right now."

I breathed ragged breaths through my nose. I couldn't help releasing one more moan and rubbing my cock against Luke's thigh.

"No, you don't, cowboy. You come on my leg, you're getting ten more."

I froze. Luke pulled the boxer briefs up, which scraped over my aching flesh like they were made of straw rather than cotton.

"Get up."

"Wait. I need a minute," I said, a tremor in my voice.

"Okay fine. Take a minute and pull yourself together. I meant what I said."

I lay there for a few moments, calming myself and getting my cock under control. I tried not to think about Luke and Noah watching me because that made the task harder. Finally, I was able to get off Luke's lap and stand on shaky legs before him. I'm sure my fucking face was as red as my ass. My cock pitched a tent in my briefs, which were soaked in front from how I'd reacted to my spanking.

Luke looked me over, licking his lips and pressing the heel of his hand against the front of his pants. He cursed Kamal but winked at me. "Don't you dare tell me you don't like getting spanked on your naked ass ever again. The evidence is right in front of me."

I cleared my throat, looking at the floor. "I don't think *like* is necessarily the right—"

Luke ignored me and looked at Noah. "Okay, ponyboy. Strip."

Noah sat up straight, took his hand out of his pants, and ripped off his T-shirt, throwing it on the floor. He breathed hard and looked desperate as he kneeled up to remove his shorts and boxer briefs.

"God, you're so beautiful," Luke murmured, watching him. "Isn't he beautiful, Jensen?"

I nodded, licking my lips, glad Luke's attention was elsewhere for the moment. "Yes. He is."

Luke stood up and started unbuttoning his shirt. "Jensen, get naked. We're going to suck our boy off together, and then I am going to make you fuck me until I get off."

"W-what?" I said. What did he mean I was going to fuck him until he came? And what if I came before he did? Which was a probable outcome at this point because I was still leaking and harder than I'd ever been.

"You having trouble with the first part?"

"Uh, no."

"Don't worry about the second part, everything will become clear. Just head over there and get his cock in your mouth. And lift that pretty red ass of yours high in the air when you do."

I looked back and forth between Noah, who lay blissfully back on the mattress, naked and aroused, and Luke who unzipped his pants.

"I want to see," I reminded him.

"What?"

"I want to see your dick in the cock cage."

Luke grinned, pushing his pants down and stepping out of them. He straightened up and put his hands on his hips.

"Is that an actual...lock?" I asked, pointing to what looked like a tiny black padlock on the clasp keeping the cage closed.

"Duh," Luke laughed. "Otherwise I could take the thing off. But the evil Kamal has the key." He looked down at himself and fondled the tiny lock with his fingers. "They don't use them in the stables 'cause we always have our arms bound. But I kind of like the lock. In a perverted *Control me, Master*, kind of way."

I stared at Luke's cock, swelling painfully against the steel bars of the metal cage. Fluid shone on the metal surrounding his glans and I found my eyes flicking up to meet Luke's. "Why does that look so hot?"

Luke smiled slowly, our eyes locking. "You want to practice on me for a second? You forget how to suck a dick?" He said this softly as if he was intent on seducing me when all he had to do was give the order.

"Won't it be painful?"

"Probably. But I'm a sucker for sexual torture. Didn't Adam tell you?" Luke lifted his chin and moved closer to me. Our fast, excited breaths synced as we stared fire at each other. Then he grinned and nodded, reverting back to Dom mode. "On your knees, cowboy."

I found myself doing what he asked without question; Luke's obedient little sub. He knew how to manage me and at this point I would probably do anything. Getting a closer look and a lick at the cage was not a hardship anyway. I dropped to my knees, finding myself at eye level with the strange device and Luke's leaking prick. I stretched out my tongue and swiped a drop of pre-come off the metal, barely avoiding Luke's swollen skin.

Luke groaned, reaching his hand down to cup his captive cock and hold it out for me. "Lick me," he said through gritted teeth.

I opened my mouth and licked along the rings, letting the tip of my tongue glide over his skin in-between. The softness of his flesh contrasted with the hard steel. Luke groaned and whimpered as I used my tongue to tease him.

"Oh fuck," Luke gasped, his hands closing into fists. "Oh, goddamn hell, Kamal, you fucking pervert. You devious fucking devil..."

I licked and teased, causing Luke's prick to swell more inside the cage. Luke groaned and fisted my hair with both hands. "God, the pressure in this cage is intense, but that's so hot. Now clean up the overflow.

I did as I'd been asked while Luke made agonized noises. Finally, his hands tightened in my hair, and he jerked my head back. "Oh fuck, okay, stop, stop."

Panting, I gazed up at him, like he was a God or some equally glorious being. While I knelt at Luke's feet in my priapic state, he could have been one.

I stared adoringly into Luke's eyes while he reflected similar feelings back, or was I imagining everything? After what he'd told me in the car, maybe this was real.

He smiled a slow, soft smile, and reached out to stroke my hair. "Good boy," he said. Why his appraisal caused the tumult of feeling in me I didn't understand. Except something in me wanted to please Luke. Something in me wanted to satisfy him the way no one had ever satisfied him before.

As if he read my mind, Luke nodded slightly and touched my chin. "Let's suck off our boy Noah over there. I think working together we should be able to do get him off in record time. Poor guy needs to come after the day he's had."

We dropped to the mattress and crawled toward where Noah had stretched out, bare from head to toe, his neck craned to watch us. But while I licked up the inside of his thigh and nuzzled into his crotch, Luke moved further and took Noah's mouth in a passionate kiss.

The kiss was so genuine and explosive I couldn't stop watching them. They came together like two flames licking a wick. The energy of their chemistry felt palpable to me as I licked my way along Noah's cock, my eyes on their kiss.

Finally, Luke broke away from Noah and beckoned for me. "Come up here. Sure, his cock is delicious but his lips are to die for." He was breathless and flushed with desire.

I crawled forward until I had stretched out beside Luke overtop of Noah who gazed at me with a combination of lust and something like awe.

Luke lifted his fingers to trace along Noah's finely shaped jaw, now giving gentle kisses to his chin and the corner of his mouth. "You want Jensen to kiss you? We can take turns..."

"Yes," Noah murmured, nodding quickly. "God, yes. Please."

I leaned down and covered his mouth with mine, drowning in the heady smells of testosterone and sweat. I remembered him as he'd been this afternoon, glowing with confidence and beautiful in his adornments and listened to him moan into my mouth as our erect cocks brushed together.

I felt Luke's lips on my cheek and turned to take his mouth with mine, suddenly desperate to be taken over by these two men. Luke undid me with his kiss as easily as he'd laid me bare with his hand on my ass. It still throbbed from his merciless assault. Then Luke pulled away from me and kissed Noah again.

I couldn't really tell who was whimpering and who was grunting, but the combination of those noises and the visual of them kissing made me almost crazy.

I kissed Noah in the curve between his neck and shoulder, then tongued my way down to the tuft of hair under his arm, taking his wrist and extending his arm so I had full access. I licked and kissed him there, hearing him gasp and feeling him wriggle under Luke's kiss. Then I lowered his arm and licked across his finely muscled, clean-shaven chest to his nipple, running the pad of my tongue over the bud several times, making it harden. I did the same to the other before licking a trail down his soft belly to where his cock curved against his stomach, leaking at the tip.

I glanced up, catching Luke's eye as he continued to kiss Noah. I held his gaze as I extended my tongue and traced a line up the underside of Noah's swollen penis.

Luke broke away from the kiss, cursing as Noah groaned and his head fell back. Luke kissed him quickly as if to apologize for breaking their connection, then leaned down, placed a hand on each side of the mattress beside Noah, bent and took the head of Noah's cock in his mouth while I continued to lick its length.

Noah half sat up and groaned as we worked him gently. His cock pulsed beneath my mouth. I remembered how his cock had looked when I'd removed the restricting cage from him. He had to be close after all he'd gone through today.

As if Luke was thinking the same thing, he circled the base of Noah's erection with his hand and started to really go at him, forcing me to back off and watch as I played with Noah's balls. The sight made my own dick leak and throb as Noah made stuttering noises and panted. His thighs parted as Luke sucked him hard, and I wet my index finger and played with his pink hole, pushing inside as Noah uttered a desperate cry and came hard in Luke's mouth. Watching Luke valiantly try to swallow Noah's release as the viscous fluid escaped his lips and dripped down his chin almost did me in. I had to grab the base of my cock to keep from coming right then, remembering Luke had other plans for me. Important plans I couldn't wait to discover.

Noah's soft cries echoed off the wooden walls of the shed as Luke sucked him through his orgasm and finally pulled off, wiping at his chin and licking his lips to get the rest of Noah's spunk. I couldn't help myself. I leaned forward and grabbed Luke's chin licking the wetness and kissing Luke hard to taste Noah's come in his warm, skilled mouth.

Luke groaned and opened to me, welcoming my invading tongue, letting me lick inside his mouth and stabbing at my desperate tongue with his own.

I felt a hand on my chin before realizing it was Noah's. He lay there looking completely blissed out, but he stroked my chin and then Luke's as we looked at him.

"Better?" I asked.

He smiled. "You're both...you're like sex gods or something."

"You inspire us. Look how gorgeous you are. And so, so sweet," Luke murmured, bending to kiss him gently on his slack lips.

I had never seen Luke so vulnerable, so enraptured. His obvious emotion made my heart hurt in a strange but not unpleasant way.

Then Luke sat up and shot me a salacious gaze. "Okay, cowboy. Now for the fun part."

I cocked my head. "Fun for me or fun for you?"

He licked his lips and shot me a coy smile. "You want to see how a guy can come wearing a cage like this?"

Uh, yeah. "Indubitably."

He raised his eyebrows. "Nice. I love a guy with a big vocabulary."

I grinned.

"Anyway, Noah can watch, or he can go to sleep, whatever he wants. But I need your cock since I can't use mine." He licked his lips as his eyes locked on my erection. "Okay?"

"Sure. Do I get to come?"

Luke laughed. "If you do everything I tell you." He gestured to the mattress. "On your back."

I rolled onto my back, hand automatically going to my cock and stroking, eager for whatever would come next.

"Can you be good and keep your hands by your head, or do I need to tie them with something?"

My stroking hand froze, and I made a strange sound in my throat. "Uh..."

"Never mind. Your reaction answered my question." Luke stood up and padded around the small shed, eyes scanning dark recesses and hidden corners. "Aha," he said, grabbing a length of old rope from a pile of junk by the door. He reached in his backpack as he passed and brought out a bottle of lube and a condom, which he tossed onto the bed beside me.

"Better use some good knots, Luke," Noah said, moving closer and trying to stifle a yawn. "He'll probably fight the restraints."

Luke grinned, his eyes glinting in the lamplight. "God, I hope so. Reach for the sky, pardner."

I gazed into Noah's calm blue eyes as I lifted my arms to reach above my head. Luke took his time with the rope, weaving the end in and out between my wrists, making sure everything was secure. When he finished, he pressed my bound wrists into the mattress as he kissed me hard, rubbing his metal-covered cock against my hip and making whimpering noises.

"Fuck, that hurts," I hissed as the metal device pinched my skin.

"Yeah, try wearing the damn thing," Luke muttered.

"No thanks."

"Figured. Anyway, I have a knife in my bag," Luke said.

At the expression on my face, he grinned. "To cut you loose if necessary, moron. Not for whatever you're thinking. Not into blood play."

"Thank God," I said.

"Yeah. I'm good with sweat and come. And maybe piss since you mentioned it." He laughed at the look on my face. "But we'll save piss play for another time. Probably work better in the shower anyway."

"Okay."

"Okay?"

"Sure."

I wasn't scared of getting a little piss on me. And the degradation could make the whole D/s thing more exciting.

"I like you, cowboy," Luke murmured, leaning close and kissing me on the lips. "I really, really, fucking like you."

I felt my chest grow warm at those words.

"Now, I am going to sheath this fat prick of yours, lube you up, and then I'm gonna sit on your dick and give myself some fucking relief. All right?"

My mouth dropped open. "Uh, yeah. Sure."

"You don't have to do anything but stay hard."

I gasped as Luke rolled the condom on me. "Not going to...be a problem."

Luke grinned and when he'd lubed my condom-covered cock and himself enough, he positioned himself over my thick erection.

"You know what they say? Save a horse, ride a cowboy?"

I groaned as Luke positioned me and sank down on the head of my cock, stopping to acclimate and closing his eyes with pleasure. Luke's captured cock swelled between the metal rings and more moisture eased from the tip.

The sight made me crazy. "Oh fuck," I gasped, pulling against the rope, wanting to thrust but knowing I needed to remain immobile.

"Good job, cowboy. Stay still and let me fuck you," Luke moaned, sinking down further.

I groaned loudly as I bottomed out. I closed my eyes because if I saw what was happening I'd come too soon, and Luke would be pissed.

"Oh God, your cock is fucking perfect. So hard. You're so hard. This is gonna work fine. All you have to do is lie there and let me do the work. Okay?"

My forehead wrinkled with the strain, but I nodded. I wanted to do what Luke said. I desperately wanted to please Luke. I wanted to make Luke come, and if Luke wanted to do this his way, I wasn't complaining.

"Okay. I'm going to start moving now. Let me know if you get close and I'll stop, 'cause I need you hard for this to work, Okay?"

I nodded again, biting my lip. "Sure."

Luke rested for another moment while I collected myself. Then he started to move. He used my cock like a dildo suctioned to the floor, lifting himself up and pushing himself down as if I were nothing but a toy.

The thought made me harder, and I had to open my eyes to watch Luke use me for his own pleasure.

Luke's eyes were closed, his face contorted in what could have been bliss or agony as he shifted for exactly the right angle. He came down hard and made a soft cry as my cock hit his sweet spot. His cock lifted the cage from his body as he came down in the same way several times, gasping out those small sounds until, finally, he sighed with relief and ground down as white fluid pulsed from the tip of his mostly flaccid penis in thick, lazy streams, dripping into my pubic hair.

Luke kept grinding down on one spot as his body appeared to gasp with relief. This strange, quiet orgasm went on for a long time, and I, feeling my own gathering climax from the sight of Luke's dripping cock, begged for permission.

"Oh fuck, Luke, I'm gonna come. Can I come? Fuck! Can I move? Please, let me move!"

Luke grinned a lazy, sated smile. His voice was tired and soft. "All right, cowboy. Show me what you've got."

I made a sound low in my throat as I began to thrust, using my hips to drive my cock into Luke. I felt my balls tighten, and the pleasure roll through me, my movements becoming ragged and my moans breaking the silence. I opened my eyes, meeting Luke's gaze as my orgasm tore through me. I pulled against my bindings but obediently kept my hands over my head.

When I'd finished, and the last tremors had moved through me, Luke slid off, dispensed with the condom, which he tied off and threw to the floor, and cuddled up next to me.

"Well done. You were so fucking perfect, and I feel so much better now," he said, yawning.

"Was that... Was that even an orgasm?" I asked.

Luke dragged his fingers through the cooling fluid on my pelvis. "Sort of. The term is ruined orgasm because your cock isn't really hard, and the feeling's not the same. Also called prostate milking." He shrugged. "Interesting sensation. But not as explosive as usual."

"Hmm."

"You wanna try milking yourself sometime? I'm sure Kamal has an extra cage..."

I paled. "Um. Well..."

"No problem. Not everybody is a pain slut like me."

"I'm not," Noah said quickly, moving in beside me. "I kind of am. But Luke and Kamal take pain to another level."

"Yeah, I'm starting to figure that out."

"You wanna sleep in those ropes, cowboy, or should I untie you?"

I held my bound hands out. "Milking you was a completely new experience for me. I always assumed if my cock went in someone I'd be in control."

Luke nodded, grinning. "Always think outside the box, Jensen. That's where all the good stuff is."

*

Noah was exhausted from his performance and our games, so we accompanied him to the bunkhouse to make sure he got there safely. Then Luke wrapped his hand around my wrist and winked.

"Come with me," he said.

He led me down a narrow path through the woods to a small pebble beach. The still water of the lake glistened in the moonlight as Luke dropped my wrist and stripped his clothes off.

"I need to get clean, cowboy. So do you."

I raised my eyebrows. "Okay, but no funny business. I'm fucking tired. That spanking almost killed me."

Luke stilled, throwing his shorts and shirt in a pile and stripping off his boxer briefs. The smile he gave me, devoid of the usual Luke mischief, was genuine and kind. I almost didn't recognize him.

"Can I kiss you at least?" he asked, hesitation in his voice. I didn't know Luke could be less than sure about anything.

"I guess so," I said. For once I didn't want Luke to suck my cock or fuck me or do anything except be with me.

In the moonlight. At the lake. Under the stars.

I finished undressing and moved toward him, ignoring his relaxed cock in the steel cage. As I examined his face I saw the notes of fatigue and uncertainty I might have missed before.

We stood like that for a long moment, mesmerized by each other after our intense coupling in the shed. Perhaps we'd finally put our desire to rest for the moment and could connect on another level.

"I know you think I only want sex from you, Jensen," he murmured, his hand coming up and cupping my chin.

I turned my head and kissed his thumb, which elicited a surprised smile.

"But I don't. It's...it's the easiest way for me to connect with someone. It always has been. And I'm good at it, and it makes me feel confident and in control."

I nodded. It wasn't like sex with Luke was a chore. I'd had more fun sexually with him than I'd ever had with anyone. But I wanted more. I wanted so much more.

"I really like you as a person, Luke. I like the way you take care of Noah and the way you protect me from—" I waved my hand in the air gently. "—my own insecurities."

His smile widened. "You do?"

I laughed, surprised that he hadn't realized. "Yeah. I do."

We were silent a little longer.

"I'm glad you came into my life, cowboy," Luke said, his face so close to mine I saw past the vibrant colour in his eyes to something else before he bent to touch my lips gently with his.

My hands settled on his naked waist as he kissed me, so softly, with a tenderness that made my knees weak. I felt like a teenager receiving their first kiss in the moonlight beside a beautiful, still lake. My heart pounded and my belly flip-flopped. I didn't know what was happening.

The sex had been great, was always great, but *this*...this was magic.

When we pulled apart, we stood there for a second, inhabiting this special moment. Then Luke urged me on, and we went into the water, splashing around like kids and laughing into the night.

Chapter Eighteen

We walked back to the bunkhouse unobserved, snuck inside, and slipped into our bunks. We were able to get in a few hours sleep before we had to wake up.

Luke had to report to the main house at ten for more time under Kamal's strict hand, and I had to be in the grooming barn to help prepare the ponyboys for the afternoon show.

This show was an exact replica of the day before, except with different ponyboys. The performances were almost as entertaining as the earlier show except for one very important element.

"It's not the same without you out there," I confessed to Noah, who stood with me by the fence.

Noah blushed and flashed me a smile.

I tousled his short hair. "I mean, Ben is a workhorse, Callum is physically impressive, and Trey is cute, but none of them have the same... I don't know...*presence* you have when you're in full pony get-up and performance mode. What I saw yesterday... You have star quality."

"Awe, Jensen. You are the sweetest."

I shook my head. "I don't feel sweet. I feel like the biggest pervert around half the time."

Noah raised his eyebrows. "You? The biggest pervert? Out of this bunch?" He waved his hand around the arena.

I laughed.

"You surprised Luke though. I don't think he expected you to be as kinky as you are."

"Did *you*?"

"Didn't really care. I only knew I liked you. But, yeah, I guess when I asked Lorraine to bring you in, I was curious."

"Oh God. Yeah... I mean, I loved that."

"I know," Noah said, looking down at the ground. "Me too."

*

While I was helping with the ponyboys after the show, Noah came into the grooming barn. He walked over to where I was attending to Callum's bridle and mask.

"Can I talk to you for a second?" he asked, glancing at Liv who was busy with Ben.

"Sure," I said, stepping away from Callum. "What's up?"

"Kamal wants us over at the house when you're done. He needs us for the final part of Luke's punishment." Noah's voice was low and held a tremor of unease.

"Oh?" I said, wondering what on earth Kamal meant. But I couldn't deny I was curious as hell.

"I'll wait outside," Noah whispered and kissed me on the cheek. As he walked away, I experienced a sudden flashback of the way he'd looked splayed out on the mattress in the shack the night before; how he and Luke had looked when they'd kissed; the vulnerable expression on his face when he'd come in Luke's mouth.

I closed my eyes for a moment, enjoying the images. My dick reacted but I blocked the memories and got back to work.

Callum remained silent and obedient while I removed his body harness. Then he said, "Thanks."

"I'm just doing my job. But, you're welcome." I grinned.

"No, I mean thanks for punching some sense into me the other day. I don't know why I was acting that way. Jealous, I guess." He looked down at the floor the way he was supposed to, but his cheeks were flushed with embarrassment.

"Um, I don't know why. Someone pretty awesome is looking at you with a lot of interest at the moment."

Callum raised his eyes to mine. I gestured toward the 'pretty awesome person'. Callum looked at Trey and smiled at him.

"Yeah, we've already sort of established we make good fuck buddies. But I don't know if there's room for more."

I hung Callum's harness on the peg and shrugged. "Ask him."

"What?"

"Ask him if he wants more. It's the only way you'll know," I said, shrugging. I removed Callum's cock cage and regarded the man's swelling penis speculatively. "You want a little...?" I made the motions indicating a hand job.

Callum shifted his feet. "Nah. Maybe I'll save it for later," he said, glancing at Trey.

I smiled. "Good thinking."

*

I met Noah outside and we walked together to the main house. The weather was cooler today, and a soft breeze ruffled the hair on my neck, drying the sweat from my exertion. "I have no idea what to expect," I said. "But that's nothing new."

"I don't really know either. I haven't had a lot of contact with Kamal. He scares me."

"Which is probably why you were assigned to Lorraine."

"Probably. I'm kind of sensitive, and I guess everyone knows."

"Yeah, well, there's nothing wrong with being delicate," I said softly. "A person can be strong and delicate at the same time, you know."

I felt a touch on my hand and looked down as Noah entwined our fingers.

*

We found Adam in his office. He flashed us a warm smile as he typed quickly on his laptop.

"They're in the upstairs board room. Go on up. Fourth door on the left."

I felt my stomach clench with nerves as we made our way up the staircase and down the hall. Noah seemed equally apprehensive. He had released me and now rubbed his hands together in an agitated way.

What we would find inside the room was a mystery except for the fact we'd be in the presence of the two most dominant men we knew. Maybe that was why I felt like turning around and dragging Noah to safety. But I was being ridiculous. This was Luke's punishment, not ours.

I forced myself to knock.

"Yes?" Kamal's voice, sounding bored and tired.

"It's Jensen. And Noah."

"Please come in."

When I pushed open the door and entered the room with Noah close behind me, my eyes found Kamal first. He sat in a chair at the head of the board room table in front of us with an electronic tablet in his hand. He turned and flashed me a broad smile that hit me right in the balls. He was a fucking attractive guy, Kamal, even if he did scare the crap out of me.

"I'm catching up on the news and doing some required reading for an online course I'm taking," he said. "And keeping an eye on your friend."

I swallowed thickly as my eyes took in the other person in the room.

"Oh. Shit," Noah whispered. I could almost smell his fear.

All the chairs except for Kamal's had been moved away from the boardroom table and stacked in a corner. Luke lay spread out face up on the polished brown wood, wrists and ankles fastened to the table legs with long straps immobilizing him. He had a black ball gag in his mouth and a red blindfold on. Saliva covered his chin and streaked his cheeks. The cage was still on his cock which swelled and leaked against the cold metal. A brown, braided riding crop lay on the table by his bound ankle. The instrument appeared old and well-used like crops I'd seen hanging in horse barns. I swallowed thickly at this juxtaposition of something so familiar to me and something so new.

"I had to gag him. He wouldn't shut up. I think he was trying to push my buttons so I'd unbuckle him and at least paddle him or something."

Luke gave an agonized moan and my cock swelled at the sound. Seeing Luke so helpless and in obvious erotic distress caused a definite reaction in me.

"How is he supposed to safeword?" I asked.

"He can snap his fingers," Kamal said, sounding bored again. "He's already used the signal once because he needed to piss. Boy, was that a production."

"Is he... Is he okay?" Noah asked.

"Luke, are you okay? Noah is worried about you," Kamal asked blithely.

Luke grunted and gave Kamal the finger.

"See, he's fine. But in a bit of a predicament."

"Yeah, okay," I said, licking my lips and trying to tear my eyes away from Luke's restrained form. "So why are we here?" I asked, worried about what Kamal's answer might be.

Kamal looked at me and then Noah, deliberately prolonging our curiosity and trepidation. Then he put his tablet down and stood.

"You're here to watch. Luke put you both in a very awkward position on Friday evening. So, I want you to see me put him in an awkward position. Several, in fact."

"Oh God," Noah murmured.

A sense of relief flowed through me. Then interest. Definite interest. "Okay. Seems fair."

Luke groaned in protest.

Kamal grinned. "Oh, he'll enjoy the experience, I'm sure. But the consequences will also be very humiliating for him. And extremely satisfying for me. Win-win."

Kamal reached out and ran the tip of his index finger along Luke's skin from his sensitive underarm to his hip as he walked half the length of the table. Luke wriggled and panted, groaning as his cock fought the cage.

Kamal glanced at us. "You can sit or stand, whichever is more comfortable. But you'll have a better view of everything if you stand."

I nodded. Neither I nor Noah took the offered chairs. The nervous tension transformed into a coiling sexual anticipation.

What was Kamal going to do? How would Luke react?

I felt like I was present at the start of a big-top show or something equally amazing and unpredictable, with the added benefit of knowing one of the performers.

Kamal picked up the riding crop and struck the tabletop beside Luke, making all of us jump.

"Okay, Luke, your friends are here. So, let's get on with this," Kamal said, running the tip of the crop along Luke's arm from wrist to underarm, making him twist and try to get away. But he was so spread out he couldn't go far.

"This is for lying to Jensen," Kamal said, flicking the tip of the crop hard against Luke's right nipple, which made him hiss and jerk. "And this is for lying to Noah." He did the same to Luke's left nipple with the same result. Then he laughed. "Nah, kidding. I know that didn't hurt at all."

He used the crop to point at something on the table I hadn't noticed before. "Noah, can you pass me those steel clamps, please?"

At his words, Luke woke up and took notice. He made a frantic sound and struggled in his bindings.

"I've clamped his nipples a few times today already. He fights nipple torture, but the results are satisfactory."

Noah moved forward and gathered the clamps before passing them to Kamal.

"Thank you," Kamal said, taking them both in his left hand and dragging the crop along Luke's side, playing the tip in the hair leading to his captive cock, and then down the inside of his thigh to tap between his legs. "How is this plug feeling, Luke? Did I forget to tell you there's a remote?"

Luke whimpered.

"I thought so. I'm going to turn the vibration on low in a moment, so you can suffer the wonderful feeling in your ass while you have no outlet of relief and while your nipples are aching with pain."

Kamal put the crop down and fished a small black device from his pocket. He held the tiny remote up for Noah and I to see, then pressed a button. A soft steady buzzing became audible.

Luke jerked his hips and gasped.

"Ah, this setting's a bit too low," Kamal murmured, pressing the button again. The buzzing became louder.

Luke's hips jerked twice more; then he relaxed and emitted a submissive whimper.

"There we go," Kamal said. "Perfect." As he moved in with the clamps, he pinched Luke's nipple quickly, making him cry out. "Watch closely, Jensen. These are a handy tool to quiet a rebellious ponyboy in the arena. Or to torture a spoiled brat in the boardroom."

"Why me?" I asked.

"Hmm?"

"Why are you telling me?"

"Oh, no reason. Except, you have the makings of a trainer. Or so everyone has been telling me." Kamal flashed me a broad smile. "If you're interested in moving further in this organization at some point."

He went about Luke's torture in the most matter-of-fact way, speaking to me about other things while he prepared to put Luke's tender nipples in some scary looking metal devices. Kamal was perfectly at home in this environment. He was a natural Dom.

Kamal leaned down and opened his mouth against Luke's right nipple, tonguing the small bud and sucking noisily. Luke writhed. When Kamal pulled away, he quickly squeezed the nipple between his thumb and forefinger and affixed the clamp.

Luke groaned and whimpered.

Kamal did the same to the other nipple until both were clamped tight between strict steel that glinted in the overhead lighting.

"Too bad Adam doesn't have anyone scheduled to use this room for a business meeting today. How provocative to have such a beautiful boy displayed this way. I'll have to approach him with the idea. We could raise our rental rates."

I didn't know if Kamal was serious but I didn't care. I was too enthralled with the way Luke's nipples looked in their clamps and the noises he made as the vibrating plug teased him.

I glanced at Noah and saw he was equally fascinated by this. Something about seeing the confident and sassy Luke in such a humiliating and subservient position at the hands of an even more dominant man was fascinating. Whether Luke would make us pay for seeing him like this, I had no idea. And didn't really mind the thought, frankly, after last evening.

Kamal picked up the crop again, tapping the leather tip at different spots all over Luke, even against the cock cage. He traced the flat end along the most sensitive places and flicked the stiff leather against Luke's skin at intervals. When he got to Luke's collarbone, he snaked the instrument gently along the man's stubbled neck, over his Adam's Apple and up to his chin, then used the tip to push at the ball between Luke's teeth. All the while Luke made small sounds that went straight to my dick.

"Do I dare remove this?" Kamal asked. "I'm enjoying a rare moment of peace. And the sounds you're making are exquisite."

Luke moaned and nodded.

Kamal sighed. "Fine." He put the crop down and moved forward, unbuckling and removing the device from Luke's mouth. "I know I'm going to regret this."

"Fuck you, Kamal." Luke's voice sounded raspy and rough. He coughed.

Kamal raised his eyebrows. "Yep."

Luke's tongue came out to lick at his lips before he said, "These clamps are making my nipples into hamburger meat."

Kamal laughed. "Quite an exaggeration although I'm sure it feels that way. You won't have any marks. Trust me."

"I hate you," Luke whined. I would have laughed at the petulance in his tone if I hadn't been transfixed.

Kamal, however, did laugh. "I doubt that."

Luke's lips pressed together, then parted as he grimaced in frustration. The red blindfold made a dramatic stripe across his handsome face. "Why are they here? Why did you bring them here? To humiliate me?"

"Partly," Kamal's voice became a soft rumble which, strangely, comforted me greatly. "But also, so you can apologize in person for the little stunt you pulled. And for educational purposes."

"You're a bastard, Kamal," Luke spat.

Kamal clicked his tongue. "All right, Luke. I know you think so, but there are still rules even though I've removed the gag. Unless you want me to leave this cage on you for a week."

Luke remained silent, forehead creasing with worry.

"I see my suggestion gives you pause."

"You wouldn't leave the cage on him so long, would you?" Noah, who'd barely said a word since we'd arrived, spoke softly. His flushed face looked anxious as he hugged himself with both arms.

Kamal smiled, picking up the crop and tapping the leather sharply against the metal cage on Luke's cock, eliciting a groan.

"I've been tasked with making sure Luke appreciates the seriousness of his actions." He looked at us with astonishingly kind eyes. "If I thought a week in the cage would help, then yes, I would."

Luke groaned and pulled at his bindings.

"How are those nipples feeling?"

"They hurt," Luke said, subdued.

"Good. I'm going to increase the vibrations a bit now. That should help."

Instead of swearing or calling Kamal names, Luke moaned in frustration. As the buzzing sound became louder, Luke's moan turned into whimpers.

"Are you sure he's okay?" Noah asked.

"Yes, he's fine. But I will have him apologize to you both." Kamal tapped Luke hard on the bottom of his foot with the crop. "Luke?"

"I'm sorry. I'm sorry, I lied to you, Noah. I'm sorry I lied to you, Jensen. Tricking you was a shitty thing to do." Luke's voice quavered whether from the pleasure of the vibrating plug or the pain of his poor nipples or both, I wasn't sure.

Kamal raised his eyebrows at us.

"Okay," Noah said quickly. "You're forgiven."

But I wasn't so ready. "Nice way to throw me off balance. When I'm so new to everything."

Luke whimpered a sigh. "I know."

"You're a bit of a prick, you know?" I couldn't help dragging this out. Kamal's amused grin made me continue.

"I know. I know," Luke muttered, squirming against his bindings. "Can't you see I'm being well punished for it?"

Now I grinned. "Oh, I see it. And I like it."

"Fuck you," Luke said, but the force of this statement was belied by the softness of his voice.

"Pardon?" I said, crossing my arms in front of myself. "I'm gonna need more than a fake apology and a curse."

Luke sighed in surrender. "I'm sorry, Jensen. I'm sorry I got you in trouble," he said with sincerity. "But I'm not sorry about everything we did together."

"I'm not either," I said. Nothing could be truer. "But don't lie to me again."

"I won't. I promise."

Kamal smiled. "Excellent. Let's move on then. I'm going to have Noah and Jensen each remove a clamp."

Luke didn't like that idea. He moaned and pulled on his straps. "Kamal, please. leave them. I'm getting used to the pain." I'd never heard Luke sound so desperate.

Kamal nodded and turned to me. "Nipple clamps hurt most when they come off as all the blood rushes to the area." He gestured to me with the crop.

I moved forward. I wasn't sure I was on board with this, but I wasn't going to say no to Kamal. And at least Luke would get the clamps off. They had to come off eventually, right?

"Take the clamp off his right nipple, and hand it to me, please."

I reached forward. "Sorry, man," I murmured as I released the clamp and heard Luke's howl of pain stretch out in agony until becoming short breathy pants. My cock throbbed and twitched, and I had to acknowledge seeing Luke in pain was legit turning me the fuck on. Maybe I should investigate the idea of going further in this organization.

"Noah?" Kamal said as I placed the metal clamp on the table.

Noah shook his head. His mouth had dropped open, but he brought his lips together, then said, "I don't want to. Can't Jensen?"

"If he doesn't mind," Kamal said gently. "I won't make you do anything you're uncomfortable with, Noah. Do you want to leave?"

Noah looked at Luke lying there, then at me, then at Kamal. "No. I'm okay watching. I don't want to do anything."

Kamal nodded. "No problem, Noah. And thank you for your honesty. I'm glad you're staying because this is going to get better." Kamal turned to me. "Take off the other one."

The muscles of Luke's ass clenched and released as he waited for me to follow Kamal's order. He frantically licked his lips as his chest rose and fell with anticipation.

I released the other clamp.

Luke howled again and arched off the table, then collapsed back with breathless whimpers and full body tremors.

Kamal reassured us. "He's all right. The intensity dissipates after a few seconds, but can be quite uncomfortable at first."

Luke hadn't safeworded, so I had to assume Kamal was right. "Okay. Good."

Kamal smiled and winked at me. "If you kiss them, they'll recover quicker."

I glanced at Kamal, wondering if he wanted to see me do this. Then decided I didn't care. I bent forward and kissed Luke's tortured right nipple, pressing gently, then moved to the left one.

Luke whimpered and sighed with relief, clenching and unclenching his fists.

"Very nice. Now I need to move him."

"Are you done?" Noah asked Kamal.

"Not quite. But soon. By the way, I can see your erection Noah. I thought Luke might want to know. And Jensen, also."

"You pricks," Luke said, but his statement held no conviction, and only made me smile and Noah laugh.

"You won't be laughing when I bend you over my knee tonight," Luke murmured, voice rough and exhausted.

"Promises, promises," Noah said, obviously feeling better.

With a casual efficiency, Kamal undid Luke's restraints and helped him stand, then bent him over the foot of the table, tying his ankles to the bottom of the table legs and his wrists to each other behind his back. Luke's caged cock jutted below the edge of the table, his ass on display for whatever Kamal wanted to do.

Which was slap his buttock a couple of times with the flat of his hand, causing Luke to whimper. Luke's skin was already pink and still had the white marks from the day before although they were faded.

"You've been such a bad boy," Kamal muttered, slapping Luke's ass hard again. "Whatever am I going to do with you?" Kamal tsked and shook his head. Then he picked up the plug's remote. "For one thing, I'm putting this on high. Because I know the sensation will drive you mad, seeing as your little prick is all caged up."

I had to give props to Kamal; he was a right bastard.

"Oh God, Kamal, you asshole," Luke muttered, groaning and twisting, thrusting his caged cock futilely into the air as the humming of the plug became louder.

"Be still. And take your punishment."

Luke whimpered. "Okay, okay. I'm sorry. Fuck, Kamal, my ass is so sore, and I need to come so bad."

"Good. Then you'll remember we don't accept lying here at the BCR. Or trespassing."

Luke made a sound like he was about to protest but Kamal cut him off.

"Or stealing. Did Adam say you could use his room?"

"No."

"Or his bathtub?"

"No."

"Or his bubble bath?"

Noah and I looked at each other.

"No."

"And will you ever use someone's room without their permission again?"

Luke huffed and groaned. "No."

"Right answer," Kamal said, bringing his hand down hard again, making Luke gasp. "I'm going to unlock you now, and I'll let this vibrating plug do the work while we all watch."

"Ah, fuck. Fuck. Okay. Whatever."

Kamal reached beneath the table and rubbed the moisture at the tip of Luke's cock, making him hiss. "You want me to keep the cage on you?"

Luke's response was immediate. "No. Please, God, no."

"Okay, then." He withdrew his finger, wiped the wet tip on Luke's hip and reached into his pocket, bringing out a tiny silver key, which he proceeded to fit into the lock on Luke's cage. With skilled fingers, he slid the device off Luke's penis and tossed the contraption onto the table. The steel made a loud thud as the cage landed beside Luke's face.

Kamal grabbed a fistful of Luke's hair and bent to his ear. "Can you smell the pungent scent?"

"Yes," Luke hissed.

"That's you. Your frustration, your fluids leaking out your soft cock, weeping for release."

My dick throbbed at the sensuality in Kamal's voice and Luke's humiliation. Kamal was a fucking artist and Luke his reluctant canvas.

Luke groaned, licked his lips, and nodded. Kamal released him and stepped back. He reached beneath the table and wrapped his hand around Luke's now fully erect penis.

"Don't come yet," he said as he stroked Luke a few times, then backed off and picked up the remote. Luke's face became a grimace of frustration as he fought back the urge to climax. He grunted as his body twisted and jerked as if attached to multiple electrodes. A shiny thread of pre-ejaculate descended from his glans and swung with his movements.

"Jesus fuck," I whispered.

"Oh my God," Noah said softly, hand going to the front of his jeans and pressing there.

Kamal picked up the remote and made an adjustment, then put the control back down. Luke's grunts increased in volume and the muscles of his arms clenched and unclenched.

"I wonder how long until he comes all over the floor with no further assistance. Not long, probably." He moved in and grabbed Luke's hair again, keeping him in place, and with his other hand nudged the blindfold up so Luke's eyes opened and fixed on us.

"You can come anytime you like now. But I'm not helping," Kamal said.

I stared at Luke, who moaned and thrashed as his body fought the release he'd so desperately craved moments ago. So brilliant, this move of Kamal's. This final humiliation of making Luke come like a mindless animal in front of his friends.

Luke held my gaze for a moment, then closed his eyes. My attention went immediately to his cock as the swollen organ arched against the table and leaked more clear fluid.

"Next time I'm going to fuck you with the dildo you like. The one shaped like a horse's cock," Kamal said.

Luke's yell echoed off the walls of the boardroom and probably reached Adam's office downstairs. His cock visibly pulsed as white fluid shot out, hitting the bottom of the table and dripping while more fountained out in thick spurts.

Kamal laughed as Noah and I stood gaping, watching Luke's epic climax with sympathy and more than a little envy, at least in my case. His body jerked as he humped the air, emptying his frustration onto the boardroom floor.

"Ah, such a mess, such a goddamn mess," Kamal muttered, shaking his head as Luke's orgasm finally subsided. Luke's breaths came hard and ragged as he sagged on the table in submission to Kamal and Kamal's wishes.

Kamal let go of Luke's hair and walked away from the table. He switched off the remote.

"You're going to clean this mess up when I release you. Do you hear me, Luke?"

Luke was silent and motionless. I wondered if he'd stroked out.

"Luke? Do you hear me?" Kamal repeated.

"Yes, Sir. Yes, Sir," Luke murmured, a subservient plaything now.

Kamal gave Luke's ass a final slap, causing an exhausted groan from the sated ponyboy. Then he turned to me.

"I'm going to leave for a few minutes, give you three some privacy. I'll be back to untie him soon."

"Okay," I said, voice hoarse. I adjusted myself and looked at Noah, who nodded.

When Kamal had gone, I moved forward and reached out to touch Luke's soft, stubbled cheek. "Hey. You might be embarrassed, but that was the most epic fucking thing I've ever seen."

Luke's eyelids fluttered open, and he let the corner of his lip quirk up. He gazed dazedly at me and sighed. "Thanks. Not my choice of position, but whatever. And I thought he'd at least give me a hand job." His words slurred a bit but his spirit seemed intact.

I laughed and Noah bent down to kiss Luke on the forehead. "I think you should be thankful he took the cage off at all. I wasn't sure he was going to."

"Neither was I. Who knows what that bastard is capable of?"

"Yeah, I wouldn't ask. Strikes me as a dangerous question," I said.

When Kamal came back in the room, he asked us to leave so he could supervise the cleanup and give Luke some needed aftercare.

I felt exhausted and drained though my dick was still hard and my heart beat faster than a kitten's. I leaned against the wall and slid down until I was sitting on the smooth wood of the hall floor with my legs stretched out in front of me.

Noah soon joined me.

"That was... That was..." I couldn't form a coherent sentence.

"Unbelievable," Noah whispered.

"So fucking hot," I finished. I glanced at him, raising my eyebrows. "Right?"

He hesitated, blushing as if afraid to concur. But he nodded finally. "Yeah."

"You still afraid of Kamal?" I asked with a grin.

He laughed and let his head fall back against the wall. "More than ever."

I reached out and ruffled his hair. "See, Kamal would never have to do anything similar with you. Because you'd be on your knees sucking his cock before he asked you. You'd be his very good boy, I know you would."

"Oh God, Jensen, stop. You'll make me come in my pants."

"Not before I do," I said, pressing the heel of my hand against my throbbing erection. "I thought Kamal said he wasn't going to punish us?"

Noah laughed. "Well, not directly."

Finally, after about thirty minutes, the door opened. Luke, in his regular clothes, stepped into the hall, Kamal close behind him.

Kamal squeezed Luke's shoulder with genuine affection. "I hope I didn't make you suffer too much."

Luke eyed him with raised brows and opened his mouth.

"Never mind. Don't answer. You deserved every bit of your punishment and you know it." Kamal turned to peer at us. "You two going to be all right?"

From this perspective he looked even more intimidating. Noah and I scrambled to our feet.

"Yeah," I said.

"Yes, Sir," Noah said.

"All right. Take him back to the bunkhouse. I think he's learned his lesson." Kamal said. "Noah, Jensen, look after him. He's a favorite of mine, you know. Adam's too."

Kamal gestured me aside as Luke pulled Noah close.

"He seems fine, but if he gets weepy and/or shaky, that's something called sub drop and you need to call me, okay? Noah is familiar with the concept so he would probably notice, but I wanted to let you know about sub drop too. I had a little cuddle with him after he cleaned up his mess to make sure he felt okay about everything. I would never push his hard limits, and even his soft limits need to be treated with respect."

I stared at Kamal, feeling inexplicably warm toward him in this moment. After what we had seen in the boardroom, to let me know Luke had not been forced to submit to anything he'd not agreed to was so very reassuring. I gave a quick nod, to show I understood.

"Still, there can be deep feelings of vulnerability after an intense scene. Please call me if he appears out of sorts, unusually withdrawn, or excessively sleepy. Although he will be tired and he needs to rest."

"Okay. Thanks for letting me know. We'll keep an eye on him."

Kamal clapped me on the back. "I know you will. Thanks, Jensen."

Chapter Nineteen

Everyone was exhausted by Sunday suppertime, so Adam put in a pizza order. Callum and Trey picked up six of the pies from the main house and brought them to the bunkhouse. Since there was a light breeze and no clouds, we all sat outside on the grass and ate together.

Although Luke decided to stand, for some reason.

"How's your ass there, Luke?" Trey asked with a grin.

"None of your business."

"Huh. Kamal was really fucking cheerful when I bumped into him at the house. I wonder why."

"Shut the fuck up, Trey."

Trey shrugged. "Hey, I'm not being mean. Anyone who can suffer at the hands of that man without sobbing and crying for his mommy, is a goddamn hero."

"How do you know he didn't?" Ben asked, winking at Luke.

Trey laughed. "Because Luke would choke on his own vomit before he would be so vulnerable."

"Well, hopefully, he'd safeword," I commented, glancing at Luke and taking a bite of my pepperoni pizza. "Or safe signal."

"Oh damn, did he gag you?" Trey said, surprised.

Callum laughed. "Probably couldn't get a word in. I'm sure Luke didn't give him much choice."

When Luke glared at Callum, the other man lifted a hand in the air. "Sorry, sorry. That was mean. I'm sorry. I'm reformed. Forget I said anything."

Luke laughed. "Well, you're kind of right. And all I can say is, Kamal is a fucking sadistic genius, and I won't be pulling any tricks like that again. At the same time, I'm wondering what he would do to me if I did…"

Noah glared at him. "Luke," he said as if Luke were a disobedient toddler.

"Oh goodness. I like your tone of voice," Luke said, winking at Noah, who smiled. "But don't forget, you're going over my knee tomorrow, not the other way around."

Some of the other men protested this was a little TMI, but Noah blushed and nodded and continued to eat, probably, I thought, because he reveled in Luke's dominance and didn't care anymore who knew.

Luke persevered until about eight thirty. I watched him try to stifle his yawns as he leaned against the outside wall of the bunkhouse with a beer in hand, pretending to be following the conversation.

I stood and walked over. "You must be bushed after the last two days. Why don't you go to bed?"

Luke blinked slowly at me and put his beer on the ground. "Come with?"

I nodded. "What about Noah?" I glanced to where Noah was surrounded by the other ponyboys in a discussion about gear and show-ring techniques.

Luke shrugged. "He's pretty popular tonight. I don't think he'll notice or care if we slip away."

I nodded. Noah glanced my way and I gestured to indicate I was going inside with Luke. He smiled and flashed me the thumbs up sign.

I followed Luke into the bunkhouse. As soon as the door shut behind us, Luke turned and curled into me, arms sliding around my waist, face nuzzling into my neck. This sudden vulnerability surprised me, but I gathered him to me out of instinct.

"Hey, hey," I said, wondering what had brought this on. Was this sub drop?

"It's not sub drop," Luke murmured, pressing little wet kisses against my neck.

I grinned even though he couldn't see my face. "What is it, then?"

"Not sure," he mumbled. "But I need to be with you. I almost lost you."

My heart beat fast and I felt something break within me. Something that had been my last small holdout against fully committing to this place. To Luke. To Noah.

"Okay. Let's get undressed. You can stay in my bunk with me tonight."

Luke pulled away slightly and gazed at me. "What you saw today, with me and Kamal."

I blushed as I nodded.

"His dominance is why I come here. He knows how to deal with me. He puts me in my place," Luke said, forehead creased with the seriousness of this statement. "I need that. From somebody."

I nodded again. "Okay. Even though most of the time you're putting me and Noah in our places?"

Luke grinned. "More so because of that. I get..." He gestured to the room around us. "I lose control very easily. And I need someone to assert control over me sometimes."

I took his chin in my hand, staring into his blue eyes. "I can be dominant too, you know. Maybe not at the same level as Kamal. But I can put you in your place."

He grinned and raised his eyebrows. "Oh yeah?"

I challenged his gaze with my own hard stare. "Yeah, I think so." I leaned forward and kissed him tenderly, feeling him give way to me. "But right now I want to go to bed." I ran my hand down his sleeve and over the top of his hand. "You want to stay in my bunk?"

Luke nodded. "Yeah."

"Okay."

We stripped to our boxer briefs and climbed into my bunk, arranging ourselves so we fit. I lay with my head on the pillow and Luke curled under my arm, his head on my shoulder.

We were silent for several moments. I listened to Luke's breathing. Then he spoke so softly I barely heard him.

"G'night, kinky cowboy."

I smiled wide in the darkness, stroking my hand along his hip. "G'night, naughty ponyboy."

*

When I woke the next day, I was alone in my bunk. At some point, Luke had left me. But I could see the outline of his elbow peeking out of the blankets of the top bunk.

He'd been so vulnerable, so affectionate, the evening before. Or had I dreamt the whole thing?

Luke was normal when we got up, acting like his usual smartass self except for the odd time I'd catch him watching me with something in his gaze. But then he'd make a cocky remark, and I'd realize he wanted back to our old way of being together. Which didn't bother me because I liked the regular Luke.

Before we went on our business, Luke cornered me in the bunkhouse. "I want to go to the shed tonight. I promised Noah a spanking."

I nodded, my cock expressing interest in this idea. "Okay."

My day passed uneventfully. I was getting so used to my stable hand duties, and to seeing and touching naked men every day. Those duties were beginning to feel ordinary and routine. They were still better than mucking stalls, by a long shot.

We left the bunkhouse an hour or so after dark with our flashlights, same as before. As we made our way along, Luke described in detail what he planned to do to Noah. By the time we got to the shed I could barely walk normally, what with my cock so hard and stiff between my legs, chafing against my jeans.

As soon as the lanterns were lit, Luke sat on the loveseat and told Noah to strip. Then he pulled him across his lap.

"You liked watching me suffer in the boardroom didn't you, you naughty boy? Did you get an erection?"

"Yes," Noah squeaked.

"Watching Kamal clamp my nipples and torture me? You got hard from that?"

"Yeah. So did he," Noah said, looking over at where I sat on the mattress, watching with avid interest.

"Guilty," I said.

"Well, maybe I'll spank him after I'm done with you then."

"Okay," Noah mumbled, blushing and glancing my way.

"You like watching too? God you are a kinky boy, aren't you?"

"Yes. Yes, I am," Noah babbled as Luke's hand came down on him again and again. "I'm so kinky. I love going over your knee."

"I know. That's why I put you there so often."

Noah moaned, rutting against Luke's leg.

"Want to see him come from this?" Luke asked me.

I blinked. "From a spanking?"

Luke nodded as if this outcome should be obvious.

"God, yes," I breathed. "Can he do that?"

"Usually. Can you come from me spanking you right now?" Luke asked Noah, running a hand lightly over his spanked bottom.

"I think so," Noah gasped. "Go a little harder and faster."

Luke grinned, flexing his fingers. "Your wish is my command."

He wrapped an arm around Noah to hold him still and spanked the hell out of his ass as his moans became louder, his breathing jerky and short.

"I'm going to come," Noah panted as Luke's hand came down on him over and over. In a moment, his whole body stiffened, and he let out a soft whine as he climaxed against Luke's leg.

"Oh yes," Luke murmured, giving Noah several more hard slaps to carry him through his orgasm. "So fucking warm and wet on my jeans. You're lucky I let you come this time. Usually coming so fast is a no-no, right?"

Noah shuddered and collapsed limply over Luke. "Right," he sighed, eyes glazed and soft as he came down from his orgasm.

"Awe, hell," I groaned. "Watching him come on your leg was hot as fuck."

"Mm-hmm. Which is why I let him get away with orgasming from a spanking sometimes."

"So, tell me something," I said, sitting forward from where I sat cross-legged on the mattress, ignoring my erection for the moment.

"Huh?" Luke said while Noah turned and blinked his blue eyes at me.

"When you guys go back to your regular jobs in a couple of weeks, what happens then?" My fingers plucked nervously at the blanket. I'd been wondering this ever since my feelings for both men had turned from lust and curiosity to something else.

"Well," Luke said, grinning at me, "we both live in Ottawa, so we keep getting together, and I keep spanking Noah's naughty little ass, and he keeps sucking my dick. It's called dating." Luke slapped Noah's ass, making him gasp. "Get up."

Noah slithered off Luke's lap and stood, grabbing his boxer briefs from the floor and putting them on.

I stared at Luke, stunned by this casual statement. "You guys... You guys date? Back in Ottawa?"

"Isn't that what I said?"

And suddenly I could picture them: *Luke taking Noah to restaurants and movies, spanking Noah after dinner, buying him Christmas presents and a cake for his birthday.* The thought of them doing these things pleased me so much. "Does anyone else know?"

"Nobody's ever asked. Except you. I wonder why."

"Ottawa isn't far from here," Noah said. "You can ask for a weekend off once a month."

"We can come here and visit you too. I know Adam won't mind, long as I behave myself. Which I am determined to do, especially if we can see you more often and maybe catch a pony show."

My brain spun with this new information. "Well, shit."

"Surprised you, did we?" Luke grinned.

"So," I said, gesturing around me at the shed. "This thing between us can be more than a temporary hook-up?"

"Sure," Luke said. "As long as things are still good between us all when our session is up. And I don't see why they wouldn't be. It'd be a long-distance thing, true, which sucks. But better than never seeing each other again."

I nodded. "Yeah."

"Now strip and get on your hands and knees, cowboy. My cock is hard as hell after spanking this slut, and I need to fuck you. And I'm gonna wear your hat while I do it, so hand that bad boy over."

I grinned, grabbing the object in question from the floor and tossing it at Luke, who put the dusty thing on and started walking toward me.

*

I thought over what Luke and Noah had said while I walked to the grooming barn the next morning. I couldn't believe I'd been this lucky. To stumble upon two of the sexiest, sweetest, most amazing men I'd ever known, in the middle of a pony-play ranch where I'd expected dust and drudgery and instead got the kink-fest of my wet dreams.

The ponyboys' shifts had flipped this week, so Luke and I had kissed Noah on the cheek as he'd lain asleep in his bunk and walked to the grooming barn together. Not holding hands but walking in a companionable silence through the morning dew.

Before he opened the back door, Luke turned to me. He gazed at the grass and spoke in soft tones. "Ask to groom me today. Please? I want you to take care of me." His eyes flicked up to meet mine as his cheeks flushed a delicious shade of pink.

I nodded. "Of course."

Liv was only too happy to let me have Luke. She had heard about Luke's punishment, and hissed when she saw the white marks on Luke's rear end.

"Oh, baby. Looks harsh," she said.

"I heard Kamal say he wasn't going to leave any marks, but I guess he meant on his nipples," I said. "From the clamps."

Liv leaned in to eyeball Luke's nipples. "They look fine. And it's not the first time we've looked after a ponyboy with welts on his ass." She walked over to the cabinet and got something out, bringing the small jar over to me. "Skip the area completely with the loofah, but when he's dry, put some of this arnica cream on him. It'll make him feel a lot better and encourage healing."

"Okay."

While I scrubbed Luke vigorously with the loofah, avoiding his genitals and buttocks, Luke made small noises of pleasure, unable to speak with the ball gag in place. For once, he appeared at ease with this treatment. I wanted to think I was the difference, but perhaps Kamal had disciplined him enough to make him malleable in the stables.

I washed his genitals softly with a cloth, then applied the cream to the stripes on his backside.

"Better?" I asked, glancing upward.

Luke nodded, his eyes calm and clear.

"You should have told me there was a cream. I could have put some on you last night."

Overhearing me, Liv said, "I'm sure Kamal put some on before he released him to you. The use of this particular ointment is a standard form of aftercare."

Her assurance made me feel better. "Okay. Good."

"But, uh, if you ever need any, there's a number of tubes of the stuff in the cupboard here. You're welcome to keep one with you in the bunkhouse." She winked at me, and I couldn't help blushing, remembering all the spanking.

I was tasked with taking the outfitted ponyboys to the arena for their training. I attached the leads to their collars and walked in front, as I'd been instructed, and they followed obediently behind me. When we entered the arena, I handed Ben and Hunter off to Michael and Hiro, who took them outside for the morning's training since the weather was nice again.

I was surprised to see Lorraine waiting for Luke instead of Kamal. Luke appeared unsure as well. He stopped dead and stared.

"Good morning, Luke. I assume no one told you I'd be taking Kamal's shift today? He had to work all weekend." She gave us an amused smile. Because of course, Kamal had been working Luke's ass all weekend.

I was trying to lead Luke forward, but he wasn't moving. He stared at Lorraine with dismay and what looked like...fear? But Lorraine was the easy trainer, wasn't she? The one Noah preferred because she had a gentle hand?

Drool dripped down his chin from the gag as he stared at Lorraine, his forehead creased and eyes wide. Lorraine held out her hand for the lead. I glanced at Luke but obediently handed him off to the beautiful woman.

"Luke." Lorraine spoke softly as though Luke were a skittish animal. "I know I'm not Kamal, but I can work with you if you let me."

Luke looked at me, then back at Lorraine, unconvinced.

"If you really don't want to give me a chance, I won't force you. I'll let Jensen take you back to the grooming barn. But Kamal is off today and tomorrow, so you wouldn't have any kind of distraction." She motioned over to a table she had set up by the wall of the arena. "I've read over your paperwork. I know what your limits are, and I won't try to push them today." She regarded him thoughtfully. "And Jensen can stay."

I waited patiently while Luke thought this over. He shuffled nervously on his feet.

"Remove the gag, please, Jensen. I would like Luke's explicit consent before I proceed."

I moved behind Luke and undid the buckles on the gag, removing the ball from his wet mouth. He licked his lips and coughed, then looked at Lorraine.

"Jensen can stay?"

"Yes."

"And you won't push my limits?"

"No. Although I would like to try something a bit different today. But I'll ask for your consent. In fact, we'll leave the gag out for this session. Okay?"

Luke considered this. "I've never had a woman dominate me before," he said.

Lorraine raised her eyebrows. "Do you have a problem with my gender?"

Luke's forehead creased. He looked at me, then back at Lorraine. "I don't think so?"

She laughed, a genuine sound of delight. "Well, there's only one way to find out, right?"

Luke smiled. "I guess so."

She shook her head. "Not good enough. 'Yes, Lorraine,' or 'No, Lorraine.'"

Luke blinked. "Yes, Lorraine." He dropped his head and stepped forward, bumping my shoulder deliberately as he passed.

I couldn't blame him for agreeing to this. Lorraine was not only sweet but beautiful as well. I might be gay, but I wasn't blind. I could appreciate a woman's attractiveness even if I wasn't turned on, exactly. Although the way her tits looked in the V-neck, black T-shirt did *something* to me. I mean, who didn't like boobs?

Lorraine spoke into her two-way radio to let Liv know I'd be busy with her and Luke this morning.

"Good boy. Adam will be pleased," Lorraine said. "And I'm thrilled you'll give me a chance to prove myself. Come on, I want to show you something."

She led Luke over to the narrow table on which sat a canvas bag. "I want to try something different with you, something Kamal has never done." She took something out of the bag and held the object up.

My eyes went wide and I looked at Luke. He stared, confused, at the leather hood. The object looked like a puppy head, with snout and ears so stylistic they would give the impression of a dog without actually trying to turn the person into one. The well-designed hood looked to be of neoprene, mostly black, with a royal blue muzzle and blue accents above the eyes and on the perked ears.

"Now, I realize this is a pony-play ranch, but your form says you don't have a problem with other forms of role play," Lorraine spoke smoothly in a pleasant tone. "I thought we might have fun with a bit of puppy play this morning." She turned to me while Luke processed this information. "There are usually lots of dogs on a ranch, right Jensen?"

I smiled. "Yep. True enough." I glanced at Luke, praying he would agree to this because I was dying to see him with the pup hood on.

Lorraine reached into her bag. "There's also this," she said, pulling out a thick black butt plug with a long rubber doggy tail waving back and forth as if excited to meet us.

"Oh fuck," I said, eyes riveted to the waving tail.

"Yes, Lorraine," Luke said without preamble. I tore my eyes away from the butt plug to glance at him. His body looked taut, like he'd gone into DEFCON 1 mode at the sight of that tail. He hummed with barely contained energy.

Lorraine nodded. "Uh-huh. Good." She put the tail down on the table and picked up the hood. "I'm going to call you Luca while we play puppy today, all right?"

"Yes, Lorraine," Luke said.

Boy, she had his attention now. I'd never seen him so focused.

"Jensen, can you please remove his arm bindings? He will need his arms free for what I have planned."

"Sure," I said, moving quickly to unbuckle the leather armbands from each other, then from around Luke's forearms. I laid them on the narrow table as Luke rubbed his arms where the bands had been.

"Come here."

Luke stepped forward until he stood directly in front of Lorraine. She gazed at him warmly for several moments, then lifted her right hand to his cheek. "So handsome. You will make an adorable puppy." She lifted the neoprene hood. "Bend your head, please. You're much taller than I am."

Luke obliged, and Lorraine slid the pup hood over his head.

"Turn around."

Luke turned and Lorraine buckled the strap in the back to keep the hood tight on Luke's head.

"No speaking, now, unless you need to use your safeword. Kamal told me what your safeword is." She turned to me. "Do you know what Luke's word is, Jensen?"

I shook my head. "No."

She smiled, a wicked, mischievous smile. "Tell him, Luca."

Luke cleared his throat as if reluctant. But he dared not disobey a direct command. "*Brat*," he said shortly, the word muffled in the leather hood.

"Very appropriate, if I do say so, although you've been nothing but lovely with me today. Maybe we can talk to Kamal about changing your safeword to something more dignified if you please me. All right. Turn around."

Luke turned to face us again and his blue eyes stared out from the black-and-blue leather hood with an adorable hesitance as if he didn't realize how stunning he looked as a leather pup.

"Wow," I said.

Lorraine smiled broadly. "Yes, that's what I thought. Those eyes of yours, in this mask, well...they are something, aren't they Jensen?"

"Yeah," I said, stunned by how sexy and beautiful Luke looked in the pup hood. "I mean...wow."

Lorraine touched Luke's Adam's apple and drifted her finger down over his chest and belly until stopping on the metal of the cock cage. "This stays on," she said, tracing the metal bands with a manicured nail as Luke stood motionless and breathed faster. "Because the cage will help you maintain the headspace of being my plaything and my very"—she reached underneath to cradle his balls in her small hand—"good"—she drew her hand back along the bottom of the cage and up Luke's torso—"boy." She pinched his nipple, causing Luke's eyes to close and a long moan to exit his throat. The sound echoed within the mouthpiece of the hood.

"What a sweet puppy, you are, Luca." Lorraine crooned as she released his nipple and pressed her hand flat against his shaved chest. "But my puppy needs his tail, doesn't he?"

Luke sighed, nodding as a shudder racked him.

"Bend over the table, puppy," Lorraine ordered.

Luke obeyed, bending himself over the edge of the wood table beside where the plug lay. He stretched his arms out in front of him, but Lorraine clicked her tongue.

"No. I want you to spread yourself open for Jensen, who is going to put your tail in."

My mouth went dry. I watched as Luke froze in place. I wondered if he would obey, or even safeword. He was still for a long moment.

"Luca, do as I've asked you," Lorraine said firmly, her tone no-nonsense and commanding.

Luke's arms bent and extended behind him, his hands moving to the globes of his ass, fingers sliding in his crack as he spread his cheeks to expose the sweet vulnerable spot between. Kamal must have waxed him there—he was so smooth and hairless. Perhaps an intimate waxing had been part of Luke's punishment and an aesthetic preference of Kamal's.

I made a noise and realized my mouth was open. I closed my lips as Lorraine beckoned me over, her arms crossed in front of her, eyes on Luke.

"There's a bottle of lube in the bag, and gloves. Take all the time you need. I've got no place to be."

I nodded, searching in the bag for the lube while my gaze kept flitting to Luke's hands holding himself open. Such a humiliating position, but he was doing it for Lorraine. For me. Still, the quicker I got this done, the better.

I put a plastic glove on one hand and picked up the tail, glancing at the back of Luke's head in the pup hood. He was facing the other way, which was probably just as well. Maybe his eyes were closed.

I squirted a ton of lube onto the plug. The object was fairly large although I knew Luke was used to the horse tail plugs of a similar girth. At least I'd done this before. But doing this to Luke was new, and doing this while he held himself open for me was blowing my mind a little bit.

I took a deep breath and moved in close. "Can I touch him with my hand?" I asked.

"Anywhere you like, darling," Lorraine said, a smile in her voice.

I looked at the plug in my hand, then at the pucker between Luke's cheeks. I put the plug down on the towel Lorraine had laid out and swiped some of the lube off it with my gloved fingers. I placed my ungloved hand on Luke's left ass cheek, rubbing with my thumb beside his baby finger.

He made a soft sound and his ass clenched, then relaxed. His fingers kept slipping on his smooth skin, so he had to readjust frequently to keep himself open. My cock moved in my shorts at the sight. I swallowed thickly, then touched my lubed fingers to the pink skin of his anus.

Luke stuttered a groan that became a sigh as I moved my fingers gently over him, spreading the slippery liquid over his sensitive flesh, and pushing one inside him to get him as ready for the plug as possible. Watching my finger slide in and out of him while he held himself open for me was incredibly stimulating as were the sounds he made and the hot sheath of his body taking the digit again and again.

I glanced at Lorraine, who gave me a wink and an encouraging nod. How this didn't affect her in a similar way was a mystery. She was all business, watching to make sure I was doing what I should be doing, but looking as though she were watching me change a tire, not prepare a human puppy for a sizeable butt plug.

I turned back to Luke, determined to ignore Lorraine for the moment. Maybe she was simply a pro and soaking her panties right this second. Or perhaps she wasn't turned on by men's bodies at all. But I certainly was. I tried to keep my breathing even as I withdrew my finger and picked up the plug, pressing the rubber point against Luke's shiny wrinkled skin.

"Spread yourself wider, Luca," Lorraine ordered. "That's a big plug he has to fit into your cute little ass."

I almost laughed at Lorraine's impertinence and how affronted Luke would have been in ordinary circumstances. But I could barely work my features as Luke's fingers spread his ass wider, causing his pucker to open slightly.

I pushed the tip of the plug into the opening he made and kept up a gentle pressure as the rubber plug went in accompanied by Luke's long groan.

"Ah fuck," I breathed as I watched his body take the object slowly as I pushed a bit and relaxed, pushed a bit more until the last inch went in and Luke's anus closed around the small neck at the flange. I rocked the plug to settle the bulk inside him, watching his fingers slide away from his cleft as his ass clutched onto the toy.

"Very good, Luca. I'm so proud of you," Lorraine said with appreciation.

Luke's arms collapsed at his sides and he lay there, breathing rapidly, the rubber tail curling over his back and quivering, wagging side to side from his small unconscious movements.

"Oh fuck," I said again, my hand going to my shorts to press against the erection there. My vocabulary was impeded this morning by things too depraved to mention.

"You keep saying that," Lorraine remarked. She laughed. "I do not think it means what you think it means."

Luke let out a muffled laugh as his body clenched around the thick plug. The tail wagged faster, and I tried to wrap my head around the fact Lorraine had quoted *The Princess Bride* to me.

"Well, actually, it means what you think it means. It means you are overcome by the sight of this adorable pup submitting to my wishes. As am I."

"Amen," I said. "But I liked the reference. Great movie."

"Yes. Where do you think I got my pet name for Noah?"

Of course. *Buttercup*. Why hadn't I figured that out?

I nodded in acknowledgement. "I see."

"Okay, Luca. Stand up now and come over to me. I need to make sure this tail is in properly," she said with a mischievous grin because she knew the object was in place.

Luke pushed himself up from the table as I removed the glove and tossed it in the garbage pail. He walked over to Lorraine, boots clomping on the wood floor, the hood making him look like a mythical being, tail wagging provocatively behind him.

"Turn around." Lorraine said, pointing to the ceiling and twirling her hand as Luke approached.

He stepped close, then slowly spun so he faced me. Lorraine proceeded to check his tail.

I couldn't see what she was doing, but from the way Luke responded, I knew she was manipulating the plug in his ass, pushing the object forward, rocking and, perhaps, twisting the item in question.

Luke grunted and tried to stay still as Lorraine moved the tail plug around, ostensibly ensuring its placement but teasing him, eliciting various sounds from Luke. Sounds that made my cock hard and my heart melt.

I watched his eyes close, then reopen as he pinned me with his gaze. He wasn't gagged but obediently said nothing, simply watched me as Lorraine played with him, slapping the rubber tail now, pulling the slim rubber back with a finger, then letting go so the tail slapped gently against Luke's back. He shifted on his feet, the only protest he could make.

She slapped him on the ass and said, "Okay, time for some basic training. Jensen, his leash is in the bag."

Oh, Dear God. His leash. I swallowed as I reached into the bag and pulled out a finely worked leather dog lead with a handle and a clip on the end. I walked past Luke and held the leash toward Lorraine.

Lorraine shook her head. "I'm going to have you do the honors. Kamal tells me you two are somewhat involved and the dynamic is generally with Luke in command?"

I saw Luke stiffen although he was facing the other direction so I couldn't see the expression in his eyes.

I nodded. "Uh, yeah, I guess so."

"Right. So, I'd like to see you take command for a change. I think the dynamic would be interesting for Luke as well." She placed a hand on Luke's shoulder, squeezing him gently. "Does my puppy have any objections to this?"

Luke didn't move for a long moment. Then he shook his head from side to side.

"I beg your pardon?"

"No, Lorraine. I have no objections," Luke said in a voice that would have sounded defeated if there wasn't a tinge of excitement there.

I glanced at Lorraine.

"Attach the lead to his collar and tell him to get down on all fours. I want to see him try to be your good boy."

I swallowed. Fuck, this was screwing with me. I figured this game was screwing with Luke too. Hopefully in a good way?

I moved around in front of Luke so he could see what I was doing. He watched me with an intent expression as I clipped the lead onto his collar and stepped back. I glanced at Lorraine.

"Tell him," she said.

I looked at Luke. His blue gaze challenged me to do as Lorraine had asked.

"On all fours, Luca," I said in what I hoped was a commanding tone.

He blinked at me as his chest rose and fell with quick breaths. Then he dropped to his knees and leaned forward on his hands in one fluid motion. His head in the pup hood bent so he looked at the floor instead of at me.

I stared down at my human lover on all fours, with the puppy mask on and the rubber tail curving over his back and wagging, always wagging. I tried not to come in my pants.

"Very nice," Lorraine said, leaning against the edge of the table, watching us. "Tell him to sit."

I swallowed, then cleared my throat. *Oh man, was I really doing this? Yes. Yes, I was.*

"Luca, sit," I commanded.

Luke obediently sat back on his heels and lifted his head to look at me. His vivid blue eyes peered at me from the pup mask.

"Nice," Lorraine said. "Now tell him he's a good boy."

"Good boy, Luca," I said, mouth going dry at the expression in Luke's eyes.

"Now, tell him to lie down."

"Luca, lie down," I said, not recognizing my own voice. Thick and hoarse with arousal, I realized this was turning me on more than I'd expected.

Luke blinked at me, and I wondered if he would do what I asked. Then, very slowly, he moved into a crouch, which was the closest a person could get to a dog's down position.

"Good boy, Luca," she crooned, walking over to him. "What a very, very good boy!" She bent at the knees so she could pet him on the shoulder. Luke's eyes closed with pleasure as her small hand stroked along his back and over his buttock. She slapped his ass and said, "Up on all fours again. We're going to practice heeling."

I saw him glance at her in surprise and a sudden flare of indignation shone in his gaze before he tamped the emotion down and obeyed. He was working hard at this, at submitting to her, to us, and I felt so proud and appreciative.

Lorraine handed me some knee pads and gloves that I put on him, then had me walk him around the arena, keeping him at my left side.

Handling Luke as a puppy was an interesting experience. I'd always supposed this type of role play would be explicitly sexual in some weird way. But the feelings rising in me, *besides* my dick getting hard at Luke's submission, were pure and protective. I wanted to take care of this man who moved slowly on hands and knees beside me, trusting I wouldn't take advantage of him. That I wouldn't lead him anywhere he didn't want to go. That I'd only ask of him what he was prepared to give.

His trust gave me a heady feeling of power, one I wouldn't abuse.

"Excellent, both of you. Jensen, you can bring him back around to me now."

I walked Luke back to Lorraine, who pulled a large metal folding table from the side of the arena and beckoned to me for assistance. "Help me set this small massage table up, Jensen. Tell Luca to sit, stay, then drop the leash and come help me."

I did as she'd asked and joined her, struggling with the folding table. We succeeded after a bit of wrangling. "Are we giving him a massage?"

Lorraine grinned as she snapped the final leg into place. "Not exactly."

She walked over to Luke and picked up the leash. "Come," she said, leading him over to the massage table. She patted the table's surface. "Up, Luca. On the table on all fours please."

Luke looked at her, then at me. He hesitated.

"Is there a problem? Do you need to safeword? I promise, the table will hold you."

I saw the turmoil in his eyes, but eventually he did as she'd asked. He climbed up onto the table and resumed his position on hands and knees. I noticed his body trembling as Lorraine approached.

"Good boy, Luca," she crooned again. "Good boy."

She ran a soft hand from his shoulder along his side and over his ass again. "I'm going to examine you for a moment, Luca." She walked over to the wood table and grabbed a couple of nytril gloves, pulling them onto her small hands.

I stared at Luke, and he stared at me, the skin of his neck and shoulders flushing pink as he took in this information. I mean, compared to what Kamal had done to him, this was nothing. But Lorraine was a woman, and this puppy play stuff apparently was something he'd never experienced before. In other words, he was used to the way Kamal treated him. Lorraine, although a milder sort of Domme, still had high expectations and no qualms about making Luke uncomfortable, only in different ways than Kamal. I could see this whole thing challenged him, but the game intrigued him as well. He was obviously aroused: from the flush on his skin, the excitement combined with caution in his eyes, and the state of his captive cock, which bulged between the metal rings of the cage and leaked shiny pre-come out its red tip.

"Face forward. Stay at his head. Hold the leash tight because he might be skittish."

I did as instructed, holding Luke's lead as Lorraine moved to stand behind him. I couldn't really see what she was doing, but when Luke's eyes flew open and he shifted slightly, I peeked around and saw Lorraine had snaked an arm between his legs and was playing with his cock in the steel cage. She reached into her pocket. My breathing sped up, and I held the leash more firmly.

"You've been such a good boy, Luca, I'm going to take this nasty thing off and see you in all your splendor. For you are splendid, you know. You are absolutely stunning in your submission and your body is a work of goddamned art. Someday, I'd like to wrap you up in ropes and suspend you from the ceiling for the afternoon."

Luke's eyes closed as she said these words. I watched her delicate hands on the cock cage, releasing the clasp and sliding the rings from Luke's penis. He groaned and struggled to stay still while her small hand stroked him quickly to fullness.

"Ah, fuck," I said, feeling my own dick throb. "Fuck, fuck, fuck."

My fingers trembled as I held onto the leash and my lust with equal determination.

"Nice, huh?" Lorraine murmured, stroking Luke with long motions as his cock filled quickly. "I've a bit of a thing for you, Luke, but I've never let on. I asked Kamal if I could have you for a session, and he agreed, thinking you might do well under a gentler hand after this weekend. Was he right?"

Luke cried out as Lorraine gathered the moisture from his glans and rubbed the clear fluid over his cock and along his perineum to where the butt plug jutted from his anus. He squirmed and panted as she teased him with her hands and her words.

"Yes, Lorraine," he sighed, voice deep from within the leather hood.

I had never seen Luke so docile—didn't know he could ever be this obedient and subdued. Maybe he was surprised too. Maybe the pup mask allowed him to be something different. I'd never want Luke to change who he was, but if he could completely relax into submission with Lorraine that was promising.

Her hand moved to the base of the tail, and she jostled the plug in Luke's ass, making him groan as a shudder racked him. "You like this tail, don't you?" she said, gliding her hand up the rubber appendage and slapping gently as Luke moaned, then grabbing the base and thrusting the plug, twisting the thick rubber.

Luke moaned, then whimpered, then sighed.

"Oh yes, my lovely puppy. I think we will have to make puppy play one of your regular things, don't you? I'm sure Kamal would like to have a loyal puppy to follow him around the stables, maybe even during your off time? When you're not fulfilling your pony duties? Or as punishment that's not really punishment?"

Luke groaned and nodded eagerly, as if he couldn't think of anything better.

"Now, I'm going to get you off, but I want you to keep your eyes on Jensen. If I see either of you look away from each other, I will stop. All right?"

I could barely breathe. "Okay."

"Yes, Lorraine," Luke said in an echoing, high-pitched, obedient quiver.

"Excellent. Such good boys, both of you. I'll be sure to let Kamal know."

With her left hand, she took hold of Luke's arching cock and began to stroke slowly. With her right hand, she rocked the base of the pup tail plug until she had Luke moaning, grunting, and squirming in place.

So many emotions flitted through Luke's eyes as I kept my gaze locked to his, until they glazed over, and he came with a shout and belly-deep groan, Lorraine milking the come out of him with skilled fingers and rocking the plug until he was done.

He sagged there, tremors running up and down his arms and legs, barely able to keep himself upright as Lorraine gently extracted the butt plug, then removed her gloves and unbuckled the pup hood. She lifted it off Luke's head.

She glanced at me standing there, shorts so fucking tight over my erection, chest heaving, and asked, "Do you need to be alone for a second?" with a smirk.

I cleared my throat and tried to think of something funny to say.

Lorraine pulled the hood off Luke and he gazed at me with those wide blue eyes, blown and dark from his orgasm, hair damp with sweat.

"Hi," I said.

"Hi," he said. His eyes raked down my torso and locked onto the bulge in my shorts.

I shrugged. "Sorry. You do this to me. Every time."

Luke looked over at Lorraine, eyebrows raised, but he didn't say anything.

Lorraine grinned. "You want me to leave for," she glanced at her watch. "let's say ten minutes? Long enough, do you think?"

Luke looked back at me while I took a moment to process what was going on. I looked back and forth between them until my brain decoded her question.

"Oh fuck. Plenty," I whispered breathlessly, eyes locked with Luke's, heartbeat ramping up even more.

Lorraine laughed. "He's been such a good boy. I'll give you fifteen. Then back to the grooming barn with you both."

She put her things on the table and walked out the side door of the arena, leaving us alone.

As soon as she'd gone, Luke climbed gracefully off the massage table. But he didn't stand. He went to all fours on the floor and moved toward me like a hungry tiger.

I took a step back but he licked his lips, eyeing my crotch, and kept coming.

"Uh, what are you doing?" I asked although I could guess what he wanted.

He didn't answer but I stood my ground as he approached. When he got close enough he rose up on his knees and grabbed my hip, pulling me forward as he pushed up my shirt and bent his face to my belly right above my waistband.

"Oh fuck," I groaned, staring down at him as he licked and bit at me, then curled his fingers under the waistbands of my shorts and boxer briefs and drew them down. My dick popped out and almost slapped him on the chin.

I barely had time to breathe before he had my cock in his mouth.

After everything I'd seen, I was as hard as a rock and leaking so much fluid I'd soaked the front of my briefs. A few more minutes and the wet would have come through my shorts. I tried to hold onto my dignity for a few moments while Luke sucked so hard my brain was about to come out my dick.

"Oh my God, fuck, Jesus, Luke," I groaned, hands on his head as he worked me, grasping at his short hair that didn't provide any handholds at all while my cock thrust in and out of his mouth.

When those blue eyes flashed up to meet mine, my lips parted on a silent scream as I came hard in his mouth, thrusting mindlessly as waves of pleasure overtook me. I stared down at this beautiful, complex man who possessed so many layers to his personality and wondered how I'd gotten this lucky.

Chapter Twenty

In the grooming barn, while cleaning Luke after this intense session, I was reminded again of his unexpected fragility. His session with Lorraine had taken him apart. The harshness of Kamal's weekend punishments affected him less than Lorraine's gentle and playful manner.

He began to shake as I hosed him down.

"Sorry, is the water too cold?" I asked.

Luke shook his head.

"Are you okay?"

Luke shook his head again.

"Liv," I said, "Something's wrong with Luke." Not even thinking, I reached up and unfastened Luke's wrist restraints. He hadn't safeworded, but I could tell something wasn't right.

By the time Liv came over, I had Luke in my arms. I'd had to drop the hose and grab him to keep him from falling to the tiled floor.

Liv put a hand to Luke's forehead. "He's not overly warm. Could be sub drop. Happens after an intense session sometimes."

She helped me wrap Luke in a huge towel and bring him to a chair by the table. He sat hunched forward when I released him, head hanging, hands finding each other and twisting together.

"He's crying," Liv said quietly to me. "Emotional breakdown after a scene is not uncommon, but I've never seen Luke lose control. Not from pony play or anything Kamal has ever done."

"We were with Lorraine," I said. "But it was nothing, only some puppy play."

Liv glanced at me strangely. "Puppy play isn't nothing. Especially if you've never done it before. Has he?"

"I don't think so. I mean, it wasn't like the stuff he does with Kamal. No pain or anything."

Liv's forehead creased. "Maybe we should get her."

"Lorraine?"

"Or Kamal. Or Adam. A trainer."

*

Within a few minutes Adam and Lorraine were there.

"Kamal is off-site right now, but he told us to text him if we need him to come in," Adam said as Lorraine approached the seated Luke.

Lorraine knelt in front of him and put her hands on Luke's cheeks, lifting his face. "Hey, look at me. What's going on? Was it something we did today?"

But Luke's eyes remained closed. He was chewing on his lip and mumbling something.

"I can't hear you, darling. What?" Lorraine said so gently I felt the sting of tears in my eyes.

"We'll bring him to the house," Adam said quickly. "I think I know what's going on, but he may not want to share the information with—" He glanced at Jensen. "—well, with anyone."

There was no way I was letting Luke out of my sight right now. They could all fight me. "I want to stay with him," I said firmly.

"I know you do. But I promise we'll look after him. Lorraine and me. All we're going to do is make him comfortable, dry him, and get him dressed. And I'll talk to him and let you know when he's ready to see you."

"No!" Luke said as his head snapped up. His eyes flashed like a frightened deer's in the bright lights of the grooming barn. "I'm fine. I'm fine. I need to talk to Jensen. Alone."

"You're soaking wet," Lorraine said.

"I'm fine. Can everyone just leave? I need to talk to Jensen."

Lorraine and Adam looked at each other. Then Adam nodded. "Of course." He turned to Liv. "Get the others finished up and on their way. And you and Adrian can have your lunch first and clean up later. Go up to the house, there are sandwiches in the fridge."

Soon they'd left and only Luke and I remained. The whirr of the air-conditioning provided a gentle, calming backdrop.

I pulled out the chair beside Luke's and sat down. He was still hunched in a defeated slump, and his eyes had closed again. At least he'd stopped shivering. I made sure the towel stayed wrapped around him.

Then Luke started talking in a voice so quiet I had to lean in to hear him. "I didn't tell you before because it really doesn't matter. Well, it matters, but none of this changes anything between you and me and Noah. I was hoping the feelings were going away and I didn't have to think about them anymore. But I guess they aren't."

A shiver ran up my spine. "What's not going away?"

Luke balled his hands into fists and spoke through clenched teeth. "These goddamn feelings...these goddamn memories! I can't get them to go away. I can't stop seeing them, and they always come at me when I'm in a *good* space. When I'm happy. I can't—"

I felt something drop in the pit of my stomach. Had he been hurt in the past? Or had *he* hurt someone?

"What kind of memories?"

Luke lifted his chin and opened his eyes—blue, glazed, and lost. "Bad ones. Horrible."

I swallowed. "Of what?"

Luke cleared his throat and looked away. "I fucking hate talking about this shit. Makes my life sound like the 'Movie of the Week'." He took a deep breath, then exhaled slowly. "So, my parents were addicts, right? They liked coke and meth and stuff."

This was bad enough, but he continued, "When I was ten, their dealer stabbed them to death in front of me."

My eyes flew open. My brain exploded. I didn't say a thing.

"Guy took a steak knife out of his pocket and sliced my mom's throat. Then he stabbed my dad in the stomach when he tried to protect her."

Now *horrible* images were flashing in my brain. "Jesus. *Jesus!*"

"He would have stabbed me but I opened the front door and ran down the street to my friend's house. His mom called the cops."

"That's fucking horrible. That's insane."

"I try to forget. I try...*so hard*. I try so hard, Jensen. I want to forget."

I leaned forward and pulled him against me, tucking his head under my chin and squeezing his shoulder. "I know. I know you do."

"Adam says I feel guilty for running away. And until I stop feeling guilty, I'll replay those events again and again in my mind. Over and over."

"Guilty? You saved yourself. If you hadn't run you'd be dead too!"

"Yeah, so everyone says," Luke commented emotionlessly. He looked up at me with questioning, empty eyes. "So why don't I believe it?"

I didn't say anything for a long time. "I don't know," I said finally. "Maybe it's not so simple."

Luke blinked and licked his lips. "What?"

I shrugged. "Guilt can be tricky. Of course, you feel guilty. You were the only one there who wasn't being attacked. Maybe you could have grabbed the guy's knife. Maybe you could have strangled him before he killed your dad."

Luke pushed me off and stood, his expression transmitting anger now instead of fear and sadness. But anger was better.

"I was fucking ten years old! Are you insane? If I'd tried anything, the freak would have sliced my head off!"

I stared at Luke, not saying a word. When he realized he had made all the arguments for his innocence, he sat down again, looking confused.

"It's not so easy."

"I know. But everything you said is true. You know it because you just explained the situation to me."

"Yeah."

"So, why are you holding onto the guilt so hard?"

Luke's face slowly collapsed, eyes sparkling with tears he fought to hold back. His right hand clenched into a fist, which he rubbed against his knee as if he were trying to wipe a stain out of his skin. "Because the guilt is all I have left. It's all I have left." His lost blue eyes pleaded silently with me to understand.

I nodded. "Okay, okay," I said as softly as I could, leaning in and pulling him against me. "I'm sorry. I'm so sorry this ever happened."

He let me do this, rubbing his forehead against my shoulder, as if he had a headache he couldn't get rid of. "They weren't very good parents, but they were mine. And they didn't deserve such a death," Luke murmured.

We remained this way for a while until I was sure he had warmed up and recovered from his mini-breakdown. When he was ready to go, I helped dry him off and walked with him to the lockers where he put on his street clothes, moving slowly and deliberately. When he finished, he flashed me an uneasy smile. "God, I feel like such a dick."

"What? Why?" I asked, moving closer and placing my hand on his arm.

"I didn't want to unload all of that onto you." He blinked quickly.

"I don't think any differently of you, you know. Except I'm sorry you had to witness such a horrible thing. And I understand you a little better. Why you need to distract yourself with misbehavior now and then. Why you need some kind of punishment for something you shouldn't feel guilty about, but do."

He stared at me, his eyes widening. "Is that what I'm doing?"

"I think so. What does Adam say?" I straightened Luke's shirt.

"Something similar."

I smirked. "Then we're probably on to something."

We gazed at each other for a long moment. "I fucking loved the puppy stuff," Luke said finally, and I knew he would be okay.

I blushed, gazing into those eyes and remembering the session with Lorraine. "Yeah, uh, me too. Quite an education."

We opened the door and stepped out into the summer day. "Hey, does Noah know about your parents?"

Luke nodded as we walked the path to the bunkhouse. "Yeah."

I looked down at my boots as I walked. "How come you didn't want to tell me?"

Luke stopped and took my wrist, making me meet his gaze. "I've known you less than a month. What if you think I'm unhinged?" His eyes questioned me, searched mine to see if I did.

I held his gaze with confidence. "Luke. I'd think you were crazy if you *weren't* fucked up about this. Anyone would be fucked up about this."

He nodded, licking his lips, and let go of me. "Yeah. Maybe I don't want to be fucked up."

We resumed walking.

Luke nodded. "Adam tell you there was something that fucked me up?"

I nodded. "After we used his room. He said you might tell me someday."

"Well, I told you," Luke said, glancing at me.

I reached out and touched his hand. "Thank you for trusting me with your secrets. And for the record? You are the most perfect, beautiful, smart, kinky, sexy goddamn fuck-up I've ever met. I wouldn't change a thing about you."

*

When we got back to the bunkhouse, Luke stripped to his boxer briefs and climbed into bed.

I went into the washroom so as not to disturb him and spoke to Adam over the walkie-talkie.

"Hey, Adam. He seems a lot better. We're at the bunkhouse. Over."

"That's great. Take the afternoon off, okay? Stay with Luke."

"Copy that."

"Let him know I'm here if he needs to talk."

"Of course."

"Did he tell you anything?"

"He told me everything."

*

Luke was still sleeping when Noah came back from the grooming barn.

"Liv told me what happened. Is he okay?" he asked, sitting where I made space for him on my bunk.

"I think so," I said. "He's calmed down and slept most of the afternoon."

Noah smiled. "I guess that's good?"

I smiled back. "I think so."

"He told me about what happened to his parents," I said quietly.

Noah nodded. "Good. He needs to talk about his past."

"Yeah."

"Especially with people who care about him."

"Yeah," I said. "I do. I care about you too. Any skeletons in your closet?"

Noah laughed softly. "Nope. My life's been pretty boring. Thankfully."

I grinned. "I don't think anyone who spends time at the Braided Crop Ranch can say their life is boring, Noah."

Noah nodded with a smile. "Yeah. True. You got me."

"Um, hey, do you know anything about puppy play?" I asked nonchalantly.

Noah's head snapped up. "What? Why?"

"Has Lorraine ever put you in a pup hood?"

Noah stared at me, turning red. "Maybe."

"Uh huh." I pointed upward and spoke softly. "Luke? In a pup hood and tail? So hot and incredibly malleable."

Noah's chin dropped.

*

When Luke woke up later, and after he had a shower, the three of us took a walk.

Not to the shed. There was plenty of time for more assignations in the shed. This time we walked the other way, past the pebble beach on a trail winding through the woods until we reached the lake again.

The water reflected the late afternoon sun, glimmering blue and silver. Luke sat on a large rock and gazed out at this vista, taking the unbelievable beauty in. Noah and I found spots near him. We sat in silence for some time, appreciating the beauty of our surroundings and the company.

"I love this place," Luke said finally. "This whole ranch. The people, the kink, the food. Everything." He glanced at me and Noah. "Even Kamal." He shrugged.

I took off my hat and wiped the sweat off my forehead, then replaced it. "I could have sworn you hated this place when I first met you."

Luke nodded. "I wouldn't be here if that was the case."

"I know," I said, grinning at him, glad his sass was back.

Noah stared at the sand and said, "You know what my favorite part of this place is?"

Luke grinned and spoke while staring at the water. "The big black dildo Lorraine likes to shove up your ass?"

Noah coughed, blushing. "Maybe. Not what I meant. I meant you guys. You guys are my favorite thing." Noah looked up at us. "Of course, I love the pony play and everything. That's why I came here. But I never expected to meet anyone like Luke. And then I met Jensen. And I think I feel like my life is complete. At least right now."

"You want a proposal?" Luke asked. "I'll propose to you right now."

"*What*?" Noah said, "No. Fuck off, Luke," Noah scoffed. "Don't be an idiot."

Luke raised his eyebrows. "You think I'm an idiot to want to keep you?"

Noah stared hard at Luke, blinking back emotion, his forehead creased. Probably trying to figure out if Luke was only teasing or being sincere. "What are you saying?"

Luke looked off over the lake, then down at the ground beside the rock where he was sitting. "I'm saying, I'm with you for the long haul. I want us to live together."

Noah was silent. He looked at me but I was as shocked as he was. And on another level not surprised at all. I smiled at Noah.

Noah stood and walked over to Luke. He leaned on the rock, facing Luke, placing his hands on either side of him, forcing Luke to meet his gaze. "You want to live with me? Really?"

"Fuck, Noah, who wouldn't want to live with you? You're quiet and sweet and adorable and sexy as all fuck. You don't even realize what a catch you are."

Noah blinked. He licked his lips, looking like he wanted to argue. "But what if we drive each other crazy?"

Luke shrugged. "Then I put a butt-plug tail in you and we do something really kinky and everything will be right again. See?" He tapped his forehead. "Got everything figured out."

"Yeah, you do," Noah said softly.

"And if things are really tough, we pack up and come visit Jensen for the weekend. He'll sort us out."

I saluted them, showing I was on board.

"Plus, it'll be easier for us to have kinky phone sex with Jensen if you and I are in one location," Luke said slyly, glancing over at me.

Noah laughed. "Fine, you've convinced me. Like you even needed to. I'll follow you wherever you go, Luke Weller."

"Jensen?" Luke said.

"Yeah?"

"You want in on this?" he asked.

"In on what?"

"You want an official part of this three-way here, cowboy? I'm not talking about the sex stuff right now. I'm asking if you want to be our boyfriend. Officially."

I took off my hat again, turning the weathered brim in my hands, thinking. Trying not to let my emotions lift me into the sky.

"I guess that would be all right," I said.

I made the statement in a casual way, like I was agreeing to go to a movie or something inconsequential. But when I looked up at Noah and Luke, I knew my eyes shone with emotion and hoped my smile conveyed everything in my utterly claimed heart.

About the Author

AE Lister/Elizabeth Lister is a Canadian non-binary author with a vivid imagination and a head full of unique and interesting characters. They have published many other books, one of which (*Beyond the Edge*) received an Honorable Mention from the National Leather Association–International for excellence in SM/Leather/Fetish writing.

Email: aelisterauthor@gmail.com

Facebook: www.facebook.com/aelister.elizabethlister

Twitter: @lizbethlister

Website: www.aelister.com

Coming Soon from AE Lister

Ponyboy

The Braided Crop Ranch, Book Two

Shadows and dim lighting made the inside of the club appear deceptively edgy. The Stocks boasted a selection of the most overrated brews and clientele in the city, in my opinion. But this particular club was one of the few places I could go to try to find the kind of man I was looking for.

"Hey, Lipke, what are you doing here again?" Sandro smiled, clapping a hand on my shoulder and taking the stool next to me. "I thought you had the real deal? You know, a nice cozy apartment with your man."

"We broke up," I said, staring at the bar and trying not to let the fact I didn't feel much disappointment about the end of my relationship bother me.

"Ah, shit, that's too bad," Sandro replied, but I saw a glimmer of satisfaction in his eyes as he motioned to the bartender. "Hey, a drink for my buddy here, Paulo." He turned back. "What are you having, Owen?"

I shook my head and tossed the dark hair out of my eyes. It was getting way too long in front. I'd been meaning to get it cut, but I was so unmotivated to do anything these days. "Thanks, but I'm hoping for some action tonight."

I never trolled for Doms with alcohol in my system. I'd learned that lesson a long time ago.

"How about a Coke, then?"

"Okay, sure. Thanks."

He was trying to butter me up because he wanted to hook up. He'd tried with me before but I had been in a relationship that didn't allow for "extras" so I'd had an excuse to turn him down.

"A Coke for Owen, please. And a ginger ale for me," he said, throwing a tenner on the bar.

"Thanks," I said again, looking Sandro over and wondering if he could give me what I wanted.

He wasn't a bad-looking guy; a little heavier in the gut, but it worked for him. He had a decent "Daddy" vibe going on and appeared to be pushing forty. Maybe he had the experience to give me something...more. Something solid and demanding and ruthless.

The Stocks was an underground fetish bar, where I'd come innumerable times to find the type of hook-up I was after. But anyone I'd ever gone home or played downstairs with, had disappointed. It wasn't operating on the down-low. The club was literally underground, which made it even darker and dingier inside than most places—almost claustrophobic.

Everyone played games. That was often the point with fetish and BDSM, and a lot of guys were perfectly happy with that. But I was tired and bored with it all.

I'd had a connection with Simon, my ex, but even he couldn't give me what I wanted in the end. I couldn't define that particular desire but I knew I hadn't fulfilled it—ever.

At night I'd dream about a Master who took total control, put me in my place easily and perfunctorily, without a thought to my comfort, yet took care of my needs like they were his own. This mystery man became a shadowy, elusive presence in my waking world. I'd never encountered an actual human being who could measure up to the Dom in my dreams. Maybe no one ever would.

Maybe I should make the most of what I could get, here and now.

Sandro handed me the Coke and winked. "So, you're a free agent tonight," he said.

I grinned. "Yep. Trolling for Doms."

He laughed, looked away, and then back. "Wanna come home with me? We could have some fun."

I picked up my glass and sipped the cold, sugary-sweet syrup, considering his offer. "You live close?"

Sandro nodded. "Just down the street. Walking distance. You can leave your car here and pick it up later, or in the morning if you decide to stay over."

It was thoughtful of him to offer me the whole night. Such an invitation was rare in this environment, where most people just wanted a quick fuck or a fun kink session and didn't give a shit what you did with yourself after.

"Yeah, okay."

"Really?"

I found his excitement flattering, if misplaced. I didn't feel like anything special these days, but I was up for a quick screw.

"Sure. But let's enjoy our drinks first. We've got all night."

Sandro had fair-to-good conversation skills. He was intelligent, perceptive, and witty. I warmed to my decision over the time it took to finish our drinks. Maybe the evening wouldn't be a washout after all.

Sandro sighed. "I wish there were more kink places in this city. I mean, this place is fine but it gets boring after a while."

I agreed with his observation completely. There were several options across the river from Ottawa in Quebec that offered more hard-core entertainment, but in terms of convenience this place was closest. And even when I had ventured as far as Gatineau or Montreal, I'd been largely disappointed.

"I hear Toronto is the place to be for this kind of scene," I said. "Maybe I should move to the Big Smoke."

"Maybe. I thought about it a couple of times. But, my family is here and my job."

"I don't know if I could sacrifice the green space," I said.

The easy access to nature was one of the things I loved about Ottawa. There were a multitude of parks and treed spaces; bike paths, beaches, and water everywhere. And the Gatineau hills were just across the Ottawa River. I enjoyed hiking and camping more than almost anything else. Spending regular time in nature was essential to my being. I doubted I'd be happy in a concrete city like Toronto.

Then again, was I happy here?

"I heard about this place in the Muskokas," Sandro was saying. "It's a ranch, but not the kind of ranch you'd expect in that touristy area."

"Huh?" I asked. A ranch? I had absolutely no interest in horses.

Sandro nodded. "It's set up like a real ranch, but instead of horses, they get men to dress like ponies."

If I had been a pony, my ears would have swung toward him. "What? No way." Something in me thrilled to the thought of it.

He laughed. "Yeah, they put them in harnesses and bridles and make them do stuff. It's all set up to make the experience as realistic as possible. At least that's what I heard."

I pretended not to be as interested as I was. "Hmm. Weird."

"Yeah, well, I guess some guys get off on that stuff. Not me. I'm happy with the regular kink experience myself, although it would be nice to have a few more bars to go to."

Men in harnesses and wearing bridles? A ranch for pony fetishists? Why hadn't I heard about this before? My balls ached at the thought of it. I'd never explored animal role-play, but the thought of being a pony at a fetish ranch rang every one of my bells. Maybe a fetish ranch was the kind of immersive experience I needed. Sure, it was still a game, but maybe they did it so well you forgot it was a game and became fully invested in submission and objectification.

I drained the rest of my glass. "Ready to go?"

Sandro beamed as his gaze raked over me. "Absolutely."

Also Available from NineStar Press

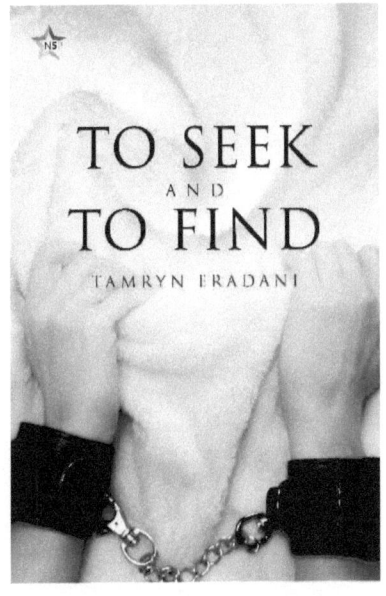

Connect with NineStar Press

www.ninestarpress.com

www.facebook.com/ninestarpress

www.facebook.com/groups/NineStarNiche

www.twitter.com/ninestarpress

www.ingramcontent.com/pod-product-compliance
Lightning Source LLC
Chambersburg PA
CBHW051606100726
47898CB00001B/245